Dear Reader:

I'm delighted to present to you the first books in the HarperMonogram imprint. This is a new imprint dedicated to publishing quality women's fiction and we believe it has all the makings of a surefire hit. From contemporary fiction to historical tales, to page-turning suspense thrillers, our goal at HarperMonogram is to publish romantic stories that will have you coming back for more.

Each month HarperMonogram will feature some of your favorite bestselling authors and introduce you to the most talented new writers around. We hope you enjoy this Monogram and all the HarperMonograms to come.

We'd love to know what you think. If you have any comments or suggestions please write to me at the address below:

HarperMonogram
10 East 53rd Street
New York, NY 10022

Karen Solem
Editor-in-chief

"DAMN YOU,"

Charles breathed, looking down into her lovely face.

"Do you refuse to dance with me?" Lettice mocked.

"Lettice, stop."

"Stop what?" Daring him, she stepped closer until less than a foot separated them.

"Your lies. Your deceit," he whispered desperately.

"I would not lie to you. I am your faithful servant now, am I not?" Her green eyes taunted him.

Suddenly his hands dug into her shoulders and he pulled her against his hard body, molding her to him, and his full mouth came down, possessing hers.

"No, please," she whispered, "I beg of you, don't."

"God, Lettice," he groaned, "why must you torment me? Does it give you satisfaction to see me driven to my knees by lust?"

Also by Candace Camp

Rosewood
Analise
Bonds of Love
Light and Shadow
Bitterleaf
Heirloom

Published by
HarperPaperbacks

Harper
Monogram

CANDACE CAMP

CRYSTAL HEART

PREVIOUSLY PUBLISHED UNDER THE
PSEUDONYM LISA GREGORY

HarperPaperbacks

A Division of HarperCollinsPublishers

HarperPaperbacks   *A Division of* HarperCollins*Publishers*
10 East 53rd Street, New York, N.Y. 10022

This book is published by arrangement with the author.

Cover photo by Herman Estevez
Quilt courtesy of Quilts of America, Inc., N.Y.C.

First HarperPaperbacks printing: September 1992

Printed in the United States of America

HarperPaperbacks, HarperMonogram, and colophon are trademarks of HarperCollins*Publishers*

10 9 8 7 6 5 4 3 2 1

One

*L*ettice idly surveyed the ball-room, her face carefully set in a look of fashionable boredom. Ennui was the order of the day, and Lettice felt she had no need to pretend in order to achieve the look. Slowly she unfurled her fan and lazily began to ply it while her cold green eyes continued to investigate the meeting. Heavens, what a crush, she thought contemptuously; if Flo had only told her how many people she had invited, Lettice would never have come. But now she would have to make the rounds and flirt and banter wittily, or else everyone would begin speculating on what was wrong with Lady Lettice. She envied Philip, who had been wise enough to refuse to come and instead had gone off to one of his gambling hells. She would have to spend at least a couple of hours here before she could slip away for a bit of gambling herself.

At the thought of the excitement of cards, a little smile curved her generous mouth, and her green eyes took on a glitter.

"Is it too much to hope that that smile is for me?" a male voice sighed fatuously in her ear, and Lettice laughed.

"Percy, dear, how could that be, since you stole up behind me so mysteriously?" Lettice turned and favored the man with one of her most dazzling smiles. Percy Fratham, resplendent in a coat of puce satin, his face a mask of adoration, had long been Lettice's most faithful admirer. He had attached himself to her when she first came out and had followed her faithfully ever since, even after her marriage to Philip. Lettice had never taken him seriously. She often declared that Percy's devotion to her was the result of laziness; finding a new object of worship would require too much effort from him. Privately, Lettice suspected that his true predilections lay elsewhere and that he used her as a safe excuse for his lack of interest in other women. Whatever the reason, Lettice nevertheless found Percy amusing in his cynical way, and she enjoyed his company.

"Thank God you're here," she said to him now. "I thought I was facing an evening of unutterable boredom. But now at least I know you will amuse me with all the gossip. Tell me, who is in love with whom today?"

Percy laughed and gracefully took a pinch of snuff. "Well, why not start with our lovely hostess, the Countess of Lysbeck? You know, I suppose, of her handsome Guards captain?"

"Percy, you disappoint me—that news is weeks old!"

"The affair is, of course, but not this: She planned this soiree tonight for him, to show him off to everyone. But it seems the captain turned stiff-necked about it and refused to attend. So Flo has gathered this horrid crowd simply to witness her humiliation."

"Poor Flo." Lettice's mouth curled downward in mock sympathy; it was a gesture she had practiced for many years, knowing full well the sensuality of it. Few men failed to respond to the dimple that would suddenly appear at the corner of her full mouth, or the delicate black beauty mark she placed strategically near her lips. Like many of the things she had practiced over the years, it came to her unconsciously now.

"I hear that your lady mother has retired to Grenwil," Percy said, his voice soft and his eyes slyly fixed on Lettice's face.

A nerve jumped slightly near her eyes, briefly disturbing her flawless face, but no friend less intimate than Percy would have noticed. "Oh? I had not heard," Lettice said airily. "She and my father must have had another tiff." She smiled and glanced at Percy, her voice turning droll. "So often I forget whether my beloved parents are merely not speaking to each other or whether they are at dagger's point. Frankly, I think it's all one and the same to them."

Calmly she turned the subject to other acquaintances and soon had her swain gaily recounting the misadventures of a certain earl on his latest jaunt to Paris. Lettice tried to ignore the pain in her stomach. Funny to think that after all these years she could feel again the fear and the tightening of her stomach that she had known as a child when her beautiful, remote parents stormed at each other in icy rage. She had learned long ago what marriage for love meant: tearful, angry battles over a mutual lack of money, regrets that they had not married to please their parents; jealous tirades over a suspected affair; passion so intense that there was no room for a child in their affections. That was why she had married Philip for his name and inheritance, not for love. Well, she had learned to regret that. Philip's grandfather had fooled them all by living to be eighty-four and still kept Philip on an allowance that left them constantly in debt.

Lettice smiled at what she hoped was the appropriate time, for she had not heard a word of what Percy had been saying. Suddenly Fratham stiffened and looked across the room in amazement. His movement caught her attention as his story did not.

"What can have riveted you so?" Lettice asked with amusement and followed the direction of his gaze.

"Good Gad!" Fratham exclaimed. "Look at that fellow! Where on earth did he come from?"

It was then that she saw the stranger. She wondered how she could have kept from noticing him earlier. Among the crowd of richly dressed aristocrats, he stood out like a crow. His skin was tanned by the sun to a shade far darker than the milk-white complexions of those around him, and he was dressed in a simple black velvet suit, not inexpensive, but hopelessly out of date and without any ornamentation. His unpowdered reddish-brown hair was pulled back carelessly into a short queue and tied with a black ribbon. He was a big man, towering head and shoulders over Sir Edward Ponsonby, standing beside him, and his square, hard face, as devoid of ornament as the rest of him, was unrelievedly plain. A large, jutting nose dominated his features, so that one did not at first notice the full, mobile mouth beneath it, or the bright blue of the large eyes above it.

"What an ugly man!" Lettice exclaimed.

"He looks much like my mastiff, Gorgon," Percy said scornfully, and Lettice giggled at his remark.

At the bell-like sound of her laugh, the man looked straight at Lettice and narrowed his eyes.

"Why, Lettice, my love, I do believe you've captured the fellow's attention. That's precisely how Gorgon looks when he's spotted a rabbit."

Lettice smothered her laughter behind her fan, even as she watched the object of their fun over the top, her green eyes dancing merrily. Now the man said something to his companion, and the other man glanced at her and frowned. They seemed to be arguing, the large man insisting and the well-dressed man demurring. Finally the shorter man shrugged and the two of them started across the ballroom toward the steps on which Lettice and her gallant stood.

"Oh, no," Lettice whispered behind her fan, her voice gurgling with laughter. "They are coming over here! Percy, what shall we do?"

Fratham adjusted the froth of lace at his cuff and said, "Why, enjoy it, of course. It has been a long while since I've seen anything quite so droll. Do you suppose it talks?"

"No, Percy, stop, you'll make me choke from laughing. How am I ever to greet them with a straight face?"

"Oh, bother, Lettice, what does it matter if you laugh in his face? No doubt he's just some boor of a colonial. You know Ponsonby—he's always bleeding for the poor colonials. A lot of savages, that's all they are."

"Shhh, he'll hear you."

The men were coming up the stairs now, and the large man's gaze was still fixed upon her. Lettice set her face in a cool, haughty mask and lowered her fan. The steady, burning intensity of the man's gaze disturbed her. Why did he not conceal his interest in her? Quite obviously he knew nothing about sophisticated manners; even a lad green from Oxford knew enough to mask his feelings a little.

"Lady Lettice Kenton, Mr. Percy Fratham," Sir Edward Ponsonby said, nodding his head at them jerkily. It was evident that he did not like the task of introducing his companion to a pair he clearly regarded as featherheads.

His attitude stung Lettice a little; she was not used to being the object of scorn. She raised her eyebrows a trifle and said, "Sir Edward?" in a tone that conveyed her total indifference to him and the stranger.

Sir Edward had the grace to flush a little at her tone, although his companion seemed to take no notice of it. However, Sir Edward went on grimly, "May I introduce to you Mr. Charles Murdock, a friend of mine from the American colonies?"

Percy rolled his eyes at Lettice knowingly, and it was all she could do to keep from laughing again. She said with false brightness, "Really? Why, I would never have guessed."

"Lady Kenton," Murdock said solemnly in the flat, almost nasal accent of the colonials, and Lettice had to bring her fan up to hide the mirth welling in her. Why, the boor had not caught her sarcasm at all!

In fact, Charles Murdock had heard too many jokes about his colonial appearance to pay any attention to them. Besides, he was too busy sweeping his eyes over the loveliness of the woman before him to notice her words. She stood there, cool and remote in pale-gold satin, the swooping décolletage of the fashionable gown revealing the gently rounded tops of her full breasts and the wide, stiff panniers on the skirts turning her waist into a mere wisp. Looking at her, Charles felt a leap of desire stronger than any he had ever felt before. Her huge green eyes glinted with amusement over the top of her fan, beckoning, promising, and keeping him at a distance all at once.

As he admired the lady, an awkward silence fell upon the group, for Lettice was too near laughter to speak and Fratham, amused by the tableau, was not about to ease matters by talking.

So, awkwardly, Sir Edward plunged in. "Mr. Murdock is visiting me while he is here from Boston on business."

"Boston?" Lettice repeated blankly. "What is that?"

"It is a city in the Massachusetts Bay Colony," Sir Edward explained with unconcealed irritation. He pointedly ignored a snicker from the direction of Percy Fratham.

"Oh, and what is your business?" Lettice asked sweetly, turning the full force of her emerald gaze on the Bostonian.

"I am a lawyer, ma'am. However, I came here to settle some matters for my late father's business; he was a merchant and purchased his goods from England, of course. Also, I was urged by my friends in Boston to bring our case before Parliament."

"Your case?"

"The plight of the colonials under the taxes imposed by Parliament."

"Oh," Lettice murmured, thoroughly uninterested.

"Tell me, sir," Percy interrupted, equally bored, "where did you acquire your apparel?"

"In Boston," Murdock replied, noticing the man for

the first time. Then the colonial caught the implicit criticism in Fratham's statement, and a dull flush mounted in his cheeks. "I take it you are jesting about my clothing?" he said, and for a moment Lettice felt a peculiar little thrill of danger—was the hulking stranger going to take exception to Percy's remark? No doubt he was mannerless enough to floor Percy right here in the middle of this gathering.

But then Murdock smiled stiffly and said, "I've always maintained that one who looks as I do only makes himself more conspicuous by adopting a peacock's plumage."

Fratham raised his eyebrows slightly, wondering if an insult to himself was hidden in those words. Suddenly Lettice felt uncomfortable and strangely guilty. Of course, the man was only some colonial yokel; still, she felt a little ashamed of making fun of him. It was something like the hot embarrassment she used to feel when her cousins baited Will Sawyer, the half-witted stableboy.

Murdock turned his face toward her, and she realized with confusion that he had somehow read her thoughts. He smiled at her, and there was a kindness and liking for her in his smile.

"Don't trouble yourself, milady. I've a much thicker hide than to be pricked by a few giggles."

Lettice was thankful for the heavy makeup that hid her blush. Heavens, she had not blushed in years! Somehow the colonial's ease of manner and his desire to reassure her made Lettice feel even worse. When a buffoon suddenly displayed manners and character, she felt herself to be the buffoon for ridiculing him.

"I am sure that is so, Mr. Murdock," she said stiffly.

"Now, if you will excuse me, I must greet our hostess. Gentlemen."

Head high, Lettice went down the stairs, aware of Murdock's blue-eyed stare steadily on her back. She would not let herself turn to look at him until she was well engulfed in the throng of people on the floor. But then, when she turned, she found that Charles Murdock was still looking at her, and his eyes met hers with a steady, inscrutable gaze. Quickly she turned away.

Fratham excused himself soon after Lettice had left the group. It would be unutterable boredom to stay with these two without someone else to share the joke with him. Murdock barely noticed the man's departure.

"Lord, man," Sir Edward said in vexation, "I would never have dreamed that you, of all people, Charles, would be infatuated with that empty-headed chit."

A slow smile spread across the big man's face as he looked down at his friend. "Come, Edward, you knew me at Cambridge. Surely you must remember that I was not entirely immune to the fair sex."

A short laugh escaped his companion, who could well remember his university days, when he had befriended the gangling, awkward colonial boy sent to England to complete his education. "How could I forget? You were like a bull let loose in a pasture!"

Murdock grinned. "Yes, I had never before known the delights of hired women. It was rather pleasant to find a woman who would ignore my face for a little silver."

Sir Edward colored a little at his friend's statement. "Now, Charles, that's not fair. You speak as if you were some sort of freak. As I remember, you were rather popular with the lightskirts."

"I was free with my coins," Charles retorted without bitterness. Although his face, quite ugly as a child, had grown to fit his great nose and large eyes, Charles had never been able to see the man and not the child, whose looks had been the butt of many an adolescent joke. Nor had he ever realized that his popularity with the ladies of the night sprang as much from his gentleness and the pleasure his expert hands could produce as from his money.

"Well, that is quite beside the point, anyway," his friend said, sidestepping the issue. "That was when you were fresh from the Puritan colonies. As I remember, you rather took to gambling, too."

Charles shrugged, and he glanced away from his friend to survey the room casually, his blue eyes again seeking out the lovely form of Lady Lettice. Sir Edward gave a snort of disgust.

"Really, Charles, you are a grown man now, with great responsibilities. You haven't the time to go mooning about like a schoolboy over some coquette who's broken more hearts than you could name."

"Ah, yes," Murdock sighed. "My duty to my people. Very well, Edward, introduce me to some more of these lords who will politely decline to help me bring my cause before Parliament."

Edward frowned a little at the other man's words. He knew that Charles was growing discouraged here—and well he might. All the weeks Murdock had been in London, he had relentlessly plodded around, being rebuffed by every official Edward had hoped could help him. In the whole time, he had been unable to secure a hearing before Parliament. Sir Edward, although a friend of Charles, was also a firm believer, as were a few others, that the American colonies were being shabbily treated. He feared that the stubborn attitude of Parliament toward even reasonable men like Charles would soon lead them all straight to disaster.

Murdock forced himself to walk around with his friend, being introduced here and there to some haughty lord who, Ponsonby thought, might listen to his cause. However, now and then he could not help but scan the room, searching for the lovely gold and white form of Lettice Kenton.

Finally even Ponsonby grew discouraged, and the two men left the great ballroom, signaling for their carriage. "Bah," Charles said in disgust. "I don't know why Warren and Adams thought I could get the English people to listen to me. I'm no politician."

"But you did go to school here," Edward reminded him. "I can see their reasoning: that you might understand our ways better."

Murdock snorted. "There are even some who claim that I am *too* friendly with England, having been educated here. If only they could see how completely I am ignored."

Ponsonby shook his head sadly and stepped into the carriage that pulled up in front of the steps. Settling back against the plush squabs, Charles stared out the window, his thoughts obviously far away.

"What is so unutterably wrong with the lovely Lady Kenton?" he asked suddenly, startling his friend.

"Are you back to her again?" Ponsonby exclaimed irritatedly. "Gad, Charles, what ails you?"

"Lust, I should imagine," Charles said lightly, but his blue eyes were dark and unreadable. "Pure lust."

"Well, forget her," Edward said sternly. "There are far easier ways of satisfying that—safer, too. For one thing, Charles, she is married."

A shadow crossed his friend's eyes. "Oh? And who is the lucky husband?"

"Those two are a matched set, believe me. Philip Kenton is one of the greatest rogues in the city. He is the heir to a wealthy duke, though one would never know it. He never stays within his allowance, and is constantly in debt. It is rumored that he tries to keep his creditors off his back by duping young fools and cheating them at cards. He keeps at least two mistresses, and I have heard that his tastes run to the . . . uh . . . perverse."

Murdock's face hardened. "Then it sounds to me as though the lady is to be pitied, not scorned."

"Huh!" His companion's laugh was mirthless. "She is no better than he. She is a Delaplaine, and not one of them has ever been worth anything; they are a careless, self-indulgent lot. Her parents have long been the scandal of England with their affairs and raging fights. As for Lady Lettice, who do you think it is that lures the innocent lads to her husband's table? She flirts and makes promises of great delights to come and gets them so befuddled with drink and lust that they never see Philip's tricks and eagerly come back for more."

"I don't believe it," Charles said, tight-lipped.

"Don't be a fool, Charles. You know nothing of the lady's character; you barely met her. Surely you don't think you can establish true character after those few words!"

"No, of course not," Murdock replied roughly. "It is just that I sensed something in her, some humanity, some caring, that the oaf with her did not possess."

"It would not take much to possess more humanity than Percy Fratham," Sir Edward responded drily. "Really, Charles, you are thinking with your loins, not your head. Lettice Kenton is a flighty, indolent wastrel, who cares nothing for anyone but herself."

Murdock envisioned the woman in question, remembering her in detail from the tip of her pearl-studded slippers to the top of her towering, powdered hairdo inset with pearls and gold ribbons. There was no way he could deny it: She was the picture of idle aristocracy, the sort of person he had always despised. And yet . . .

"Perhaps," Murdock said, a faint smile playing upon his lips, "perhaps you are right. I saw her for only a few moments in a crowded ballroom; I could not judge her properly. I think I should call on the lady tomorrow afternoon and observe her more closely, for a longer period of time. Surely her tarnish will show then."

His companion gave a muffled groan. "Oh, Charles, you are behaving like a schoolboy."

Charles smiled sardonically. "Where is the harm? I am accomplishing nothing in tramping around from politician to politician, office to office. My cause will suffer no harm, I think, if I take a few moments out for my own pleasure. I must leave soon; already the captain of my ship grows restless and tells me that he and his men wish to leave soon. They are worried about their loved ones back in Massachusetts. So I have told him that we will set sail

Wednesday morning. How complete a fool can I make of myself in that short a time?"

"Only complete enough to break your heart, I fear," Sir Edward replied heavily, "and lose money at Philip's game, as well."

Murdock chuckled. "You needn't worry about that. Gambling no longer interests me. Besides, I believe I am expert enough at it to protect myself. Don't forget my years at Cambridge."

They were silent for a few moments as the carriage rumbled noisily through the cobblestoned streets. At last Charles spoke, his voice low and thoughtful. "You think I don't know that the lady is not for me? I know what I look like; I realize that she thinks me an uncivilized oaf. But, you know, Edward, when I saw her tonight, standing there so icy and beautiful, something stabbed through me. Call it lust, love, whatever you will; I felt a trembling in my soul that no other woman has ever caused. I must see her again, if only to satisfy myself that I was wrong."

"This isn't like you, Charles."

"I know," Murdock replied simply. "All my life, I've been a sober, upright, industrious citizen. When other lads were out playing or flirting with girls, I was always studying, or helping my father at his office. Since then I've worked hard at my profession, as well as trying to keep Father's business alive after he died. The rest of my time I spend in serious political discussions with Sam Adams or John Adams or some of the others. Don't you think it's about time I did something just a little bit foolish?"

* * *

Lady Lettice was sitting in her drawing room with her cousin Victor Delaplaine the following afternoon when her butler stepped into the room to ask if she was at home to a Mr. Charles Murdock.

"Who?" Victor asked, knitting his brows. "Never heard of the fellow. Have you, Letty?"

Lettice grimaced, destroying the lovely line of her mouth. "Yes. He's some fool I met at Flo's last night. No one you would want to meet, Victor." She turned to the servant. "Please tell him I am not at home."

"Yes, milady," the butler intoned and stepped back out into the hall.

Lettice rose and walked across the room to the decorative Italian mantel, tapping her closed fan against her dress in an impatient tattoo.

"The lout seems to have disturbed you, cousin," Victor said, idly placing a pinch of snuff on the back of his hand and sniffing it.

Lettice sighed. She could hardly tell Victor of the strange, smothering guilt that rose in her at having refused to see Murdock. Doubtless he would see through the lie, and know that she had no wish to see him. But what did that matter? She had given the same excuse countless times before without a qualm. Why should she care what Charles Murdock thought?

Lettice swung around, her eyes lit with the fierce green light that often rested there. "Let's do something exciting tonight, Victor. I feel unbearably bored."

Her cousin's eyes danced with amusement; he rarely disagreed with Lettice's wild ideas. "Shall we mask and go to the Vauxhall Gardens?"

Lettice made a face and shook her head. "Too tame by half, Victor."

"I know. There's a new gambling hell that I went to the other night. Of course, your reputation would be in shreds if I took you. You should have seen some of the types who were there."

Lettice's eyes sparkled. "Victor, that sounds like just the thing! I can dress up in a boy's costume, as I did once before—remember? I still have the clothes I wore."

"Capital!" The two cousins smiled at each other, the same fear-heightened excitement coursing through their veins.

Lettice yawned and opened her eyes sleepily; her head was pounding cruelly and she felt as if she had hardly been asleep. She cast an accusing glance at her maid, who had shaken her awake.

"What the devil do you think you're doing, Elly?" she snapped fiercely. "I can't have slept three hours, I know."

"No, milady, it's barely eight o'clock. I'm dreadful sorry to wake you up, but it's his lordship. He wants to speak to you. Right away."

Lettice sighed. She could hardly blame the girl for obeying Philip; he was a wicked man to cross, and at the very least it would mean the girl's dismissal if she did not fetch her mistress to him.

"All right, don't look so anxious. I will come, and I promise I won't bite your head off either. But what is Philip doing up at this hour himself? Surely he went out last night."

"Oh, yes, milady, he did, and he just now came in. He said he wanted to talk to you before he went to sleep."

Lettice grimaced. Trust Philip to think of no one but himself. "Well, fetch me my dressing gown, then."

She sighed and sat up, swinging her legs over the side of her bed. Hammers were pounding in her head, and her mouth felt as dry as cotton. Last night she and Victor had gone gambling as planned, and stayed out far too late and drank far too much. She did not know why exactly; but she had felt the need of some distraction after the wretched gathering at Flo's the night before last, and after that American had come calling yesterday afternoon. Not that she could be criticized; he had gotten just what he deserved—how could he think she would welcome a bumpkin like him? My heavens, imagine what Mother would say to her, the descendant of Norman lords, a Delaplaine, no less, entertaining some farmer's son—no, merchant's—from the colonies.

Elly brought her a pale-blue French sacque dress, which tied up the front with white satin bows and hung loose and flowing in the back. Because Philip was an impatient man, she did not bother with her hair, but slipped into shoes and went straight down the hall to his sitting room.

"Gad, you must have been asleep like a rock, the time it took you. I would have said that the chit must have found you *en flagrante* with a lover, but then, we know that wouldn't be like you, would it, my love?" her husband said, his voice soft and sneering.

From years of experience, Lettice ignored his taunt and merely sat down across from him. Philip, his thin frame richly dressed and as immaculate as always even after a night of revelry, studied her thoughtfully. One hand, with a bright pigeon's blood ruby flashing on his finger as it moved, tapped softly against his cheek. Lettice knew his tactics well enough by now to realize that he was trying to unnerve her before delivering some blow. Well, he had never yet managed to defeat her, she thought defiantly; let him see that he never would. She returned his gaze with apparent calm, though her mind raced, turning over possible reasons for his summons.

"A bad night?" he asked smoothly, his voice offering false sympathy even as he implied a criticism of her appearance.

"I am used to more than three hours of sleep, Philip; I am rarely up at this ungodly hour."

"I understand that you have a new admirer." His voice was silky; it amused Lettice that she had once thought it soft with affection. She had found out since that his voice softened when his cruelty expanded.

"Who? What are you talking about?"

"I learned last night that you met a colonial who was enchanted by you. Why didn't you inform me of it?"

Lettice affected a yawn. "Is that what you have awakened me for? To ask why I did not tell you I met some colonial boor at Flo's party? If I had known you were so interested in colonials, I would have brought him home and introduced him."

Philip chuckled. "Lettice, you've learned to bite. You know, I think you are far more interesting than you once were. Perhaps I shall sample your wares again some night soon. Have you new tricks in bed as well?"

A shiver ran down her back at his words, but she hid it and said tartly, "Not enough for you, milord."

Her husband smiled, reminding her of a cat with its prey. "Lettice, if you had but thought of it, surely you would be aware that I am always interested in a fool with a great deal of money."

"Oh, you mean you want to cheat Mr. Murdock at cards? Well, I doubt he has the wealth for you, Philip; he certainly did not show it in his clothes."

"You never look beyond appearances. No doubt you once thought me as handsome inside as out."

"Silly of me, wasn't it?" she retorted coolly.

"Well, it happens that you are very wrong about your Mr. Murdock. It seems his father was a wealthy merchant in the colonies, with a nice fleet of ships to carry his goods, and he died, leaving it all to Mr. Murdock, who holds you in such esteem."

Lettice shrugged. "He is a friend of that dreadfully dull Sir Edward Ponsonby, and I frankly don't see how you will get him into a game with you, with his friend to advise him against it."

"Ah, but that is where you, my charming wife, come in. I want you to invite the bumpkin to a small, intimate party here—without Ponsonby, of course. And you shall ply him with wine and soft, sweet words; let him fumble at your bosom a time or two. Then, when he is eating out of your hand, we will suggest a friendly little game of cards. How can he refuse? Especially when you pout so prettily and ask it of him?"

"No! I won't do it!" Lettice snapped, leaping to her feet.

"What? Don't tell me you have a fondness for this boor?"

"Don't be idiotic, Philip. I simply refuse to go along with you any longer. I will not be a lure for you to snare some poor, ignorant man into a card game so you can strip him of everything he owns. I think it is loathsome, and I refuse to help you again."

She whirled and started for the door, but Philip's lazy voice brought her to an abrupt halt. "It's been a long time since I've come to your bed, hasn't it, Lettice? I know how little it pleases you, so, like a gentleman, I have stayed away. And how long has it been since you've had a lover?"

"Lover!" She faced him furiously. "I never had a lover! Just some man you forced upon me, and whom I hated as much as I hate you!"

Philip laughed. "Come, come, is that any way to speak about your husband? After all, Lettice, I do have a right to your bed."

"You have no right to force me into the bed of some old roué like Danby, just so you could—" She broke off, choking back her furious words.

"I hardly forced you, Lettice. I simply explained to you that I owed old Danby so much from cards that we would be ruined if he collected, disgraced before all the world and reduced to abject poverty. And since the senile fool was so hot for you that he was willing to forego the debt for one night in your bed, I advised you to take him up on the offer."

"Oh, yes, I had a lot of choice, didn't I? To let him take me, or spend the rest of my life in everlasting hell with you!"

He raised his eyebrows contemptuously at her tone. "Really, Lettice, it isn't as if you had any morals. Or any love for me. Why should you care whether it was I or Danby or that other fellow, what was his name?"

"Leslie Evanton," Lettice said colorlessly.

"Yes, that's right. Got me that position with the government. That brought us a few pounds, didn't it? Anyway, why carry on so? You despise me, so why should you be faithful to me?"

"Believe me, my reluctance is from no desire to be faithful to you."

"Surely you can't claim to have principles? Scruples? A Delaplaine? Don't make me laugh. There isn't a soul in London who hasn't had an affair or two, including your esteemed parents, my love."

"You think I don't know that?"

"And since you do nothing but lie there like a stick, anyway, I can't see why it should be any worse with one fellow than the next."

"I am not a whore, Philip!"

"No?" Again his eyebrows lifted lazily. "All women are whores, Lettice, but only the poor, honest ones are named so."

"Why are you saying all of this? Surely you aren't suggesting I sleep with Murdock to bring him to your card table."

"No, I am just pointing out that for well over a year, I've left you all alone in that great bed of yours. But if you cross me, if you refuse to go along with me—well, that just might change. God knows, I prefer my mistresses to you; they have more passion in one finger than you do in your whole bloodless body. But wait, perhaps I shan't have to make the sacrifice myself. The other day Sir Harold offered me his matched pair of bays in exchange for a week with you at his hunting lodge."

"How dare you discuss me in that way with that

filthy—I won't do it, Philip. I promise you, you can threaten me with anything, but I will not do it."

"You won't have any choice, my love. Someday when you are out riding in our carriage, the driver will simply leave London and take you to your rendezvous with Sir Harold. He wouldn't mind your unwillingness; he always likes a little resistance, to stir his ardor. And of course I shall not report you missing." Her husband smiled at her coldly, baring his teeth without humor.

"Damn you, Philip!" Lettice hissed, seething with fury and frustration. How she hated men—all men. Their clumsy pawings, their painful domination of her body. Old Danby had been bad enough, and Evanton—she had endured that night as if in a trance. But Sir Harold! He was of a kind with Philip; she could tell from the way he looked at her and his furtive pinchings of her breasts and buttocks. He liked pain in his lovemaking, and that was the worst kind of man, she was convinced.

"All right. I will do it. I will have a party next Tuesday and invite Mr. Murdock," she said tightly.

"Good girl. I knew you'd see the light." Philip stood and walked to the door of his bedroom, then turned to look back at his wife. "Poor Lettice. We made a bad bargain, didn't we? You married me for my money, and I married you because I desired you. And here we are; my damned grandfather won't die, so I am penniless; and you—you are the coldest woman I've ever had the misfortune to bed with."

With a dry laugh, he left the room, and Lettice turned away, blinking back hot tears. It was useless to cry. Besides, a Delaplaine would never stoop to tears. Head high, she sailed out of the room. Poor Mr. Murdock, he was about to be thrown to the wolves, she thought, then amended scornfully to herself: Fool that he was, he was enamored of one of the wolves.

$\mathcal{T}wo$

$\mathcal{L}$azily, Lettice's fan moved through the air, as she stared vaguely at the wall, only half aware of what the other three people in the room were saying. She was thinking of the warm note she had penned to Charles Murdock that morning, apologizing for being out when he called and asking him to allow her to rectify that by coming to a small party she was giving the following Tuesday evening. She wondered if Murdock would have the sense to smell deceit there; she hoped he would send her back a note regretting that he could not attend. That would spoil Philip's plans nicely. Perhaps she should have worded the note more sweetly, so that its falsity would seep through.

"What do you think, Lettice?" Caroline Southam asked.

Lettice looked at her, startled, and her fan snapped shut. "What? I'm sorry, Caro, I'm afraid I wasn't attending properly."

"That's obvious," Caroline laughed. "What is it, Lettice? Dreaming of a new beau?"

Like most of the *haut ton* of London, Caroline Southam suspected the flirtatious Lettice of taking a steady string of lovers. After all, who could bear to be faithful to a man like Philip Kenton? Although everyone suspected much, no one was ever able to prove anything about Lettice's amours, and London society decided that in this one respect, at least, Lettice Kenton was discreet. There were those who declared that Lettice's handsome wastrel cousin, Victor Delaplaine, was secretly the love of her life, but Caroline, having seen the two together often, rejected that theory. Victor and Lettice were more like brother and sister than lovers. There were even times when Caroline thought that *all* the rumors must be untrue. After all, she was Lettice's oldest and dearest friend, and Lettice had never breathed a word even to her about having feelings for any man. However, she joked slyly, as they all did, about Lettice's lovers. After all, one day she might reveal something.

Before Lettice could make her usual flip reply to Caroline's question, her butler stepped into the drawing room and intoned, "A Mr. Charles Murdock, milady."

Lettice uttered a soft, vivid curse. She could hardly avoid the fellow after sending him that warm invitation, but she still did not want to see him, and certainly not today. In the reverse thinking that people commonly indulge in, she disliked him and was uncomfortable around him because she knew she was doing him a wrong. However, knowing there was no other out, she smiled tersely and commanded the man to show Murdock in.

At that statement, the callers already seated in her drawing room stared at her with astonishment. They had all by now heard Percy Fratham's droll account of Lettice's meeting with the colonial, and they couldn't imagine why she would let him step foot in her house. Caroline Southam narrowed her eyes and studied Lettice: What sort of sly game was she playing now? The two men in the room, Fancher Willoughby and Kit Summers, both adoring swains of Lettice, surmised that she had done it to make them jealous, and they silently determined to put on a good show of jealousy to convince her of their admiration.

In truth, Lettice noticed little of her companions' reaction. She was wrapped up in her astonishment that Murdock was even plainer and more unfashionable than she had remembered him. He wore not a speck of jewelry anywhere on his person, and his dark brown clothes, less formal than the other suit she had seen, were of plain broadcloth and so severely cut that he looked exactly like a shopkeeper or farmer. The blunt squareness of his features, in no way softened with the beauty marks or powder affected by dandies of her acquaintance, was even harsher here in the daylight than it had been by kind candlelight. His short hair was unpowdered and clubbed back carelessly with a plain ribbon. If he had been a savage Indian, he could not have looked more different from every man she had known in her life. In fact, she decided, his skin was so dark that he could well be a savage.

Murdock stopped just inside the doorway, brought up short by the sight of a roomful of people. It had not occurred to him that Lady Lettice would have other visitors. He greeted her briefly, then stood awkwardly, dwarfing the delicate room with his size, and when finally he thought to sit down, everyone watched in fascination as he perched on a fragile-looking French chair, expecting any moment to see the dainty legs snap off and Murdock come crashing to the floor.

Lettice's lips tightened, but she forced herself to say, "I am so glad, Mr. Murdock, that you came again. I was devastated when I returned home and found that I had missed you."

Murdock smiled at the warmth in her light, teasing voice. He could not take his eyes off her; today, in sea-green silk that deepened the color of her eyes, she seemed more beautiful than before. He noticed all over again the purity of line about her face and the slender elegance of her figure. Charles had never liked the heavy white makeup used by fashionable women, or the red rouge that brightened their lips and cheeks, or the powder that covered their hair; these things hid the real woman. But they could not hide the true loveliness of Lady Lettice, though he longed to see her without such devices. He did not even know what color her hair was beneath the thick white powder. Raven black? Flaming red? Spun gold?

"I came as soon as I got your note," he said, and Lettice felt the faint nausea of guilt at the earnestness in his voice.

How could he expose himself so, she wondered. She had learned as a child to hide her feelings, so that others could not crush them or use them against her. There were jungles other than geographic ones, and Lettice had learned to combat the savage jungle that was the *haut ton* of England. Murdock might think that this aristocratic world built weaklings, but in the qualities that counted here—beauty, wit, equanimity amidst vicious rumor, battling for position, display of wealth—one also had to be strong and quick to survive. Lettice had survived and, to all appearances, had prospered. It did not occur to her that the world in which Murdock lived might use different standards, so she judged him weak and stupid.

"Why, Mr. Murdock, you are teasing me. Be careful, you are likely to turn my head."

He smiled, not knowing how to react to her raillery. The two other men in the room, however, had little difficulty in doing that, and soon they and the two women were engaged in their usual light, bantering conversation, teasing, flirting, trying to top each other with their witticisms. Murdock, watching them, rued his coming. He could think of no way to enter the conversation, and he felt like a dolt. No doubt he looked like one, too, he told himself moodily. He had foolishly expected to have Lettice all to himself, and he was paying the price of his naïveté.

However, Lettice grew bored with the conversation. She often did; her boredom had inspired many of her more adventurous episodes—her crazy pranks and outrageous flirtations, her gambling and partygoing and the scandalous disguises in which she wandered the streets of London with her cousin Victor. Besides, the colonial was the man she had to attract, not the others; she could not have him leaving her house thinking that she was not interested in him.

So Lettice turned to Murdock and said sweetly, "Now, Mr. Murdock, I am afraid that I did not entirely understand what Sir Edward said the other night about your reasons for being here. What is it that you are doing?"

Warmed by her interest, Charles said, "I am here to beg the Parliament to reconsider their policy toward the colonies, particularly toward Boston and the Massachusetts Bay Colony. Early in May we learned of the Boston Port Act, and I agreed to come to England to plead our cause. However, when I arrived here, I was shocked to learn that Parliament had passed even more acts to destroy Boston and the Massachusetts Colony. I have tried to speak before Parliament about our grievances and the explosive situation in the colonies, but they will not give me a hearing. I have been meeting privately with the Members and arguing our side of the issue, but—" He sighed. "I'm afraid to say that I seem to be having little luck. It is as though everyone here is determined to force the colonies to knuckle under, even if it means destroying Boston. What I can't make them understand is that we in the colonies are Englishmen, too, and value the English liberties and rights just as strongly as the people here do. I am afraid the colonials simply will not stand for this treatment."

Lettice looked at him, startled. "But what choice do they have? If Parliament has enacted laws and you can't get them to change them, how can the colonies not stand for it?"

Murdock looked at her seriously and said, "They can do the same thing that Englishmen have always done in defense of their liberties: take up arms."

Now Lettice and the others stared at him in amazement. "You—you mean that they would fight? Rebel against their own king?"

"I hope it doesn't come to that. No Englishman on either side can wish that to happen. And yet, what the government is forcing on us—quartering soldiers in our homes without our leave, closing the port of Boston, taking away our right to select our own governing council or judges, even jurors—these are acts the people will resist to the utmost!"

"Oh, come now, Murdock," Fancher Willoughby drawled contemptuously. "Surely you can't expect us to believe that a lot of rag-tag merchants and farmers in the colonies are going to stand up to the King's soldiers. That would be sheer madness."

Charles's mouth was grim as he replied, "I am afraid that you people here in England have no real understanding of the colonies at all. I am talking about independent, free-thinking people, people who have wrested the land they live on from savages and in the face of much hardship and danger. Ask a man who has seen his wife and children slaughtered and scalped by the Indians if he is frightened by British soldiers."

Caroline Southam gasped at his statement, and he said, "I am sorry. I should not have mentioned such matters in front of ladies. But you see, in America, ladies not only hear such things, they also see them."

"I imagine they find it difficult to remain ladies in that case," Lettice said drily. "I am sure I would."

"Lettice," Caroline said, her eyes sparkling with laughter, "I have heard that you find it difficult to remain a lady here in London."

Murdock was startled that her friend would make such an insulting remark, but Lettice laughed merrily. Willoughby and Summers stood to take their leave, clearly bored by the conversation. Murdock felt that he too should leave, that it was probably impolite to stay any longer on a first call, but he hated to go.

Lettice's soft voice, the smile she flashed at him, the flirtatious way she looked up at him through her thick lashes, the bold thrust of her breasts against the bodice of her dress, all stirred his blood until he longed to take her in his arms. When he realized that after Tuesday night he would see her no more, a strange, dull ache sprang up in him.

Charles forced himself to stand and say good-bye to her, taking her soft, dainty hand in his and raising it briefly to his lips. Then he turned and hurried out of the house, leaving Lettice looking after him, bewilderment mingling with amusement on her face at his sudden, graceless departure.

When Charles reached his friend's home, Sir Edward jovially invited him into his study for a drink before dinner. Charles joined him and silently held out Lettice's invitation. Sir Edward had not been home when the note had arrived, sending Murdock hurtling out of the house to call on Lady Lettice.

"What's this?" Edward looked up from the notepaper to stare at his friend. "I thought yesterday she refused even to see you."

"Her butler said she was out. I thought that meant she did not wish to see me. But according to this, she was truly not home."

Edward quirked an eyebrow suspiciously. "Surely you're not going?"

"Yes, I am," Charles replied evenly.

Sir Edward sighed and tossed the card upon a table. "Charles, you are too bright to fall for this. Can't you recognize a trap? Why should Lady Lettice, who was so cool the other night, suddenly wax so warm in her affection for you? It's obvious: They want to strip you of your gold."

"Ah, Ned, you are a gloomy one, indeed." Charles chuckled. "I am going home the following day, Ned. What can happen in so short a time? Maybe her husband does wish to play me at cards, but as I said before, I am not entirely a novice.

"I know I have to go home. Boston is suffering already under the Port Act—where is their food coming from without the lifeline of shipping? Doubtless my stepmother needs my help, as do my other friends. I fear greatly what lies before us; I think it will be a long period of suffering and hardship. So at least allow me this one small pleasure before I leave: to look upon Lady Lettice's beautiful face again."

Ponsonby sighed and poured himself another drink. "I don't know, Charles. I just don't like it."

Lettice sighed and examined her reflection in the mirror. She did not like what she saw. She had had trouble sleeping lately; her sleep had been full of angry, disturbing dreams, and she would awaken feeling little better rested than when she had gone to bed. For some reason she seemed to be subject more and more to the bad feelings that had plagued her since she was a little girl: the bitter rush of loneliness, the sadness and emptiness, the desperate lack of love and shaking doubt of her own worth. Since she had grown up and married, she had evaded such feelings by flinging herself into the social life of London, dancing and gambling and drinking to escape the dark demons of her youth. But recently the usual remedies had not been working. Her activities merely made her more tired and they enlarged the dark circles under her eyes.

The only remedy was to thicken the heavy white makeup beneath her eyes and pray that in the soft candlelight the smudges would not show. But now, as she looked still closer at her reflection, it seemed to her that she looked not only tired, but also far older than she was; the heavy powder was merely weighing on her skin, pulling it down and creating wrinkles where none existed. Or did none exist? She was only twenty-three, she cried to herself. But, her mind went on relentlessly, wasn't she remembering the way she had looked at seventeen, when she had left her country home for London, taken the season by storm, and ended the year in triumph by marrying England's most eligible bachelor? Six years had passed since then, years of constant late nights with never enough sleep, years haunted by the creditors always nipping at their heels, years tainted by Philip's demands. That lovely, fresh-faced girl had vanished, and in her place sat a hardened, bitter sophisticate, a woman whose knowledge extended far beyond her age, and whose eyes reflected it.

Angrily Lettice whirled away from the mirror. What idiocy she was indulging in—and all because she felt bad about deceiving the American. If only he were not so trusting. He was like a child or a puppy, putting his heart entirely in her hands. Well, the more fool he! He would just have to go back to Boston a little wiser. She could not risk Philip's wrath in order to honor Charles Murdock's silly trust; after all, she had to live with her husband the rest of her life. Besides, what if it was wicked of her to deceive the fellow? Hadn't the Delaplaines been successfully wicked for decades? Why, it was a family tradition, no less. She remembered what Victor used to say when she described her troubled feelings to him: "Bad? My dear Tice, what other way should you feel? We Delaplaines have been an unprincipled lot ever since we came over with the Conqueror and stole land from the poor Saxons. Why, people used to joke that our family motto was 'For ourselves.' Look at your parents—or mine. You might as well own up to it—we always turn out to be the bad apple in the barrel."

Lettice swept from the room and went quickly downstairs to make a last-minute tour of the dining room. Everything had been laid out to perfection. As always, the butler had followed her instructions to the letter, including her order to place Mr. Murdock's name card at the seat next to hers. Then she firmly fixed a slight smile on her face and went toward the drawing room, where Philip was already conversing with the guests that had arrived.

Charles Murdock had been the first to come, and had spent an excruciating half hour with Philip Kenton. He had arrived so unfashionably early that he had spent several minutes cooling his heels all by himself in the entry hall until Kenton came downstairs, his smooth manner covering his irritation that the boor's premature arrival had forced him to complete his toilette in haste.

Murdock had disliked the thin, elegantly dressed Kenton on sight. He had, up till then, rather successfully kept the thought of Lady Lettice's husband out of his mind, but once presented with the man in the flesh, he had to admit his existence and therefore the insuperable impediment he presented to Charles's feelings for Lettice. Moreover, Charles had to face his violation of his own strict moral code: He was lusting after another man's wife. Worst of all, Kenton seemed to him a snake, an oily, evil man. Now Charles could well believe all Sir Edward had told him about the man, and it made his fists clench to think that the lovely Lettice had to endure living with him. Charles thought of her naked beneath Philip's hands, forced to accept his caresses, and he churned with helpless rage. There was nothing he could do. No doubt Lettice had been forced to marry Kenton by her parents; arranged marriages were common among the aristocracy of England. But since she was his wife, no one could protect her from him; Charles could in no way help her to escape.

Of course, Sir Edward would have laughed at that thought and assured him that the lady had no desire to escape her husband. "A matched set," he had called them. But there Edward was wrong, Charles thought. He had to be. Lettice was stunning, yes, but there was something more to her; there must be. Surely there was some sweetness, some goodness in her nature that attracted Charles.

Lettice entered the drawing room, pausing at the doorway for effect, and Charles sprang to his feet, dazzled all over again by her sumptuous beauty. She was dressed in stiff pink brocade, the skirt flattened in front and held out to the sides by a hoop, making her waist appear ridiculously fragile. The boned bodice pushed against her breasts, making them swell alluringly above the square neck of the dress. A diamond drop lay against her bare chest, diamond bobs danced in her earlobes, and here and there a diamond winked in the intricate swirls of her powdered hair.

She spread out her lacquered white-and-gold fan and held it before her mouth in mock embarrassment, her eyes glinting above the lacy semicircle. "Can you ever forgive me?" Her voice implied that they already had, simply because she was charming. "I am horridly late, as always. But then I could hardly appear without trying to make myself pretty for you."

Immediately the men chimed in that she could not help but be lovely, no matter how little time she spent at her dressing table. She gave them a tinkling laugh in recognition of the expected compliment, while her eyes obviously circled the room, as if looking for something. They paused on Murdock, and she smiled.

"Mr. Murdock, how glad I am you came. I was afraid after your most militant remarks the other day, you would not grace a gathering of Englishmen." Her voice was gently teasing and her green eyes sparkled at him.

Charles stepped toward her and said in a low voice, "Madame, I could never harbor any militant feelings toward you."

She touched him playfully on the cheek with her fan. "Why, Mr. Murdock, take care. If you stay here much longer, we shall turn you into a gallant, and then what will they think of you in Boston?"

He laughed. "Doubtless they will think me much improved. I fear many, such as my little sister, find me dreadfully dull."

"Oh, surely not. Dull?" she said, her voice plainly mocking.

Charles flushed and said, "I realize, madame, the sort of appearance I must make. I am not quick of tongue, nor turned out like a dandy, as are most of the men you know.

But I pray that there is finer metal beneath the paint than first appears."

Something softened in her eyes, and there was a hint of wistfulness in her voice as Lettice said, "I am afraid that with most of us, there is only paint and no metal at all beneath it."

For a moment they looked at each other, and it seemed to Charles that the lady's eyes were dark pools of sadness. He moved to take her hand, but they were interrupted by her husband, and behind him a servant with a tray.

"Here, Murdock, try some of this. I vow it is the best wine I've had smuggled in from France yet."

Chagrined at the intimate moment they had been discovered in, Charles took the wine and sipped at it while Lettice resumed her inconsequential chatter. Time and again a servant returned to fill his glass, but Charles was too engrossed in Lettice to bother with drinking, and he turned him away.

As the company moved into the dining room for their dinner, Philip took his wife's arm in a cruel grip and whispered, "What is the matter with you? The fellow has hardly had two glassfuls all evening. Have you lost all your ability to charm?"

"I have tried!" Lettice snapped back. "Whenever the footman comes by, I urge him to fill his glass, but he always refuses. Can I help it if he is a Puritan?"

Philip tightened his grip painfully. "Just try harder. You'd better persuade the oaf to gamble with me, or it will go hard with you, my girl."

Tears started in her eyes at the pain of his grasp, but Lettice said nothing, just nodded her head briefly. At the table, she turned her full charm on the man beside her, listening intently to what he said, showing by her eyes and her very posture that he interested her greatly. In truth, she hardly heard a word Murdock uttered, for all the while her brain was registering the level of his glass and the look of desire in his eyes and the effect of her every move and glance on him. Flirtation was an art in itself, and Lettice could orchestrate an enticing conversation to perfection. There was no room for feeling in the delicate planning she did; a mind racing to analyze a man's desires and reactions and to perform the gestures that would spark his interest had no time for romanticism. Once, as a girl, she'd flirted with excitement; now the only exhilaration in it was the thrill of outwitting another human being.

Although she cunningly kept his glass filled with wine, she could not make him drink much of it, and as the meal progressed, he remained sober. Charles, stunned by his good fortune, had little interest in food or drink. He was completely wrapped up in the woman beside him. She was amusing, charmingly frivolous, and utterly ravishing. When she leaned close to him, the subtle scent she wore was dizzying, and once she accidentally brushed her bosom against his arm; his skin flamed where she had touched it, even through the cloth of his coat. Sweet heaven, but she was delicious—her soft, white breasts, bound by the stiff bodice, always seeming about to burst out of their confinement; the pink mouth that parted slightly in her interest, the lower lip full and sensual, begging to be kissed; the graceful hands, with their long, slender fingers, that slid idly up and down her wine glass until he envisioned them sliding over his skin. No woman had ever affected him like this; halfway through a dinner conversation surrounded by other people, he was stiff and pulsing with passion. At that moment he felt he would gladly have consigned all else to hell, Boston included, to be alone with Lettice and free to make love to her.

After dinner, the group retired to the drawing room for after-dinner drinks and conversation. Lettice, recalling her duty to her other guests, said that she must circulate among them, and left Charles. But wherever she moved, his eyes followed, so intent on her slender form that she held his attention as fully as if she had sat with him, and all the while he ached to have her back. The party broke into small groups of two or three as the evening progressed, and Lettice flitted back and forth among them. It was her intention to let him feel her absence, so that when the gaming started, he would stay to be near her. Once caught up in the game, surely he would be unable to leave. It was always Philip's trick to catch an opponent's interest by letting him win at first.

Her ploy worked. Shortly after she returned to Charles, Philip suggested that they retire to the gaming room. Everyone assented eagerly but Charles. He remembered what Edward had said, and he had no wish to get involved in Philip's nefarious activities. But when he demurred, Lettice turned to him, her large eyes liquid with regret.

"But you can't mean that you are leaving? Please stay, do."

Put to him that way, he could not help but play. He had no desire to leave Lettice, indeed felt that he could not tear himself from her, but if everyone else retired to the gaming room for cards, he could hardly remain and not play. Besides, he doubted that it would do him much harm. Although he might seem a bumpkin to most of these sophisticates, he knew that where cards were concerned, he was their match. At Cambridge, he had been quickly shorn of his allowance when he first came, and after that he had applied himself with his usual diligence to mastering the cards. Through college and his legal studies, he had played cards constantly in his free time, learning to recognize and dodge cheating, and to win routinely.

Tonight he played well and won consistently, for the skill came back to him quickly, even though he had used it little since he'd left England. However, he found himself at a table with Philip and several strangers, while Lettice was at another table. He soon grew impatient, since his only interest in staying was to be near Lettice. Away from her, his head cleared a little, and he recalled that his ship sailed the next morning and it would behoove him to get to bed early. Soon he stood and took leave of his host, gathering up his winnings.

"Come, now, man," Philip said cheerfully, his smile wolfish, "you can't leave while you're winning. Stay, and give us a fair chance to win back some of our coin."

Lettice watched, fascinated, as Murdock refused her husband's blandishments and the cajoling of the others at the table. She had never before seen a person strong enough or canny enough to escape Philip's grasp, and she felt a giggle rising up in her at his defeat. Apparently neither his easy gains nor the opinion of the others at the table could sway him, and a strong spurt of admiration darted through her. He bowed to her, solemnly taking his leave, and his hungry eyes swept over her, as though he wanted to hold her in his mind forever.

On impulse, she sprang up and hurried after him, catching up with him in the entry hall. "Mr. Murdock!"

He turned toward her, and his blue eyes were warm with affection. "Lady Lettice."

"Will I see you again?" She stopped, feeling suddenly, inexplicably shy.

His eyes darkened. "No, I am afraid not. My ship sails tomorrow."

"So soon?" Lettice felt strangely downcast. Without thinking, she said, "Then take this parting gift from me," and she stretched up on her tiptoes to gently brush her lips against his.

At the touch of her mouth, all Charles's restraint crumbled, and his arms shot out to draw her against him. He bent his head to kiss her hard, deeply, passionately, as if to draw her very soul from her. Lettice could feel the trembling of his body against hers, his raging need barely held in check. She had been kissed by other men, but never had she felt a kiss quite like this mingling of violent desire and gentleness. His mouth pressed against hers, warm and velvety, yet brooking no resistance, and she heard a barely suppressed moan from deep within his throat, as though he were torn.

Suddenly he released her and stepped back, his knuckles white as he clenched his fists. For a moment he hung in the balance, his reason fighting the wild hunger within him.

"Really, Murdock, how brash of you," came Kenton's lazy, mocking voice from the doorway, and they both whirled to face him. "You've won our money, insisted on leaving without giving us a chance to get it back, and now I find you fondling my wife. Did no one ever tell you that was rude?"

Lettice felt the color drain out of her face as she looked at her husband. He would take out on her his frustration at Murdock's leaving. A spasm of fear shook her.

"You've spent the evening making sheep's eyes over my wife; the least you could do is grace the poor husband's card table," the mocking voice continued.

Lettice wet her lips nervously and said in a colorless voice, "Yes, please stay."

Charles looked from Kenton to his wife, and suddenly suspicion pierced the haze of desire that had befogged him all evening. Firmly he turned Lettice to face him, and on her coldly set white face, he saw stamped the confirmation of his suspicions.

"So it was true, then, what Edward told me: You are the lure to entice green boys into your husband's net." Anger flushed his face. What a fool he had been, dancing to this lady's tune, naïvely swallowing her bait, so pounding with desire for her—a desire she had cleverly stoked all evening, he could see it now—that he had not seen the wickedness in her, so apparent to others. How could he have believed she was interested in him—great, lumbering, ugly thing that he was! As well believe that she desired a bear or an ox. Why had he not been able to see through her sweet words and clever flirtation? "You lying, deceitful bitch!"

Anger flared in Lettice, and she raised her flushed face to stare at him. "You are a fool and a coward, Mr. Murdock," she said coolly. "A fool to believe I invited you for your *beaux yeux*, and not your fortune. And a coward to run from the settling up."

Hot, black anger coursed through him at her words, and he hated her—hated both of them, the smiling, superficial aristocrats, sneering at him as they led him to the fleecing, laughing scornfully at his honest emotions. Damn them, damn them all—selfishly, blindly following their greed, not caring who was trampled in the process. He wanted suddenly, harshly, to defeat them, to take their game and shove it down their throats. Let the wolves choke on the sheep they thought to devour!

"All right," he said, and his voice was deadly cold. "I will settle up. Let's return to the cards." Abruptly he strode past them back into the card room.

Three

$\mathcal{M}$urdock played shrewdly and calmly, although he seethed with anger. He was possessed of the same collected calculation—driven by flaming hatred but remaining separate from it—that sometimes came upon him in court or in a political discussion with those unfavorable to the colonial view. He saw Lady Lettice, as coldly beautiful as a stone statue, standing behind her husband as he played, and he despised them both with the heat he had earlier felt in desire for her. But his emotions did not interfere with his play; his mind worked like a machine, discovering Kenton's weaknesses and playing upon them, recognizing the methods he used to cheat and cleverly blocking them.

The frustration of the man across from him was tangible as the pile of money in front of Murdock grew larger and his own dwindled. The others at the table gradually dropped out, declaring Murdock too clever for them. But Kenton was like a man obsessed. The irony of losing heavily to the dupe whom he had plotted to shear was too much for his pride to bear, and with each loss he grew more feverish to win. In his frustration and anger, he made mistakes, bet too high a stake for the cards he held, and threw away cards that he should have kept.

They went from whist to faro to loo as the nighttime hours dwindled away, and still the two men faced each other across the table, the only players for some time now, while everyone else crowded around the table to watch. There was little sympathy for the upstart colonial, but at the same time, few felt any pity for Kenton. They had played too often with him and lost, suspecting somehow that he cheated, but not knowing his method. All of them had felt the lash of his scornful tongue, his arrogance, his sarcasm, and there was a fillip of pleasure in seeing him defeated by a bumpkin whom he had plotted to cheat. Even Lettice, who knew she would bear the brunt of her husband's anger at this humiliating defeat, and who would suffer with him the consequences of the financial loss, felt a thrill of pure delight to see someone trounce him so. How gloriously paradoxical it was that the American should beat him after all Philip's miserable plans to lure him into a game. It seemed a fine reward for the way he had forced her to bring Murdock to the cards.

Philip's eyes glittered threateningly as they began their last hand; he was certain he could win this one. The only problem was that his stack of money was too small to bring much of a win; he needed a big wager on this hand to recover a chunk of what he had lost. Given a little time and some of his money back, he was sure he could beat this crude oaf. The luck had been running against him so far; that was all.

Casually he said, "It seems I am temporarily out of funds. May I give you a chit for it?"

Murdock's laugh was short and ugly. "You think I'd

trust a piece of paper with your name on it? I've heard of the worth of your debts, sir. No, thank you."

Kenton raised his brows contemptuously, indicating that he might have suspected such rudeness from a churl like Murdock. He stripped the ruby ring from his finger and held it up to the light. "Then perhaps you would take this bit of jewelry as a pledge. You can see it is a valuable gem, worth far more than the amount I wish to bet."

Charles curled his lip. He was tired, and if he was to get any sleep before the ship left, he needed to return home. Besides, the bitter anger that had driven him had drained away, leaving him cold and sick inside. "No. Haven't you had enough? I won't take everything from you."

The casual contempt in the man's voice stung Kenton past bearing, and he snarled, "Then perhaps you will take something I neither want nor need."

He reached back and grabbed his wife's wrist, pulling her forward abruptly. Charles stared at him in disbelief. At last he said, "You mean—you are putting up your wife as a wager?"

"Why, yes. You seemed to like her well enough earlier this evening. What would you say she's worth to you? A thousand pounds? That sounds fair enough to me. You put up a thousand pounds, and I will put up the fair Lettice."

Lettice swallowed and stared fixedly above Murdock's head, rigid with humiliation. Philip had done many vile things to her, but none so degrading as this: To offer her like an object, an animal or thing, as a wager to a man who despised her, a man whose pride and heart she had cruelly hurt just hours before, and before a roomful of acquaintances, too. Only her pride kept her upright, as it had done when she was a child, frozen in dread and mortification, facing the punishment of her nurse or governess.

Murdock looked from the thin-lipped, arrogant face of Kenton to the woman beside him, who stood as still as a statue, her face revealing nothing. How could any man be so lacking in decency as to subject his wife to this treatment? Or perhaps she did not mind; Edward said she had slept with many men; perhaps she regarded it as no more than an adventure. Revulsion shook him. Did they think themselves so noble, so far above the common herd that anything they chose to do was unquestioningly correct? Or did they do it to gain a little more amusement from him, to laugh at his petty merchant's morals when he refused the bet with horror?

"I hardly think a thousand," Charles said, his tone purposely cutting, "but if that is how you wish to value her, I will accept."

Philip bared his teeth in a thin smile, and picked up his cards. Beside him, Lettice was aware of nothing but a roaring in her ears. Dear God, what was she to do? If the Bostonian won, and he seemed bound to, would he really take her with him? Could he be so cruel, so vengeful? But how silly—of course he could; he was a man after all. Philip would let her go, would throw her out, in fact; she had no doubts there. He would be so angry at his loss that he would hate the sight of her. So she was to be passed from her husband to another man. Oh, he had done it before, but not so publicly. And she was to suffer the very fate that would have awaited her had she refused to lure the American into Philip's clutches!

There was a loud oath from Philip, and his chair turned over with a clatter as he jumped up. "Damn your eyes! I'd swear you are a sorcerer, the way you've won tonight! Take her with you then, and I wish you well of her. I would as well take an icicle to bed!"

A dull flush mounted in Lettice's cheeks, and Murdock was sure that he had never in his life hated a man as much as he hated the sneering Kenton. It was all he could do to keep from leaping across the table and seizing him by the throat. Barely in control, he swung on his heel and left the room, summoning Lettice after him with a brief motion of his hand.

Humiliated further by his summary gesture, Lettice followed him from the house, hating him and all men, but especially Philip. Once outside, Charles walked rapidly and in silence, in too much turmoil to speak. He had been surprised when Lettice followed his gesture, coming to heel behind him like an obedient puppy; he had thought her too proud. But it was becoming more and more obvious to him that he knew her not at all. He wondered if Kenton was feeling any remorse or regret over what he had done. It was hard for Charles to believe that any man would be so nonchalant about sending his wife to a stranger's bed. The more he thought about it, the angrier he grew, at Kenton, at Lettice—and at himself, for the lust that still curled in his abdomen at the thought of bedding her. He wanted her, and he despised her, and he loathed himself for feeling both.

Lettice was too frightened to pay much attention to their surroundings, but when Murdock came to an abrupt halt, she was surprised to see that they were at the door of an inn—and one near the docks, too, if her nose told her anything.

"What is this place? I thought you were staying with Sir Edward?" Lettice said blankly.

"You want me to bring you to my room at Sir Edward's house?" he said coldly. "Is your reputation so worthless that it doesn't matter?"

Lettice glared at him in silence. A fine thing for him to be sneering at her reputation, when he was set on blackening it. Her head high, she stepped past him into the inn.

Murdock must have paid the fellow well, for the innkeeper, with a sly glance at her, showed them to a large, well-kept room. To hide her embarrassment, Lettice strolled to the window and looked down. The inn was indeed close to the docks, for she could see the ships' masts from the window.

"Which is your ship?" she asked, stalling for time to recover and think her way out of this.

"It's the *Sally Blue*. You probably can't see it from here." His tone closed the discussion.

Lettice drew a deep breath and turned to face him. There was no point in hiding now. Murdock still stood across the room from her, leaning casually against the door. His eyes roamed her hungrily, and she tensed herself for his attack.

But unexpectedly he spoke. "Do you do this often?"

"What?" she retorted, her face defiant.

"Sleep with men to pay your husband's debts."

Lettice curled her hands into fists to resist the urge to slap him. "No."

"Why did you do it tonight? Just because it added a little spice to your life?"

"How dare you! I did not do anything. You and Philip arranged this, not I."

"You came with me when I left."

"I had to then. It was a matter of honor."

"Honor?" His voice was derisive. "You call it honorable to commit adultery?"

"Philip gave his word. I could not dishonor a gambling debt."

Murdock snorted with laughter. "You people here have a strange sense of honor, it seems to me. But then, what do I know? After all, I'm just a lout of a colonial. I have no knowledge of the finer things in life—like trying to fleece novices at cards, or seducing a man so your husband can cheat him, or offering your wife's virtue as a wager in a card game."

Lettice wanted to burst into tears at the bitter contempt in his tone, but she bit her lip to stop the trembling and blinked away the moisture. All she had was pride; all she had ever had to sustain her was pride. She had endured Philip, and she had endured the men he had forced upon her. She could endure this one, too.

Charles started toward her, and she saw the dark passion in his eyes. Her fingernails bit deeper into her clenched hand and she shook, but she waited like a trapped animal for her fate. His big, blunt hands came up to rest on her shoulders, and he pulled her to him slowly. Murdock's wide face loomed larger and larger in her vision, and then his mouth was upon hers, the sensual lips digging into hers, hot and insistent, opening her mouth to the possessive touch of his tongue. Lettice felt helpless, smothered in his grasp, and she quivered with revulsion at the thought of his broad hands fumbling at her breasts and squeezing them cruelly as Philip was wont to do. It was all she could do to keep from crying out when his hands slid down her back and one hand crept insidiously around her waist and up to the tender flesh of her breasts, exposed above her gown. But surprisingly, his hand was gentle, and he only teased with his fingertips across the crest of her breasts.

Charles raised his hand and took her chin firmly in its grasp, tilting her head back until she was forced to look into his eyes, and he said harshly, "So, because of your honor, you are now mine to do with as I will. Suppose I take it into my head to take you with me when I sail tomorrow—does your honor stretch that far? Or if I should tire of you and decide to sell you to another, will your honor send you with him? Or is your honor served only by being subject to my command, to undress if I say so, to pleasure me in any way I tell you?"

Lettice could not speak; her mouth felt as dry as cloth, and her heart thudded sickeningly in her chest at his threats. Never had she felt so alone, so helpless. What did he want from her? Did he expect her to beg, to crawl to him? Never would she do that, she told herself, and yet she feared that in another moment she would be on her knees before him.

He searched her face for a moment, and then, with a disgusted sound, flung her away from him. "Go on, get out. Go back to your snake of a husband."

Lettice stared at him in disbelief, unable to stop the shivering that shook her body. "You—you mean, you aren't going to—"

He turned to her, his face thunderous. "Of course I am not going to take you. Did you actually think that I would force you to bed me because your husband was so crude as to wager you in a card game? Good Lord, among all you aristocrats, have you never known a gentleman? Well, no matter what the men of your acquaintance would do, I am not one to terrorize a female. I only wanted to unsettle you a little, to make you look at the consequences of the rash things you do. Perhaps next time you will think twice before you set out to trick a man into loving you."

Lettice hesitated for a moment, then scampered to the door. She turned to look back at him, and wanted desperately to say something to him, to beg his forgiveness, but the words stuck in her throat. Quickly she turned the knob and left.

For a moment Charles stared after her, his heavy-lidded eyes blue pools of pain. Then slowly he drew himself together and followed her. He might as well get his bags from Sir Edward's house and board the *Sally Blue*.

The eastern sky was paling with the approaching sun when Lettice wearily let herself into the house by a side door. She felt unutterably tired and despondent, despite Murdock's generous release, and she thought with longing of leaving her home and going to the country. Perhaps she could coax an invitation out of Jenny Courtland, who was at her country home waiting out her pregnancy. She and Jenny were not the fastest of friends, but doubtless the poor thing was bored to tears there and would be grateful for some company. Or she might go up to Grenwil and join her mother, although it was all too likely that they would be at each other's throats within a few days' time. But she must go somewhere; she could not stand another day here.

Softly she went up the stairs and down the hall toward her room. No doubt Philip was either gone from the house or soundly sleeping in his room, but she did not wish to take the chance of his hearing her and waking up. She was far too tired to deal with him—and far too awash emotionally. All kinds of strange feelings were alive inside her—gratitude at Murdock's releasing her, yet anger that, knowing he would release her, he had frightened her so; fear and horror as she had hurried home through the dock area of London, sidestepping sleeping beggars and tramps; hatred of her husband and the cruelties he inflicted on others; vague dislike of herself and her life; a longing to be different, to be away. She was desperately confused, but too tired and frightened to sit down and try to sort out what she felt. All she wanted to do was sleep; things would be better in the morning.

However, she was not to be so lucky. As she tiptoed past his door, Philip whipped it open and stood looking at her, his gray eyes as icy as death.

"So, he sent you back," he said, and laughed cruelly. "He found he did not want you after all, eh? No doubt he liked your coldness no better than I."

Anger welled up in Lettice and she snapped, "Oh, shut up, Philip. He let me go because, unlike you, he is a gentleman."

"A gentleman! That scrubby merchant? Don't make me laugh."

"Jewels and satins don't make a pig into a gentleman."

His nostrils flared at her remark, and one hand flashed

out to take her wrist tightly in his grip. "Come in here, Lettice. I want to talk to you."

Fear touched her eyes, and she held back. "No, please, Philip. I'm tired. Haven't you done enough tonight?"

"No, not nearly enough. You see, you have gotten us truly in a fix. The creditors were beating down our doors before, but now we haven't got a shilling to our name. We need to make some plans, my girl."

"*I* have gotten us into a fix! It was you who insisted on playing cards with Murdock. I was against it, if you will remember."

"*You* did not do as I instructed, and get him fuzzy with drink. And you sat down at another table, instead of hanging over him and distracting him. And then you revealed our trickery to him."

Philip pulled her inside, his voice hissing her wrongs. Lettice tried to pull free of him, but he was too strong for her. With a solid click, the door closed, and Philip locked it, then dropped the key into his pocket. A dry sob caught in her throat. After everything else, she did not think she could take Philip's hurtful lovemaking.

"I am sending you to Sir Harold," he said peremptorily. "Doubtless he will give me enough cash for your favors that I can flee to the Continent."

"The Continent?" Lettice repeated dully.

"Yes, the Continent. God, Lettice, what is the matter with you? If I remain here, I will be in debtors' prison. Don't you understand? We are completely, utterly destitute!"

"The jewels . . ." she murmured.

"Oh, Lord, Lettice, you know they're all paste. Every

damn one of them is a glass imitation of something we've already pawned. We haven't a thing that's real."

"Yes, that is true, isn't it?" Lettice said vaguely, staring past him. "There is nothing about us that is real, is there?"

His voice was acid with irritation. "What on earth is wrong with you? This is no time to go soft on me. Pull yourself together, girl. No matter what else, you've always been a game one up till now. Don't turn into a witless ninny when I need you!"

"I am all right, Philip."

"Good. You'd better be. Now, listen to me: Go pack a few of your more enticing frocks and meet me at the stables. It's almost dawn, and I want to get away before the collectors start pounding at our door. Soon the servants will be all over the place and they'll see us fleeing. The less they know, the better."

"And where are we going?" Her voice was grim.

"To Sir Harold's, as I just told you. Now, hurry up."

"No, I won't go."

"What do you mean?" he said, his voice dangerously low.

"I will not do it. I will not go to live with Sir Harold like some cheap tramp. I am tired of it, Philip, and I refuse to do it anymore. I am not some mare to be sold by you to your despicable friends."

"Damn it, I am your husband, and you will do as I say!"

"No, I will not! Don't you understand, Philip? You cannot make me. You can divorce me and cause the biggest scandal you want, but I will not do it. You can starve me or beat me or haul me up before the magistrate for wifely disobedience, but I still will not do it. And more than that, I will tell everyone what it is you want me to do—friends, judge, people on the street. I don't care any longer! I'll make your name stink to high heaven—" Her voice rose hysterically, and was abruptly cut off as Philip lashed out with his hand and slapped her hard across the cheek, sending her stumbling backward.

"Damn you, I'll teach you to defy me!" her husband roared, his face white with fury, his eyes glittering cruelly. "By God, by the time I'm through with you, you'll be begging to be sent to Sir Harold!"

He struck out at her again, and Lettice dodged the blow, darting to the door, only to find it locked. And the key was in his pocket! There was no escape! Like an animal at bay, she turned and faced him as he charged at her. Fighting now for her very survival, she defended herself by attacking. Doubling over, she ran straight into him, and, by the very unexpectedness of her attack, bowled him over. The blow enraged him past reason, and Philip ran to the wall and seized his riding crop from where it hung. Lettice ran from him with the terror of one facing the insane, but he was quickly upon her, raining down blows with the small whip, slicing into her heavy brocade dress and splitting the skin of her arms and hands as she tried to shield her face. With an oath, he brought the whip down on her head by the wrong end, stunning her with the knob of the handle.

Lettice sagged weakly, and Philip seized her by the throat, his long fingers digging into her neck, and shook her hard, again and again. She struggled wildly, gasping ineffectually for air, then threw herself against him so that they staggered back, crashing into his small desk. Her lungs were on fire, and black spots danced before her eyes: around the edges of her vision, a red mass was growing and spreading. She realized with astonishment that he was actually killing her in his rage, and somewhere in her mind she laughed that she should come to such an end, even as she beat wildly at his head with her fists.

He bent her back over the desk, and Lettice helplessly felt the redness obscuring her vision, felt herself slipping away into eternal blankness, and then her faintly flailing hands touched cold, hard stone. Her fingers curled around it and her hand flew up, crashing into her husband's head. The grip on her throat eased slightly, and she struck again and again, sometimes missing, but hitting him once, twice. . . . Suddenly the pressure on her throat was gone, and sweet, blessed air rushed into her tortured lungs. She pulled herself up from the desk, her head spinning, her vision still unclear, and the roaring in her ears growing stronger. Hardly knowing what she was doing, she staggered toward the door and grasped the cold knob, and slowly she sank to the floor. She was fainting, she knew, or was it that she was still dying?

Curled up into a ball, she fought the weakness, and slowly it subsided, leaving her cold and nauseated, her head still numb and confused. But at least the room was no longer whirling around her, and thought penetrated her brain. The door was locked, and the key was still in Philip's pocket, she remembered. It terrified her to go to him, for he might come to and attack her again, but she knew she had to or be trapped in this room with him. On her hands and knees, she crawled across the floor to where he lay sprawled on the elegant Aubusson carpet. With shaking fingers, she dug into his pockets, not daring to look at his face. At last her hand closed on the cold metal of the key, and she pulled it from his pocket. She could escape now to her own room and lock the door against him. His head would doubtless ache when he came to, but perhaps he would have returned to rationality.

For the first time, she stole a glance at Philip's face, and what she saw chilled her. His face was covered with blood; two great bloody spots stained his wig, and a gash ran across his forehead, thick and sticky with blood. His face was ashen, and his pupils rolled back. Lettice felt bile rising in her throat, and she clamped her hand across her mouth, fighting against the nausea. She looked down at his chest and saw no rise and fall. Dear God! She swallowed hard. She had killed him!

Four

For a long moment, Lettice knelt beside the body, paralyzed, and then she began to tremble violently. She looked down at her hands, and for the first time saw her husband's blood on them. Frantically, she wiped them against her skirt, but she could not get it all off. What was she to do? What was she to do? Hysterical sobs began to rise in her throat. How could he have died from her blows?

Her eyes fell on her weapon, which lay beside the body: the heavy Carrara marble paperweight that Philip kept upon his desk. Doubtless that was heavy enough to crack a man's skull. *But I did not mean to,* she cried inside. *It was just that he was trying to kill me! I had to do it!*

But who would believe that? And who would help her even if they did? She scrambled to her feet, her mind racing. She knew she stood no chance here in England. Philip's grandfather, the Duke, was a powerful man, and Philip was his only heir. He had disapproved of Philip's ways, but she also knew that he would not rest until he avenged the blow to his family. He had always hated her, anyway, blaming Philip's wildness on his connection with the Delaplaine family, who had always been wicked. No, the Duke would have no pity on her; he would move heaven and earth to see that she was hanged for murder. And who was to say that her story was true? No one had witnessed their quarrel and the ensuing struggle; the servants were all safely away in their rooms. But there were ample witnesses to what Philip had done last night in a drunken rage, and they would all report the humiliation he had brought upon her, humiliation enough to cause a wild, proud soul like herself to return and murder him.

Quickly, quietly, she moved to the door and unlocked it, then stepped outside and relocked it with trembling fingers. She darted softly into her own room and began to tear off her dress and many petticoats, her brain buzzing, trying to come up with a plan. She must escape, she knew that. She could catch a ship to the Continent—but no, that was not far enough away. The authorities would be bound to catch her. The Duke had quite a bit of influence in France, as well. First things first: She would dress up as a boy; that would enable her to move more freely, and keep her from being recognized. She had done it before, just a few days ago, a wild lark with Victor, and she still had the boy's costume she had had made up for herself.

She flung herself haphazardly into the thin, white lawn shirt and black satin breeches, pulling on white stockings and black, buckled shoes, and then donning the heavy, loose-hanging brocade coat that did much to disguise her soft, rounded form. She had no time to fix her hair or face; thank God men wore the same heavy white powder on their faces. She jammed the hat down firmly over her hairdo, hiding all her hair, and pinned it securely in place. Over the costume she flung a long black cloak, and she was ready.

For a moment she paused, glancing all around the room. Was this all? Was her life so easily left? She had no money to speak of, or any real jewels. She had nothing, in fact, but herself.

Lettice picked up her key, tossed Philip's key on the floor, and left the room, locking the door behind her. That should slow things down a bit. The servants were not likely even to try their doors before noon; they knew their master and mistress's hours, and knew too their tempers when awakened. Then the locked doors would cause them more long hours of indecision before finally someone took the initiative to send for a locksmith. She would be far away by that time.

But where? Even as she slipped down the stairs and out the front door, mindful of the servants already stirring in the kitchen, she still did not know where she was to go. Her cousin? No, Victor was good for a lark, but she did not trust him to see her through something like this. Grenwil? No, that would be the first place anyone would look for her. For the same reason, her closest friends were useless.

Then suddenly she remembered the American and his kindness in letting her go. Oh, he had teased her and frightened her, to be sure, but when it came down to it, he had not hurt her. And his desire for her had been obvious, until he discovered Philip's plan. Might he not help her through kindness—or in return for her favors? He certainly had no reason to feel any liking for Philip. And the colonies would be the perfect place to escape to.

They would never find her so far away. It was said that countless criminals had escaped there.

Her heart leaped, and she hurried toward the docks, keeping her hat low over her forehead, and trying not to arouse the interest of the sleepy people who moved through the early-morning streets, cleaning off the sidewalks, opening up their shops, laying their wares out for sale in their carts to be peddled through the streets.

When she reached the docks, she almost despaired of finding the *Sally Blue*. Mast after mast stretched before her; the docks were huge, and it would take her hours of going from ship to ship to find the right one. By that time, it would probably have already sailed.

Then, pitching her voice low, and summoning up every ounce of haughtiness she possessed, she called out to a passing lad, "Here, you, where is the *Sally Blue*? A colonial vessel out of Boston."

The boy regarded her with a surly look for a moment, and then said, "About six ships down," jerking his thumb in the proper direction. Lettice barely nodded at him, as a young blade would, and proceeded in the direction he had shown her. As she drew closer, her heart pounded in her chest. What if it had already sailed? But then her eye caught the name *Sally Blue* in fading paint on the prow of a ship. She had reached it.

Knees weak with relief, she went up the gangplank, both hands firmly on the rope. Unused as she was to ships, the sway of the vessel and the narrow, steeply rising walkway made her feel desperately unsure of her footing.

On board, she paused, uncertain where to turn, and not wanting to draw attention to herself by asking. The ship was a hive of activity, with men scurrying about on the sails like cats, and no one threw even a glance her way. She preferred it that way, but she also needed to find Charles Murdock. Casually, she sauntered over to what appeared to be a doorway, and found steps leading down to a narrow passageway. Below, she found herself in a short hall with several closed doors. Any one of these, she supposed, could be Murdock's quarters. She knocked timidly at one and received no answer, then proceeded to the opposite one, and so on down the hall. Silence greeted her until the fourth door she tried, and there she heard the familiar nasal tones of Charles Murdock, telling her to enter. With a sigh of relief, she opened the door and stepped inside.

To say that Charles Murdock was surprised to see Lady Lettice Kenton entering his room in a young man's garb would have been a supreme understatement. He had settled into his quarters and was undressing to crawl into his bunk when the knock sounded, and the last person he expected to see enter the door was Lady Lettice. He had imagined she was home fast asleep, blissfully oblivious to his departure. No doubt it would be some time before he could think of the woman without a churning cauldron of emotion inside him, but he was certain that *she* was more than happy to see the last of him. So, to turn and see a stripling lad who tilted his head and pushed back the brim of his hat to reveal the face of Lettice Kenton stunned him past speech. Could this be some outlandish charade?

Then the apparition spoke, and the soft, musical tones of Lady Lettice convinced him that he was not mistaken:

"Hello, Mr. Murdock. Pray, do not look so amazed. It is just me, Lettice."

"What in the hell—" Charles began, then remembered that he was undressing when she came in and was clothed in nothing but his trousers. Blushing, he broke off and hastily put his shirt on.

Even in her predicament, a giggle bubbled up from Lettice at the sight of the huge man reddening like a schoolgirl and covering his naked torso modestly. Her laughter made the flush rise even higher in his face.

"Just what are you doing here, Lady Lettice?" he said stiffly. "This joke may rebound on you if you aren't careful; we are due to set sail any moment."

"But that is what I want," Lettice said soberly, cursing herself for that silly, half-hysterical laugh—there was nothing to be gained by setting his back up. "I have come to ask you to take me with you."

His brows drew together thunderously. "I have had enough of your mockery. I warn you, you should learn to curb these adolescent escapades of yours."

She wet her lips nervously. "No, please, Mr. Murdock, I am serious. Have pity on me. I—I am in grave danger, and I must flee the country. I need to go to the colonies immediately. Please take me with you. Hide me; help me to escape."

"Escape? Danger?" Murdock snorted. "You must think me a total fool. Get out of here, please, or I shall have to eject you forcibly."

"No, you don't understand!" Lettice cried, her voice teetering on the edge of hysteria. "Don't send me away! They will hang me! You can't, you can't be so cruel."

Murdock glowered at her suspiciously. He knew she

must be lying, playing some idiotic trick on him, no doubt for a bet, but her voice was so plaintive that he could not but hear her out.

"What are you talking about? Here, make some sense. Pull yourself together."

Lettice clasped her hands together tightly, fighting for control. She had to convince him to let her come; this was the most important task she had ever undertaken.

"I—I killed my husband."

"What!" Murdock exclaimed. This had to be a jest—or else the girl had gone mad.

"He was quite angry when I returned home. He blamed me because I did not get you drunk or distract you while you played. He said that we were penniless after his loss to you—"

"Oh, so that is what it is," Charles said, his voice heavy with sarcasm. "You came to persuade me to give the money back."

"No! That isn't it at all!" Lettice cried. "We quarreled terribly, and he was vile, as always. And he said that he had to flee the country to escape his creditors. He said that—well, that doesn't matter. What matters is that I defied his will, and he grew insanely angry. He attacked me with his riding crop. He knocked me almost unconscious, and then he began to choke me. Here, see!" Lettice pulled off her gloves and held out her slender white hands to show the bloody welts where his whip had hit her. "And here." She untied her cloak and pulled open the neck of the shirt to expose her neck, blotched by the purpling bruises Philip's hands had caused.

"My God," Charles breathed with horror and reached

out to touch the livid marks, then snatched his hand away as though her skin burned him.

"I managed to pick up a marble paperweight on his desk, and I hit him on the head—more than once. I did not mean to kill him, but I could not breathe. He was killing me in his rage. So I hit him, and he let go, and then I saw that he was dead."

Lettice stood before him, white as paper and trembling, bruised and broken, and suddenly he longed to take her in his arms and comfort her, to kiss and caress away her pain, and assure her that he would protect her. But he steeled himself against the treacherous feeling; that was disaster, and he knew it—she had pulled the wool over his eyes before. She was a clever actress, and she was heartless.

"It sounds to me as if you acted in self-defense then. Why not go back and face up to it? I can't imagine a judge and jury executing a beautiful woman like you for defending herself against an insane husband who was trying to murder her."

"You don't understand. I have no money and no power. My family has social position, true, but no influence and no wealth. Besides, everyone knows that we Delaplaines have always been a bad lot; we've provided England with more than one juicy scandal over the years. No one saw what happened; we were alone, and the servants were asleep. Why should anyone take my word? Why not think I murdered him for the insult he handed me last night? His grandfather hates me; he says *I* ruined Philip." She laughed shortly, scornfully. "As if Philip could be ruined; he was utterly corrupt when I married him. But the Duke would make sure the courts pursued me with a vengeance. I know he would get me; I know it. That is why I have to flee."

"Don't be a fool," he said shortly, to hide his emotions. "If you leave the country, everyone will be convinced that you murdered him. 'Why else would she run like that?' they will say. The smartest thing to do is to stay and face them down."

"That's easy for you to say! You are not the one who will feel the noose. And you don't know his grandfather as I do. There is no way I could win against him. I am lost if you refuse to help me. Lost!"

He looked at her, his face set and closed against her, and she felt as though the ground were giving way beneath her feet. He did not mean to help her. He was going to send her away. Then what could she do? She was lost, helpless! The horrors of what she had just gone through—the emotional earthquake she had felt, the physical punishment and nearness of death, the accidental killing of her husband—boiled to the surface, breaking her fragile control. Suddenly, hysterically, she began to cry; bitter, wracking sobs tore through her slender body, and she sank to her knees, weeping as though her heart would break.

"Please, I beg of you. I have never begged in my life, but I beg of you now: Please don't leave me here. Take me, save me. I shall die here, I know it. Isn't this enough salve to your pride—that I am broken and begging before you? I promise you, I will do anything you ask, if only you will save me. I'll be your mistress, if you want it, or your servant. Please, please . . ." Her words strangled in sobs.

Charles could not bear the sight of her crumpled on the floor, abject with hopelessness. Without thinking, he went to Lettice and pulled her up, cradling her gently in his arms. Tenderly he rocked her, his hands stroking her back, his voice murmuring reassurances. Slowly her sobs subsided, and she grew still in his arms.

"Now, I want you to lie down. You are safe here, I promise. I can feel the ship moving underneath us; that means we are already underway. You will be safe. Just lie down and try to sleep."

He guided her to the lower berth, which he had already turned down for himself, and set her down. Then he knelt to remove her heavy shoes, and took her coat and hat off and tossed them aside. Like a puppet she lay back at his command, exhausted from her storm of weeping, and he pulled the covers up over her. Lettice did not notice the flinch of his hand when it grazed her breast through the thin lawn shirt as he adjusted the blanket. Quickly, he snatched his hand away and stood looking down at her, as her weary eyelids drooped and closed. In an instant she was asleep.

Lettice slept nearly the whole day, lulled by the rocking of the ship and a new, peaceful feeling of security. So soundly did she sleep that when she awoke she had no idea where she was; she started in fear in the strange, dark cabin. Then she remembered, and relaxed. She had escaped, and was safely on her way to America. She thought about the events of the night before; they seemed almost unreal now, after her sleep. It was impossible that she could have killed Philip. But she knew it was no dream; it had happened, and she felt sick at the thought. Not that Philip was any loss to humanity; there was no one who would truly mourn him. But the fact that she had actually killed another human being made her shudder; never would she have imagined it possible. Remembering the thud of the stone against his head, the sight of his face covered with blood, made her feel queasy and lost, as though she were a stranger to herself.

The soft sound of breathing in the berth above her reminded Lettice that the American was there, too. Thank heavens he had not shared this double-berthed cabin with another passenger, and thank heavens, too, that they would not have to share a bed—unless, of course, that was the price he demanded for his help. Tiny doubts began to nag at her: Had she done the right thing to flee? Might it not have been easier to have stayed and faced it out, as Murdock had suggested? After all, she was persuasive, and she did have the truth on her side. Surely people would realize that if she had meant to murder Philip, it would have been far easier to shoot him with one of his dueling pistols than to attack a man far larger than she with a paperweight.

Having fled, had she gotten herself into worse trouble? For one thing, she had to face the prospect of a long sea voyage with a man who desired her and held great power over her. There was no doubt in her mind that he would demand her body in return for his help. And when they reached the colonies, she would be alone, friendless and penniless. How was she to keep from starving to death? Poor women managed to keep alive somehow, she knew, but she had not the skills for employment. She had never cooked or cleaned a day in her life, nor had she learned how to sew anything but dainty embroidery. Charm, good looks, and a witty tongue were good only for catching a husband. Doubtless she could easily ensnare some bucolic oaf, but she dreaded the thought of tying herself to another man, particularly some colonial. And how would she live until she found someone and inveigled him to the altar? Well, there was always beggaring and whoring, which were far worse than marrying, even. Perhaps Murdock would be so pleased with her that he would make her his mistress, but that seemed a miserable way to eke out her life, always at some man's beck and call, without even the privileges of a wife.

Her head ached, and her eyes were puffy and sore from crying. She hated the way she had broken down in front of Murdock. No doubt he had loved to see her so debased. It wounded her pride to think that she had cried in front of him, collapsed before him in utter despair. Her insides twisted with hot shame as she imagined what her mother and father would have said at such a display. She remembered crying once because she had wanted her mother to stay at Grenwil for her birthday instead of going back to London, and she had received a blistering setdown from her parents. The worst sin for a Delaplaine was a common display of emotion. And here she had completely exposed herself in front of a man who no doubt greatly enjoyed her shame.

For a moment she wished angrily that she had not been such a fool as to come, and then she thought of Philip's bloody face, and knew that her choice had been the right one. The Duke would not rest until she hanged. Surely she could endure a little humiliation to escape Newgate and the scaffold.

Cautiously she eased out of bed; the floor rocked most peculiarly under her feet. She felt violently hungry, but nauseated at the same time. Lettice sighed and sat down again; she had never been a good sailor. She had gone once to France, and that choppy ride across the Channel had convinced her that ships were not her preferred mode of conveyance. Even Paris had not held a great enough allure to draw her back over the water. Friends had told her that the Channel crossing was worse than the open sea, but from the way her stomach was beginning to feel, she had her doubts. Oh, Lord, she could not be sick for days in front of Murdock! How farcical. How maddening!

Above her, Charles awoke at her stirring and sat up. "Lady Lettice?" It seemed absurd to share a cabin with her and address her so formally.

"*What?*" Her voice was harsh with annoyance at the way she felt.

Charles grimaced and swung down lithely onto the floor. He was beginning to think he had been played for a fool. The more he thought about it, the wilder the lady's story seemed. Before he had drifted off to sleep, it had occurred to him that it was all a piece of fine acting, and that she had left her husband after a tiff, vowing to make him regret what he had done. If her story *was* true, and if the Duke was so powerful, then doubtless they would track her down even in Boston, and her fleeing would have proclaimed her guilt. And now he would be an accomplice to it. It could even be that she had cold-bloodedly murdered Kenton; nothing in his experience with her would support her story. It was not at all unlikely that he would be seized by the British authorities for abetting the escape of a murderer, or at least for abduction of a nobleman's wife! That would be a fine predicament; he would be a disgrace to himself and the whole colonial cause.

Irritably, he groped to the stove and, fumbling in the dark, struck his flint to tinder, igniting the fire. Even in summer, the North Atlantic was chilly in the evening. He took a cone of paper and lit it, then lit two candles. The muted light that had earlier entered through the porthole was gone, and Charles guessed that it must be evening.

In the flickering light of the candle, Lettice looked awful. Her powdered hair, through sleep and the rough treatment it had received, had escaped its careful moorings here and there, and hung straggling untidily about her face. The heavy white makeup she used was old and caked, streaked with her tears. She looked not a beautiful sophisticate but a ragged whore.

"I spoke to the captain about you. I said you were a lad who was an acquaintance of my brother, and that with all the trouble between England and home, you had fled your school and begged me to let you return home with me. I said you were in fear, on account of having run away from school, and would not be showing your face. It seems an idiotic enough story, but he believed me." His voice turned bitter as he went on. "Of course, he has no reason to think I would lie to him. I was a very honest man until I met you."

His words stung Lettice, and she said baldly, "Well, I imagine you will extract full payment from me in bed for your help."

"Damn it, I told you I was not the miserable cur of a male that you are used to. I would not use a woman's helplessness against her." Murdock's irritation was only fanned by her attitude. Why, she acted as though *he* were forcing *her* to accompany him. "Besides, the way you look, believe me, I have no desire to bed you. Here, look at yourself!"

Angrily, he grasped her shoulder and pulled her to the small looking glass on the wall, forcing Lettice to peer at her face up close. His voice was heavy with disgust as he said, "It is a crime, what you have done to yourself. You've abused that lovely flesh of yours, going like a whore from one man to another. Once, God knows, you must have had real beauty, but you cover it up with paint and powder. Do you even know any longer what color your hair is?"

Lettice swallowed against the nausea and rising tears. His words slashed at her pride, and she hated him for it. Damn him, what did he know of what she had done and what she had had to do?

"Puritan," she said sneeringly. "No doubt beauty is a sin where you come from. And no doubt you always preach to women while you make whores out of them."

"You did that to yourself, milady, not I." His blunt face hovered close above her, distorted with fury and other emotions he could hardly name. "I have some demands to make on you, Lady Lettice, that is true. But they do not include sharing my bed. I have never taken an unwilling woman, and I never shall. Perhaps I am crazy—I must have been to let you talk me into hiding you—but when I met you in London, and this morning when you wept on the floor like a child, I thought I glimpsed something good, something fine somewhere beneath all that paint and dissipation. No doubt it was a pipe dream, but I intend to find out. By God, if there is anything worthwhile left in you, I'll discover it on this journey. I am going to try to turn you into a decent woman."

Lettice gasped at his effrontery, and her green eyes blazed. She forgot her rebellious stomach as she launched into a vivid, oath-spattered diatribe against Murdock's manners, character, family, and looks. Grimly, he grasped her by the shoulders and pulled her over to the washstand, where he splashed water from the pitcher into the washbowl. He dug one hand firmly into the hair at the back of her head and shoved downwards into the cold water, effectively choking off her comments. When he pulled her head back up she was sputtering and gasping in outrage. He wet a washrag, applied soap, and set to scrubbing every last vestige of makeup from her face. By the time he rinsed her face in the same unceremonious way, her skin was flushed and stinging from the scrubbing, and she was too angry to speak.

Satisfied with his work so far, he began on her hair, ruthlessly tearing the pins from it and tossing aside the paper rolls and hair pieces added to give it height. Charles grabbed up his hairbrush and roughly pulled it through her hair, bringing bright tears of pain to her eyes. Lettice, rigid with fury, endured it silently, but silently vowed that this upstart would pay for his handling of her. When at last he had brushed most of the powder from her hair, he bent her again over the basin and wet her long hair thoroughly, then soaped it up and rinsed it. With a thick towel, he rubbed her hair furiously, then stepped back.

"Here," he said shortly, handing her the brush. "Dry it by the fire, or you'll catch cold."

She snatched the brush from him, stalked to the small

iron stove, and began to brush the knots from her long, fine hair, pointedly staring past him as she worked. Charles watched her, a knot in his throat that he could not seem to swallow. Free of the makeup, her face was beautiful, flushed from her anger and the rough washing. He saw the color of the hair that he had longed to know: Wet, it was golden, and as it dried and separated, it became a pale silvery gilt; not gold, not white, not silver, but a delicate, subtle combination of all three. Brushed and dried, it was the texture of fine silk cascading across her shoulders and down her back.

Never had Lettice looked so desirable to him as she did now, standing defiantly by the fire in the boy's garb that showed off her long, slender legs and let her full, ripe breasts be seen through the thin lawn, with her hair shining down her back, and the natural, clean lines of her face naked to his eyes. He felt desire thickening in him, and hoped shamefacedly that she would not notice. For all his rough words, here he was, as quickly stirred by her as a schoolboy. She had called him Puritan, but he was not, and right now he felt little religious impulse at all. The only thing that kept him from her was the scorn he knew she would heap on him and the stern sense of fairness that he had always held. He would not prey upon the weak. But, oh, how he cursed himself for making her loveliness shine forth more than ever, and turning his situation into a pure, living hell for the rest of the voyage.

Five

Even her pride could not contain the queasiness that gnawed at Lettice's stomach. The fact that she had not eaten that day did nothing to improve her nausea, but the very thought of food made her feel even sicker. By the time she finished drying her hair and calmed down enough to think of a few remarks to set Mr. Murdock back on his heels, her roiling stomach betrayed her. She cast an agonized glance at her companion, then made a dash for the washbasin.

When at last the spell of nausea was through, she wiped her damp face with the washrag and staggered weakly to her berth, too ill and ashamed to do anything else. No doubt, after that display, he regretted ever letting her come aboard; she was certain any man would be thoroughly disgusted and would lose whatever desire he might have felt for her.

To her surprise, he came to her and knelt by the bed, his hard face softer with compassion. Gently he brushed the hair from her forehead, and his hand slipped back to rub her neck.

"Why did you not tell me you were ill? I would not have handled you so roughly. Don't worry, it's just a little seasickness. It quite often happens to people their first day out. Before long, you'll get your sea legs, and then you'll feel fine, I assure you. The best thing for you to do is just relax and try to sleep a little."

Her seasickness lasted for several days, and Lettice found during that time that she frequently wished she were dead. At other times, she decided that she was already dead and had gone to hell. Patiently Murdock nursed her: holding her head while she was sick, wiping her face with a damp, soothing cloth, murmuring reassurances to her when she moaned that she was dying, spooning broth into her mouth whenever she could swallow it.

Had she felt strong enough, Lettice would have been shocked at his behavior. She had never imagined any man would do such things for her; seeing her so unlovely, so horribly human and unmysterious, most men would have abandoned her. She certainly could not imagine Philip or any of her admirers nursing her so competently and without complaint or revulsion. Yet this man, whom she had betrayed and who had shortly before treated her with such cold, rough familiarity—nay, such dislike and disgust—now nursed her tenderly, with never a word of reproach or a gesture of revulsion.

Charles had lived with too many childhood upset stomachs and seen too much seasickness to be offended by her illness. He was a practical man, and it never occurred to him to do anything but help the poor woman as much as he could. He had always had compassion for the weak and helpless.

Gradually the illness lessened; she was able to hold her food down for longer and longer periods of time, and even the nausea subsided. Finally she awoke from a nap to realize that, though she felt weak as a kitten, her stomach was calm. Wanly she smiled, relief flooding her, and announced that she was hungry. Murdock smiled back at her, and for the first time Lettice noticed how his smile lightened his features and made his plain face more appealing.

Another day or two of fortifying meals brought her back to her full strength, and with her returning health came a flood of memories. She marveled at Murdock's kindness to her during her illness and blushed to remember how weak and vulnerable she had been; she could recall begging him to help her and holding on to his hand as if it were a lifeline. He had seen her at her very worst: when she was sick as a dog, when she was frightened and fleeing for her life, when she tricked him into playing cards with Philip. No doubt he thought her capable of nothing but deceit and weakness, and again she found this thought made her angry with him, as though he had somehow connived to make her betray herself. She recalled, too, the rough way he had treated her before she got sick, washing her face and hair as though she were a recalcitrant, dirty urchin, reviling her and telling her that he would make her "a decent woman."

Who was he, she thought contemptuously, to tell her how she ought to look and act? After all, she was Lady Lettice Kenton, a leader of London society, while he was nothing but a bumptious, ill-dressed colonial! She looked at him where he sat across the room, engrossed in reading a book. He was as plain as ever, a square-faced brute without a tenth of the charm or looks or elegance of a Delaplaine; why, her cousin would make him look like a jester. And, yet, something formed in her chest, like a great block of ice, and she felt a strange, swirling horror of regret and pain and loneliness, and she fought an urge to burst into tears.

"I am bored!" With those words she jumped into the cavernous silence, more to still the tumult inside her than out of a desire to converse.

Murdock looked at her inquiringly. Lettice sat on her berth, still pale from her sickness, her features molded into a look of hauteur. He sighed, for the millionth time wondering what in the world he was to do with her. She was beautiful and deplorably alluring in her close-fitting boy's garb. He could not be unaware of the shape of her long legs in their breeches or of the full breasts that pressed against the thin white shirt; truth was, he could think of little else. Looking at her now, her pale blond hair tousled and free-flowing, her soft underlip drooping a little petulantly, her great green eyes dark with feeling, he wondered how he would ever make it through this journey. It was the subtlest of tortures to be confined in a small cabin with the most desirable woman he had ever met and to know that she considered him a rustic fool.

And as if that were not bad enough, she was also a selfish, vain, spoiled aristocrat, who probably looked upon him as something of a servant who ought to provide for her and keep her entertained. He dreaded the thought of spending weeks with a vapid, foul-tempered, self-centered English lady. In his anger, he had vowed to bring out something decent in her; in the cold light of day, he had to admit to himself that there was probably nothing there to be brought out. However, he certainly did not intend for her to get the upper hand in this situation; he would not play peasant to her proud noble.

If he gave in to her now, it would be hell to pay the rest of the trip; she might as well get a taste of what things were to be like.

"I am afraid that is of little concern to me, Lady Lettice. You are the one who asked to come on this long voyage, and you shall have to entertain yourself," he replied coldly and went back to his book.

Lettice stared at him, amazed at his rudeness. Doubtless he had decided to get his sweet revenge on her by being as openly disagreeable as he could be; probably he hoped to make her cry or crawl to him for kindness. Well, he would soon find out what sort he was dealing with. She had brought more than one man to heel.

Humming softly, she rose from her berth and crossed the room to pick up his hairbrush. He purposely kept his eyes on the pages of the book and so did not see Lettice stealthily undo the first button on her shirt. Slowly, languorously, she began to pull the brush through her long, silken hair, and the crackle of each stroke pierced Murdock like a knife. He would not look at her, but he imagined the brush sweeping through her long hair, and the thought set him afire. He sat as taut and aware of her graceful body as if she had undressed before him. She was teasing him, he knew, using her sensual power over him to get her way, and suddenly he realized that he was doing precisely what she wanted, forcing himself not to look and by that very act proving how totally, longingly aware of her he was.

So he looked up, his face calm and slightly derisive, and settled himself comfortably in his chair to watch her. He let his gaze wander over her without restraint, enjoying the luscious curves of her body, the grace of her stance and movement, the beauty of her hair tumbling like liquid fire across her shoulders. He noted that she had unbuttoned the top of her shirt, so that the tops of her breasts peeked temptingly above the cloth. Now she bent over to brush her hair up from the back, and he could see the full swell of her ripe breasts, barely contained by the shirt.

His mouth was dry and hot, and his hands ached to reach out and touch her, but he kept his voice cool and unconcerned as he said, "Why, thank you, my dear, what a splendid show. I never expected you to keep me so well entertained."

Lettice stopped, nonplussed. Instead of turning him hot and begging, as she had planned, he had merely enjoyed the display of her body—as if she were trying to please him! Angrily she flushed and put down the brush, then stalked to her bed, rigid with embarrassment.

Murdock spent most of his waking hours up on the deck for the next few days. He found that was the only way he could retain his control where Lettice was concerned. Every moment he was with her she either drove him to the brink of blind rage with her childish, selfish ways or turned him to liquid fire inside by the sight of her smooth, luscious body. Now that she was free of her heavy powder and getting adequate sleep, her skin had acquired a luminous glow and a softness that made her more beautiful than ever. And her hair—Charles could hardly take his eyes from the golden fire of her hair falling softly across her shoulders. When the sun coming through the porthole hit it directly, it shone like silver, and in the soft candlelight it glowed like burnished gold.

His fingers ached to sink into the silken mass, and he longed to bury his face in her hair, to kiss and caress it. The only release from this misery of longing was to leave the room for the windy deck and to walk for hours, until the pain lessened.

Sometimes Charles wondered what had happened to him, that he had become so insanely enamored of this shallow aristocratic beauty. Once, he thought, he had been a sensible man, one who knew his role in life and his wishes and the goals he could hope to obtain. Now he was like a child crying for the moon, wanting what he would never have and what he would not want, surely, if he could obtain it. Lettice Kenton was not for him; no doubt she would laugh scornfully at him should he take her in his arms and tell her of his passion for her.

As for the object of his desire—she was bored. Lettice could not leave the cabin for fear her disguise as a lad would be found out; so she sat in her room all day, longing for something to do. Her companion was gone most of the time, tromping around outside where she longed to be, and during the short time he was in the cabin he sat in a corner with his nose buried in a book. Not that he was exciting to talk to, Lettice thought, but at least he would have been better than this dreadful, lonely idleness, and it infuriated her that he left her alone so much of the time. It pricked her pride, too, to realize he had lost all interest in her; she was not used to a man being indifferent to her charms.

When she complained that she was bored, Murdock just laughed and told her to read a book. As if that would relieve her boredom, Lettice snorted to herself; she had despised her governess and every second she had been forced to stay in the schoolroom when she was a child. She had always wanted to be outside, free to run and explore, not cooped up with some dull tome about English history or the French language. Books seemed to her the dullest objects in the world, and she had vowed never to open another one once she was free of childhood.

However, she was bored enough that she would have welcomed almost anything, even a chance to paint or play the piano or embroider—any of the ladylike things her stern governess had taught her. She even went so far as to pick up some of Murdock's books when he was out and to read the titles; they were about law or government or the flora and fauna of the southern colonies, and Lettice quickly put them down again. She longed for a card game, but Murdock had no cards; or for some witty conversation, but he would hardly speak to her at all.

With all her free time, she found herself thinking far too much of dreadful things, things she usually was able to avoid. She thought of her childhood home and of her parents, who were rarely there, and who, when they were at home, saw little of her. She remembered the pain and the loneliness, which she had successfully submerged beneath her gay life in London. And she remembered all the bad times with Philip: her loveless courtship; her trembling, virginal fear on their wedding night and the way Philip had laughed at her and roughly initiated her into the male-pleasing rites of sex; the times he had reviled her for her unresponsiveness; the times he had forced her into the arms of his friends. Worst of all, she remembered that final wild quarrel and saw over and over again her husband's bloody, lifeless face.

At other times, her unoccupied mind dwelled on the

future, and she became filled with a heart-pounding fear. What would she do? Where would she go when they landed? She would be all alone, friendless, penniless, hopeless . . . At such times, she tried to tell herself not to think that way. Something would turn up; it had to—it always had. But her mind returned to it, like a tongue seeking a sore tooth.

It was while she was brooding over such thoughts one day that she happened to look up and catch Charles, who she had thought was reading, watching her. His blue eyes were as dark as midnight and filled with desire—no, more than that, they were full of an intense longing, so hungry and naked that it almost took her breath away. He wanted her, she thought, and a strange chill rippled through her, part excitement, part fear. Immediately his eyes went blank and he returned to his reading, but Lettice contemplated him, her heart pounding rapidly. She could not mistake the look of lust in his eyes; she had seen it too often in the eyes of other men. And there was more, so much more there, emotions she had never seen in other men, fathomless—longing, frustration, pain, just what she was not sure. What she *was* sure of was that he had looked at her the way a man lost in the desert would look at the mirage of a pool of water.

Could it be that he still wanted her? But surely not, or else he would have made some move toward her before now. He would at the least have murmured soft endearments in her ear or tried to steal a kiss—but then, being an unsophisticated colonial, perhaps he did not know how to flirt with or seduce a woman. In that case, surely he would have tried a more direct approach, such as grabbing her and pulling her down into bed with him.

Unless—yes, that was probably it—he was still so angry with her over her deception that he would not give her the satisfaction of knowing that he desired her. Philip, of course, knew her well enough to know that sex would have been the ultimate punishment to her and would have taken her to express his anger. But this man did not know her that well, and he might think it would please her or at least puff up her pride.

She smiled. Well, it did puff up her pride somewhat; she had not realized until now just how miffed she had been that Murdock seemed unaroused by her. She was used to men wanting her; it was the source of her power, even if she did dislike the outcome. And it was nice to know that she still held that power, even without her makeup and rich clothes. Somehow she would be able to use it to survive in the colonies; she could catch a wealthy husband. After all, there were some men with wealth there—why, Philip had said that Murdock himself was wealthy, despite his plain dress. So there were men with money, who would no doubt be easily caught by a woman with wit, beauty, and sophistication. Why, a bumpkin certainly should be easier to snare than a wily English lord.

Speculatively, she looked across at Charles. He was ugly, of course; she shuddered to think of having to endure his manhandling whenever he pleased. But, then, surely it would not be any worse than what her suave, handsome husband had done to her. All cats were gray in the dark, so they said. She knew for a fact that she had not enjoyed the touch of any man. Why should Murdock be any worse? God knows she did not want to marry and be subject to a man's whim again, but what else was there for her to do? She was trained for nothing but gracing a man's house with her looks and charm. And perhaps he would be more malleable than Philip, more adoring of her, so that she could evade his lovemaking more easily. He might believe her excuses, feel sorry for her headaches or tiredness. Besides, he was a Puritan, and everyone knew that they thought sex was a sin. Why, come to think of it, that might be one of the restraints preventing him from taking her now. If that were so, then he would be all the more likely to marry her if he desired her, rather than just make her his mistress. "Better to marry than to burn"—wasn't that what they believed?

Lettice felt a shiver of excitement. It just might work; things were not really so bleak after all. She had all this time alone at sea with a man who already desired her; surely she would be able to entice him to the boiling point, so that he would forget his anger toward her. Being guided by his Puritan upbringing, he would marry her in order to have her (helped, of course, by strong hints from her). Then, once she had him where she wanted him, she could marry him and have his money and the security of his name and yet keep him from her bed much of the time.

For a moment, the thought of the way he had handled both her and Philip after he discovered her deception deflated her. He had easily outwitted her devious husband and calmly scared her out of her wits before he threw her back to Philip. Then her spirits rose as she reasoned that she had not really been trying before, when she had flirted with him only because Philip demanded it. Now, with her mind put to it, she was confident that she would be able to lure him and yet hold him off, to play the delicate game of courtship and win.

The first thing she had to do, of course, was capture his attention. She could not hope to catch him if he spent all his time on deck or hidden behind a book cover. She must get him to look at her and talk to her.

"Mr. Murdock," she began, making her voice soft and hesitant. He looked up, surprised. "I know you do not like me, and I guess that you have ample reason, but I am so dreadfully bored and I wondered if perhaps you would talk to me a little."

Charles felt a twinge of suspicion at her almost humble words and soft, open face. What sort of game was she playing? "What would you like me to say?" he returned stiffly.

Lettice shrugged. "I don't care. I just want to hear a human voice. Tell me—tell me about your mission in England. You know, Boston and all the grievances you hold against the King."

Charles sighed. He had spoken of this subject to her before, when he had foolishly believed she had some interest in him, but obviously what he had said had passed quickly through her head. It seemed a waste of time to tell the bubble-headed lass again.

"Please," she pouted prettily.

Again he sighed and began, "Well, basically all we want are the rights of an Englishman, the rights obtained by the Magna Charta and Bill of Rights."

Lettice had some vague idea about the Magna Charta—something about the barons overcoming wicked King John—but the Bill of Rights meant nothing to her, and she knew that now she had to understand what he said to sustain any conversation at all. So, risking his censure, she asked, "What is the Bill of Rights?"

Murdock stared. Why, even his little sister Molly knew all about the Bill of Rights, and she had been to no more than Dame School, whereas this woman had doubtless had a full-time governess, and was actually one of the nobility of England.

"Don't look at me like that!" Lettice snapped, angered by his astonishment. Who was he to look so amazed and pitying? "What good would history have done me? I learned to paint and sing and dance and play the piano, to make witty conversation and dainty stitches, not to remember dull bills."

"Then why should you care now?"

"Because I am bored to tears and I will still be bored if I listen to you talk about something for ages when I don't know what it is you are talking about!" she answered, resentment making her frank.

Murdock laughed at her honesty. "All right, then. In sixteen eighty-eight, the nobles of England forced King James II to agree to a Bill of Rights, which gave Englishmen certain basic rights, such as the right to bear arms or to be free of having the King's soldiers quartered upon them. You see, the English people took from their King much of the power he had had over them. Many people are completely ruled by their royalty, but the English have the right to be free of restrictions unless they are placed on them by their Parliament."

"What difference does it make?"

"Why, this: The people elect their representatives, and the representatives are answerable to them. If they make a law the people don't like, the people can elect new representatives."

"So it is almost as though the people were making the laws themselves?"

"Exactly, or as close as you can get to it in a country of this size."

"Then what is the problem? After all, Parliament is making the laws, not the King."

"Yes, but we colonials are not represented in Parliament."

"But of course you are. You are Englishmen, aren't you?"

"Yes, but our interests are different from Englishmen who live in Great Britain, and unless we have representatives elected by the colonies, our interests are not really represented. You see, the people in England place taxes on the colonials, which hurt the colonies and help England. The Parliament's interests and ours are not the same."

"But everyone pays taxes," Lettice reasoned.

"True, but Englishmen have some say in what their taxes are; we do not. And now Parliament has gone far beyond that. England is trying to cripple Boston and the Massachusetts Bay Colony. Parliament has passed acts that take the right of electing the Massachusetts Assembly away from the people and allow the royally appointed governor to appoint our representatives. They have closed Boston's port to all ships, virtually destroying our economy. Another act permits the King's troops to quarter in the homes of our citizens without permission. And they have sent thousands of soldiers to Boston, as if we were an enemy country, not a colony!"

"But surely after you Bostonians dressed up like Indians and dumped all that tea into the harbor, you must expect some punishment. You defied the government, after all."

Charles looked at her suspiciously. "You show a good deal of knowledge for one who doesn't even know what Boston is."

For a moment Lettice frowned, puzzled, and then laughed. "Oh, that! I only said that to stir up Sir Edward; he is such a sanctimonious, patronizing man! Of course I knew about Boston and your infamous 'Tea Party'; after all, I am not quite a fool. Everyone has heard of that incident; it was the talk of London for days."

Now it was Charles's turn to frown in puzzlement. "But surely it would have surprised Sir Edward more if you had displayed your knowledge than if you pretended to be ignorant. All you did was reinforce what he believed; I fail to see how—"

"As if I cared what a ninny like Sir Edward Ponsonby thinks of me!" Lettice said scornfully. "He would have thought me ignorant even if I had admitted to some slight knowledge of Boston; he was already prepared to believe that. But by pretending to total indifference, I shocked him and made him angry, and it amused me to shock such a prude."

"I don't think I understand you at all," Charles said.

Lettice smiled at him, her mouth curving alluringly. "Do you really have to understand me, Mr. Murdock? Isn't a woman more appealing with some mystery?"

He felt desire stab through him like a white-hot knife, but he answered quietly, "I was under the apprehension that we were conversing on politics, not discussing your womanly wiles. But I see now that I was mistaken. You are incapable of being interested in anything but yourself."

Rage shook Lettice and her fingers itched to slap his plain, smug face. The man was impossible. "It's no wonder you do not understand me. You can't see beyond your own narrow little world. You think nothing exists but Boston and your cause and your pious Puritanical morals. You have no idea about my life or the world in which I lived. You think I should have learned history and concerned myself with politics and the colonies; you think I should have stripped myself of makeup, worn plain brown clothes, no doubt, and put my hair up in a mob cap. How arrogant you are, to think I should have modeled myself on a person and way of life I have never seen, just so you would approve of my character!"

Charles rose, a little shaken by her words. She was right; he had no claim on her, to expect her to meet his standards. He had no knowledge of her life or the forces that had worked on her; yet he was judging her. The woman angered him, and he wanted to lash out at her. But he controlled himself with great effort and said evenly, "Perhaps you are right. I do know nothing of you, and it was wrong of me to expect you to conform to my standards instead of your own. Why don't you tell me something of your life?"

Lettice stared at him, stunned. She had regretted her words as soon as they were out of her mouth, fearful of his anger and rejection. But instead of raging at her, he had admitted the justice of her accusations. Now she felt confused and foolish and a little ashamed.

She shrugged and said hesitantly, "Oh, there is little to it, really."

Her sudden shyness touched him, and he said softly, "Please, I should enjoy hearing about your childhood. Where did you live? What were your parents like?"

"There is really little unusual about it. I lived at Grenwil, the Delaplaines' country estate, until I came out when I was seventeen. My parents were quite elegant. Mama was a renowned beauty, and Father was something of a rake, I believe. They preferred the excitement of London, of course, so I did not see them often, only when they came up to hunt or if one of them had fought with the other." She smiled, trying for an amusing tone. "They are great fighters, you see; Mama was always at Father about some affair or other, and he was the same with her." Her voice trailed off, unconsciously wistful. "They were very much in love, of course. Theirs was a famous love match. Both of them possessed looks and splendid names, but neither family had a farthing to fly with. They married for love and have spent the rest of their lives trying to stay one step in front of their creditors. They are always angry with each other, though, for not having any money, and they were terribly jealous, but sometimes when they looked at each other—" Lettice stopped, horrified at the tears that sprang to her eyes. What on earth was she doing, talking like a silly schoolgirl to this man who already thought her beneath contempt?

Charles felt a pang of sympathy for her—what a lonely childhood she must have had. It was no wonder she knew little of deep feelings. "I am sorry . . ."

Brightly she said, "Oh, don't be. I was lucky enough

to learn at a tender age that one regrets marrying for love. So I married for money instead."

"You did not love your husband?" he asked.

"Love Philip?" Lettice said and laughed mockingly. "As well love a snake. No, Philip and I had a very satisfactory agreement. I made a very fashionable, desirable wife, and he was the grandson and heir of a Duke. Except the old fool hadn't the grace to die at a normal age, and Philip was kept quite penniless."

Her tone was brittle and sarcastic, effectively turning aside any attempt at sympathy. Charles grimaced; it was next to impossible to talk to the woman on anything but a superficial level. He hardly knew whether to pity her or be angry with her—or take her tempting body into his arms. A woman who married for money; a woman who had obviously never learned how to love. Dear God, why must he want her so?

Grimly Charles excused himself and left the room. Once alone, Lettice slumped down onto the berth, feeling strangely shaken and bereft.

Six

$\mathcal{A}$ few minutes after Murdock had left, Lettice went to the small bookshelf and picked up a book on South Carolina. She did not know exactly what drove her, whether it was Murdock's sneer at her lack of learning and her self-interest, or whether it was the only way at hand to escape the troublesome thoughts and feelings left by talking of her childhood. Whatever her motive, she sat down on her bunk and began to read. Soon she was engrossed in a witty, literate account of the tribulations of an Anglican minister in the backwoods of the Carolinas. She laughed at his appalled description of the morals and manners of the poorly educated people who scraped a living from the earth in the wilds, and soon she became engrossed, as the author himself had, in the problems and inequities suffered by the farmers; their agitation had eventually burst into the near rebellion, a few years back, known as the Regulator movement. Remembering what Murdock had said about the injustice of taxation without representation, she applied it to this vivid account of the backwoodsmen, taxed by the Tidewater-dominated government of the colony but without any voice in the legislation and suffering the indifference of the royal governor.

For some reason, she quickly hid the book when she heard Murdock's returning steps. She did not want him to glean any satisfaction from seeing her reading. But as soon as he left again, she pulled the book out and once more began to read. She was almost sorry when she finished it and went in search of another book, hoping it would prove to be as interesting. Unfortunately, it was a rather dull volume recounting the early exploration of the coast of North Carolina. She soon abandoned it and plunged into a small treatise written by Thomas Paine. From there she went to a book on government by John Locke, hoping it would clarify for her some of the issues Paine had written about. Here she bogged down thoroughly, and found to her frustration that, no matter how hard she tried, she had difficulty understanding it.

Lettice refused to give up and went back time and again to the book, until at last she was convinced that she truly was too shallow to understand it. Finally, after she had sat frowning over it for a full hour without getting anywhere, she threw the book across the room with a shriek of frustration.

At that moment, Charles entered the room and checked at the sight of her hurling a book at the wall. "What in heaven's name—"

"Oh, I cannot understand it. My governess always said I was too frivolous to live, and I suppose she must be right," Lettice said, too angry to care what her companion thought of her. "I have been trying and trying to understand it, and I just can't. Once I grasp part of it, something else eludes me. Why doesn't he write so an ordinary person can comprehend his meaning? No, don't tell me, I know; it isn't meant for lightweights like me."

Murdock went to pick up the book. Seeing its title, he smiled. "You might try starting out with something a little less difficult." He paused and glanced at her. He could not imagine what she had been thinking of; surely she did not really want to read John Locke. And yet, if she had put forth so much effort, she deserved a little encouragement. "Would you mind if I helped you with it?"

Lettice hesitated. Getting help was like admitting defeat—but, then, had she not just admitted that she would never master the book? At least this would provide a reason for them to talk, and he might warm toward her a little. Certainly nothing she had done so far seemed to have furthered her scheme of luring him into marriage; he had been, if anything, even colder and more aloof since their talk the other day.

"All right," she said cautiously, and he sat down on the berth beside her.

They started through the book, and each time she came to a difficult passage, Lettice stopped and asked for his assistance. To Charles's amazement, he found that she had a quick mind and soon grasped the concepts he explained, even at times putting up a fair argument against them. He would never have thought her capable of analytical thinking; still less would he have dreamed that she could be interested in such things. That fact astonished Lettice herself. She had always thought government and history the dullest subjects imaginable, and she was most surprised to learn that she now found the stuff intriguing. From then on she looked forward to their sessions every day, noting with pride that they became less and less study sessions and more and more discussions between equals. Charles was quick with his praise, and Lettice, who had always thrived on admiration, worked harder and harder, trying always to surprise and impress her mentor.

From books and government their talk slid easily into more personal matters. Lettice had always been an interesting conversationalist, and she made Murdock laugh at her descriptions of people and of pranks she had played. She did absurd imitations of everyone, from Lord North to the chimney sweep who worked in her London townhouse, capturing mannerisms and accents exactly. Charles could not remember when he had been so entertained.

As for Lettice, she found herself enthralled by Murdock's account of life in the American colonies. Never had she imagined that families lived as his did, close and warm and loving. She tried to imagine a mother who laughed with her child and sang lullabies to him and even taught him to spell, but she could not. She caught the dislike in his voice when he spoke of his stepmother, but there was warmth when he told her of his younger half-sister and half-brother, whom he had helped to raise.

"Margaret—Molly, I call her—is a shy little thing, like a bird or a deer. A servant dropped her when she was a baby and ever since then she's had a limp. It is a slight one, but she is very sensitive to it. Her mother doesn't help her there, for she is always harping on her to stand straight and look pretty and captivate people with her conversation. Molly is a dear, but I fear she is so reticent with people that she will never find a husband—and that's a pity, for she is good with children.''

Listening to him talk, it occurred to Lettice that it must be a very warm, secure feeling to be loved by this solid man, as Molly was loved by him. She thought that if she had had a brother like that, her childhood would have not been half so anxious or lonely. Molly probably did not realize how lucky she was, Lettice thought, and then smiled at herself. Imagine her, Lettice Delaplaine, wishing she were kin to this plain colonial.

It was even more ridiculous in view of the fact that she had decided to seduce him into marrying her. In the warmth of their talks and their blossoming acquaintance, Lettice had pushed the unpleasant thought of marriage to the back of her mind. However, as the ship came closer to port, her fears began to rise again and clamor inside her. If she did not induce Murdock to marry her, she had no idea what would happen to her; it seemed most likely that she would starve or have to turn to prostitution.

Marry Murdock, that was the sensible solution, she told herself, resolutely beating down her strange guilt. What did it matter to her whether she deceived him? He was a grown man and able to take care of himself, after all. If he succumbed to his lust, as other men did, enough to marry her, then that was his lookout, not hers. And the fact that they had spent some pleasant hours together should make her *more* willing to marry him, not plagued with guilt. After all, it meant that she might find marriage more enjoyable than she had envisioned it; at least she and her husband would be able to talk.

Nevertheless, a niggling question ate at her: What would happen if Murdock fell in love with her, if she enticed him into marriage by appealing to his lust, and then he found out that he had been deceived? How would he feel if he realized that she did not love him? Would he not be hurt and miserable when he discovered her utter lack of response? It was deception to let him marry her without knowing this crucial flaw in her—no, worse than 'let,' to persuade him to marry her. And if she grew bored, as she so often did, and decided to leave him for a better situation, what would happen to Charles then? And how would he feel if she played one of her silly pranks and thereby hurt his reputation among his own people? Those were the cruelties she would inflict on a man who had been kind enough to take her with him to America after she had deceived him, who had helped her learn and made her realize for the first time in her life that she was not just a flibbertygibbet, as everyone had always told her, as she had always thought.

Then the terror would seize her; she would imagine being alone and friendless in a strange country, having to stay alive however she could, with no asset but her looks. Marrying Murdock, she concluded, was the only answer. So, swallowing her self-contempt, Lettice began to try to attract him.

It would have taken less than she realized to stoke Murdock's ardor. The weeks they had spent in close companionship had only made him desire her more. He found, in fact, that he was spiraling helplessly into love with her. She made him laugh as no other woman had ever done; the stories she told were at her own expense as often as not, and he felt, once the laughter had died, a sympathy for the dislike she had for herself. It tugged at his heart to glimpse the lonely, frightened child lurking in her stories, or the unloved society beauty she grew up to be. Charles felt he had seen more deeply into her character than anyone else had, and he had found the untapped good his instincts had told him was there. Beneath the paint and powder, the cynicism and manners, the laughter and boredom, there was a woman of heart, who must have spent years wanting desperately to escape her life and not knowing how.

He longed to release her, longed to bring forth the warm woman inside. And he wanted—oh, God, how he wanted—to see her smile at him with passion, to feel her smooth arms around him and her lips soft on his. The sight of her sitting cross-legged on her berth—her face alive with curiosity or humor, her pale blond hair shimmering, her firm body barely concealed by her clothes— sent waves of delicious fire through him. The tight boy's trousers clung to her slim legs and rounded buttocks, and through the thin lawn shirt he could see quite clearly the darker circle of her nipples and the luscious curve of her breasts. To look at her and know she did not want him was a curious blend of heaven and hell, and when she called him to her side to read a passage and he was so close to her that any movement would touch her flesh, he trembled with the effort of restraining his passion. Charles dreamed of her at night and woke up thinking of her, only to find the loveliness of her reality greater than what he had dreamed. He tried to walk away his passion up on deck, tried to reason with himself, tried everything he could think of to calm this raging tide of desire, but nothing worked.

When Lettice began to try to entice him, it was almost more than Charles could endure. The things she did were so subtle—a mischievous yet sultry glance; a stretch that pressed her bosom hard against the sheer cloth of her shirt, followed by a sleepy smile—that he did not even realize she was making a conscious effort to seduce him. All he knew was that he ached for her constantly, unbearably, until he thought he might go mad.

Lettice was in despair. Although she could tell from the stark hunger in his shadowed eyes that he desired her, he would never speak of it, never give her a chance to guide his thoughts toward marriage. What Lettice did not realize was that his passions were held so tightly in check that the visible signs she noticed were a mere inkling of what lay inside him. Because he was certain she would never welcome his attentions, Murdock did not broach the subject of his feelings for her. Instead he tried to keep them firmly under control, repressing his longing with such severity that when at last his control did break, his desire came raging out in a wild flood, unreasoning and uncontrollable.

When Charles told her that the ship was only a few days away from its destination, Lettice realized that she must act quickly if she was to spur him to a declaration. Driven by the thought of the fate that might await her, she smiled at him, her lips dipping down in her old provocative way.

"Thank you," she said softly. "I would never have made it if you had not taken pity on me and let me come with you. You have no idea how much it means to me."

As if on impulse, she leaned forward, her breasts barely grazing his arm, and kissed him lightly on the mouth. For an instant after she drew back, there was a charged silence, and then his hand fastened like iron on the back of her neck. She stared at him, her lips slightly open in faint astonishment. His eyes were a dark midnight blue, hard and unreadable, and suddenly she felt a thrust of fear. This was not the man she knew, the gentle man who encouraged her reading and talked about his childhood. No, this stern man, whose skin seared like fire where he touched her, whose eyes turned heavy with lust, this was not Charles Murdock!

"No," she breathed faintly and tried to pull away, her apprehensive gaze going involuntarily to his full-lipped mouth.

Slowly, inexorably the hand on her neck pulled her toward him until at last that mouth fastened on hers, and she knew that she was caught, unrelentingly caught. His other hand came up to cup her face, while his lips branded hers. Then his mouth moved from hers to explore her face and throat, softly kissing her flesh, gently nibbling at the tender column of her neck.

"Lettice," he groaned against her skin. "Lettice, my love."

Vainly Lettice struggled against him, stiff and almost mindless with the same horror she had always felt, the terror that Philip sneeringly termed her coldness. Her breath stuck in her throat and she screamed silently that she could not bear this, not again. Wildly she began to fight him, clawing and twisting, but he wrapped his arms around her tightly, easily lifting her from the floor and holding her helpless against his broad chest. Again he kissed her, his lips hard and demanding, and his tongue possessed her mouth, roaming freely, drinking in the sweetness of her.

Still holding her captive against him, he sank to the

floor, pressing her back against the hard planks, his huge body fully on top of her. Blindly she pushed up against him, but the movement served only to excite him more, for with a moan, he plunged one hand down the front of her shirt, tearing at her already-strained buttons until they popped and the full lushness of her breasts lay exposed to him. His weight shifted, and Lettice tried to wriggle free, but quickly he pulled both her hands behind her back and, kneeling astride her, wrapped his legs around her, effectively pinning her to the floor.

Lettice looked up at him, her green eyes swimming with tears of frustration and fear. She hardly recognized him; his face was flushed and his eyes glittering as he looked down at her with raw animal hunger. How huge he was, how strong—dear God, what would he do to her? She closed her eyes, praying that it would be no worse than Philip.

"God, you are beautiful." Murdock's voice was hoarse. His hands began to caress her breasts, lovingly sliding across her chest and stomach, teasing her nipples to hardness with his fingers.

He tugged hurriedly at the fastenings of her trousers, his fingers rough with haste, and pushed them off her hips. His breath was hard and rasping in his throat as his eyes roamed her pale, slim body, and his manhood was stiff and throbbing, straining against the cloth of his trousers. Quickly he took off his trousers and parted her legs, then eased his pounding, tormented flesh into her. Slowly he began to move within her, luxuriating in the silken feel of her body, and again his mouth took hers in a kiss.

Lettice lay rigid and unyielding beneath him, hating

him for violating her and hating herself for not foreseeing what would happen. At last he shuddered and collapsed against her, his skin trembling and cool with sweat.

"Lettice," he murmured thickly, burying his hands in her hair. She felt him go slack against her. He had fallen asleep, of course, the great clod—just like all men.

Angrily she shoved at him, hard, and he rolled off her onto the floor, blinking with surprise. "You great oaf!" she cried, careless in her fury. "I thought you were different! Sweet Jesus, what a fool I was, to think that any man had any thought or feeling except between his legs!"

Fingers fumbling with anger, she retied her trousers and attempted to fasten her shirt. That was beyond repair, so she tied it in a great knot at her waist.

Bitter words tumbled from her mouth, spurred by her disillusion. Not stopping to consider that she had encouraged his lust, Lettice could only think furiously that Murdock had turned out to be like all other men. Imagine her thinking he might want to marry her! Of course he would not—she was no virgin fresh from her come-out, and that was the only sort men married from desire. She had been an idiot to think that he would do anything but take her, penniless as she was, so much in his debt and in his power. He had no regard for her wishes or thoughts; she mattered not at all to him. He was a man, after all, and he saw her as nothing more than a receptacle for his seed.

"Damn you! Damn you and all men! You told me you were a gentleman, and I believed you. I thought you had some regard for me, some respect, because you listened to me and helped me with those books. But now I see that all you ever wanted was my body, just like Philip, just like all the others. I hate you! Do you hear? I despise you!" Her voice broke on a dry sob, and she turned away, holding herself.

Charles returned foggily to full consciousness, his thoughts still blurred with the remnants of passion, and began to pull his clothes back on. Suddenly, seeing her thin, shaking shoulders, the full force of what he had done hit him.

"Oh, dear God, Lettice!" He staggered to his feet. "Lettice, I'm sorry." He choked on the inadequacy of his words. He had raped her. Like a filthy animal he had taken that delicate, beautiful woman by force. For the first time her struggles penetrated his consciousness and he winced, as if from a physical blow. In his passion, he had seized her and kissed her and taken her. Raped her. She must hate him; she had every right to. Miserably, he wiped his hand across his face.

It seemed to Lettice then that she had hit bottom. Her last hope was gone. The man she had come grudgingly to like, even admire, was a pig like all the others. He would probably take her a few times more, until his thirst was slaked, and then he would toss her out. Before her loomed starvation, degradation, and—somehow worse than all else—the betrayal of this one man.

"Why did you have to be like that?" she mumbled brokenly. "For a while, with you, I felt like a person. You made me think I wasn't just a face or a body, useful for nothing but satisfying a man's lust. What a joke. You deceived me well. For a while I forgot that's all I am. All I'll ever be."

Suddenly she ran to the door, pulled it open and stumbled through it. Charles stared after her for a moment in astonishment. Where on earth . . . Then for some reason he thought of the limitless dark sea that lay out there, and he rushed out of the room after her.

Seven

*L*ettice hardly knew what propelled her out the door and up the steps to the dark deck, or even why it should hurt so that Murdock was merely a man like other men.

It seemed as though a lifetime of suppressed pain and bitterness had risen in her like gall, and she longed suddenly, desperately, never to have to feel again. She ran across the deck to the rail of the ship and looked out over the water. Dark and surging, the ocean plunged beneath the ship, here and there glittering palely under the moon. She stared as if mesmerized, then slowly pulled herself up onto the wooden rail and swung her legs over the side. She closed her eyes and took a deep breath, then leaned forward into the empty air . . . and suddenly an arm clamped around her waist, hard as iron, and jerked her body back against a broad, firm chest.

"Lettice, no!"

She heard Murdock's agonized voice in her ear, and she slumped against him, silvery teardrops oozing out beneath her closed lids.

Easily Charles swung her into his arms and carried her back down to their cabin. Lettice rested her head against his chest; she felt so tired, so numb, and it was reassuring to feel the warmth of his skin beneath her cheek and hear the steady rhythm of his heartbeat. Once inside the cabin, he laid her gently on her bed and sat beside her, holding her hands in his. Lettice could feel the slight tremor in his hands and wanted to ask him the cause, but her tongue felt too thick to talk and her brain too slow. All she could do was close her eyes and slide into sleep.

Sleep did not come so easily to the man who sat looking down at her. Softly he pushed a stray lock of hair back from her face. He could think of nothing except that his actions had almost killed the woman he loved. With a sigh he rose and went to sit in a chair across the room. Throughout the night he sat and stared, his blunt face brooding as he went over the events of the evening.

Charles was more appalled by his actions than Lettice; before meeting him she had expected little of any man, but he—he had acted in complete disregard of his beliefs. He had raped a woman, had taken her without any thought of her well-being or desires; no, worse than that, knowingly against her desires, for he knew full well she had no feeling for him. He remembered her words; indeed, he thought that he would never forget them: "For a while, with you, I felt like a person . . . You deceived me well." She had come to trust him, to think he regarded her as a human being, as no one else ever had, and then he had shattered that trust.

All his life, Charles Murdock had been in control of himself, had studied, worked, supported his family, done what others expected of him and what he expected of himself. He had never claimed to be a saint, but at least he had thought he was a man who considered before he acted, who was in control of himself and his destiny. Steady, his friends called him. Dull, his sister teased him. He got things done; he was the haven in the emotional storms of everyone he knew. There had been times when he wished that others did not regard him with such placid dependence. Still, he had also prided himself on the way he ran his life.

Now, bitterly, he saw how false his pride had been. On that long, dark night, he looked deep within his soul and saw there the violence, the turmoil that had long dwelled in him and that he had long denied. It had taken Lettice Kenton to bring it out of him. The lovely Lettice, who had set his soul aflame with her beauty, who had attracted like a magnet all the roiling passions inside him. He had reviled her for her frivolity and her deceit, had with superior scorn promised to make her "a decent woman," had held himself better than she.

He laughed to himself without humor: Had he hoped to make her a decent woman by raping her? He was no better than she; worse, if anything. Charles knew now that there lived inside him a raging, elemental man, a being beyond reason, who was driven by anger or love or passion and paid no heed to whomever might be hurt by his actions.

Murdock walked to the berth where Lettice lay and stood looking down at her. Even now, the need for her pulsed in him; he would have given the world for her to wake and smile up at him and hold out her arms in invitation. Charles knew that he had to have her; it did not matter what she had done before he met her, how she had lived or whose bed she had graced. He had proved tonight the wretchedness that he was capable of;

she was certainly no greater sinner than he. But she stirred him: body, heart, mind, and soul. She had brought him to life, unleashed all the wild, bursting hunger in him that he had never before admitted. The consequences had been grim; he hated himself for his deed and he swore that in the future he would manage to harness this new flood of emotion. But neither could he bear to lose the heat, the beauty, the life that burst alive in him. Lettice was its wellspring, and he must keep her. No matter what it cost him, no matter how hard he would have to work to restore her trust in him, no matter how bitterly she despised him, he must keep her with him.

Lettice awoke feeling much restored. She was far too pragmatic a person to wish that Murdock had not succeeded in pulling her back from her intended watery grave. Whatever lay before her, she really had no wish to die quite yet. Cautiously she sat up and glanced about the room. Charles sat bolt upright in his chair, sound asleep; his face was drawn and lined with fatigue, and Lettice suspected that he had not slept much that night. Thankful that he was not awake yet, she lay back and tried to assess her feelings. How strange it was that she really did not know how she felt.

Murdock had been a brute last night, of course, and proved himself to be no better than other men. However—a slight smile curved her lips—who would have thought him capable of it? She could not help but feel a thrill of excitement that she had inspired such passion in his calm breast. Besides, he had not been as bad as other men, not fumbling like old Danby or cruel as Philip always was. She had scarcely enjoyed it, of course, but those other times had been much worse. It was her own fault, after all, for not having been clever enough to realize that her enticements would only spur him to attack, not to marriage. She had been an idiot to try to enflame his passions as she had, considering their isolated situation and her dependence on him.

It was gloomy to think of the future; God only knew how she would get by in that strange land. Still, she would rather be facing it than the fires of hell. Murdock had saved her; she had to be grateful to him for that. It would have been far easier for him to let her go; then he would not have had to face her recriminations or the fear of her creating scandal for him. Many men would have done so. At least he was no coward. And at least he was no frozen Puritan; he had proved that.

Her thoughts were disturbed by the scrape of the chair, and Lettice sat up to see Murdock advancing on her, his face grim. She faced him squarely, determined not to show any fright, although her heart began to pound within her chest. Was he going to take her again? Certainly there was nothing to stop him.

However, when he halted and looked down at her, she saw how deeply etched were the grooves around his mouth. To her amazement, she realized that his blue eyes were dark with remorse and pain.

"I am sorry, Lettice. I know there is no way you can actually forgive me, but I hope you will accept my apology." He closed his eyes, and suddenly his face twisted with anguish and his words burst from him as if torn: "Oh, God, I'd give anything if I could only make it right, make it as though it had never happened. I was an animal, a savage; I hate myself for it. Please, please forgive me."

Lettice stared at him in complete disbelief. Never in her wildest dreams would she have imagined a man apologizing to her for hurting her. The men she knew took their pleasure arrogantly, without regard to the feelings of their partners. In her experience the only concern that stopped a man was fear of her male relatives or of public censure, and neither was applicable here. A warm wave of feeling rose up in her chest, and she felt a strange urge to comfort Murdock.

"To think that I drove you to the brink of suicide—" he said brokenly and stopped, his hands clenching into fists.

"Oh, no," Lettice cried and seized one of his hands. "No, really, don't think that way. That was a foolish thing for me to do! You are not to blame for that. And anyway, you saved me, kept me from doing it. If it weren't for you, I would not even be here. I would be floating face down back there, in the sea—no, I would be facing trial in England!"

Charles wrapped his powerful hand around hers and squeezed it gratefully. She was no angel, he knew that; but few women would be so understanding and reasonable.

"I stayed awake for a long time last night, thinking about what I had done. There is no way I can excuse myself. But if you will let me, I will try to do what I can to make up for it. I want to marry you, Lettice."

"Oh, Charles," Lettice said, and buried her face in her hands. He wanted to marry her. She had suddenly, unexpectedly gotten what she wanted, what she had been scheming for. She had enflamed him to rape, and now Charles wanted to marry her. Out of guilt. Out of remorse. It left a taste as bitter as ashes.

Charles, mistaking her reaction, knelt beside her. "Lettice, I know how you feel. I know you don't love me; why, after last night, you probably fear me. I don't ask that you feel anything for me. But allow me to give you the protection of my name. Allow me to look after you."

Looking at his sincere face, Lettice wanted to cry. He was offering her what she had been angling for. Here was her chance. Why did she feel so miserable? Why did such a lump form in her throat, blocking her words of assent? Damn him—if only he were not so honorable, she would accept his offer in a second. But in the face of those sad blue eyes, she could not do it. Perhaps for the first time in her life, Lettice was swept by a guilt so strong she could not deny it. She had tricked him into asking her to marry him, had stirred his passion so that he could not control himself and then he, out of self-condemnation, had felt obliged to offer to marry her. It amazed even herself, but Lettice could not make advantage of him.

"No, Charles," she sighed. "I won't marry you. I cannot do that."

"But, Lettice, think: What are you going to do? Do you know anyone in the colonies? Do you have any money to live on?"

Miserably Lettice shook her head, lowering her face so that he would not see the tears that sprang into her eyes.

"How else are you going to live? I know it is not a very palatable solution for you; I am no aristocrat, nor even a man of great wealth by your standards. Certainly my actions last night did little to endear me to you. I know what you must think of me: I am an ugly, clumsy bear of a man, with no sophistication, no refinement, scarcely the sort you could find happiness with. I swear to you, if I could think of any other way, I would. But how else are you going to live? Please, Lettice; you must be practical."

"No!" Lettice almost shouted the word, and turned away from him, angry with herself for throwing away this opportunity, angry with him for arguing. He would hardly be so importunate if he knew how she had tricked him. "I tried marriage, and I found I did not like it," she continued, striving for a light tone.

Charles rose and walked away from her. Turning his back, he said in a muffled voice, "Is it that I disgust you? That you loathe the thought of this face beside you each night? If that is it, then I promise you I will respect your wishes. I will never touch you if you don't wish it. I promise I will not ever force you again."

"Oh, stop it," she snapped, exasperated at his self-abnegation and generosity. "Please, I simply do not wish to marry you. Can't you leave it at that?"

"No, I can't!" he thundered back. "My God, woman, I dishonored you. I can't just leave it at that!"

Oddly, it angered her, this insistence on making amends for his taking her. Not that he loved her, not that he wanted her for his wife; oh no, it was only that he had to do the correct thing. He would have married anyone in this position! Lettice felt an itching desire to slap his pious face.

"How many times do I have to tell you?" she yelled back, appalled at the sound of her own voice. "I do not want to marry you. Be grateful! Thank your stars that you escaped! Have you no sense? No eyes in your head? I tricked you! I wanted you to ask me to marry you because I am penniless, without any prospects. I was frightened of starving. So I posed and smiled and did a dozen little things to seduce you. And you fell into my hands like a ripe plum. It did not happen in quite the manner I had planned, but the outcome was the same. I tricked you! I set it up!"

She stopped, panting for breath, and for a moment they looked at each other in stunned silence. Finally Charles drew a long breath. "Then if you planned it, why do you not leap at my offer now?"

"Because last night taught me that nothing was worth marriage!" Lettice retorted. Before the contempt in his eyes, she would not let him know the guilt that kept her from taking advantage of him.

His face was cold and stark, and his eyes were the blue of a frozen lake. "So—it seems I have played the fool. Again."

Lettice swallowed and said nothing. There was a frozen block in the pit of her stomach that she feared she would never be rid of. She had thrown away her last hope, alienated the one man who might have helped her, all for the sake of some silly, last-minute compunction.

Murdock turned and began to pace the room. Finally he stopped and said, "Doubtless I should have known that you were incapable of being dishonored. However, no matter what part you played in this, I cannot excuse my own conduct last night. I must be responsible for what I did—and for the child you could be carrying. I might add that there was no need for you to perform that little drama at the ship's rail to bring home to me what I had done."

"Drama!" Lettice repeated wrathfully. "I did not pretend that. How dare you—"

Murdock looked at her, one eyebrow raised contemptuously. "Do you really expect me to believe that?"

Lettice started to retort; then, realizing the futility of it, she swallowed her words. What did it matter if he thought she had faked a suicide attempt as well? It was obvious that his opinion of her was too low to be endangered.

"I cannot in good conscience abandon you to your own devices when we land. And should you prove to be with child, we would, of course, have to marry."

"We would not 'have to marry.'" Lettice mimicked his stern tone bitterly. "I would not for the world be a burden to you. In fact, I think I would do almost anything rather than marry you!"

Murdock overrode her words as calmly as if she had not spoken. "Therefore, Lady Lettice, you shall accompany me to Boston and take up residence in my house as a guest."

"Nor will I be your mistress," Lettice said flatly.

"Never fear," he said dryly. "We shall be well-chaperoned. I reside with my stepmother, my sister, and my brother. I assure you, your virtue will be quite safe."

Lettice set her mouth stubbornly, but refused to rise to his sneering tone. "It may seem a little strange that we should entertain an English guest," he went on imperturbably. "However, I shall tell my stepmother some tale of your being robbed of all your possessions and temporarily destitute. I came upon you in port—I think it more prudent to leave out our traveling together on board ship, don't you? I imagine that you can be a sort of companion to my sister Molly, teach her some of those delicate feminine arts you learned. As long, of course, as you do not try to persuade her to emulate your behavior."

She longed to slap him for his mocking words and the cold, snide smile that played on his full mouth. It would have served him right if she had accepted his marriage proposal; from his tone, anyone would suppose *she* had done *him* some great wrong, instead of letting him out of her trap. Lettice would have liked nothing better than to toss his new, degrading offer right back in his face. Lady Lettice Kenton—companion-governess to an obnoxious brat! However, at the moment, she did not have that privilege. His offer was her best chance for survival in the colonies, and she would stay there no longer than it took her to figure out some better mode of living.

"You must realize how little I like the prospect of doing what you propose," she said haughtily, trying to match the severity of his tone. "However, I have little choice at the moment. Therefore I will accept your 'kind' offer of hospitality, and I promise that I shall do my utmost to school Miss Margaret in some of the more feminine arts—without, of course, altering her strong moral fiber."

Murdock looked at her coldly. "I am well aware of your love of jests. But I warn you that I am deadly serious in this. I would toss you out in the cold before I'd see you harm Molly in any way."

"Don't be foolish. What advantage would it give me to influence your sister to evil?"

"I count on that as the only consideration that would restrain you."

* * *

Her future was settled, at least for a short time, and Lettice could breathe a little easier. However, Murdock spent the last few days on ship in a mood so icily distant that Lettice found it hard to endure. She was profoundly grateful that at least she would be better able to avoid him in his house than in this tiny cabin. Otherwise, she was not sure that she would have agreed to his proposal, no matter what the alternative. She thought it unfair that he should treat her so rudely when she had done him a favor, or that he should assume her despairing dash for the sea had been false. As far as she could tell, he did not have any right to judge her.

Reason had little to do, however, with Murdock's feelings. He had been betrayed again by Lettice, and this last betrayal wounded him deeply, coloring all her other actions. He told himself that she had never been interested in his books or the other topics they had discussed; she had merely been fattening him up for the kill, intellectually seducing him. Her smile, her brilliant laugh, the way she seemed to value his opinion—all mere playacting. Even her refusal to take the final, deceitful step of marrying him he saw in the worst possible light. Charles did not recognize kindly impulse, only a loathing for marriage to him that was so strong she could not go through with it. She despised him; no doubt his touch made her flesh crawl, so that the thought of sharing a marital bed with him was unendurable. That was why she had struggled against him that night; it was not morality, merely revulsion. He cursed his plain face and hulking size, knowing, with shame, that he would have accepted marriage with Lettice, whatever her motive. He still ached to have her, his hunger seemingly only heightened by their brief consummation. He thought he would have paid her, crawled to her, whatever it took to have her again—except the only way open to him, to seize her again with force.

Since the port of Boston had been closed by General Gage, their ship docked in nearby Salem, and from there Charles and Lettice had to take a coach to Boston. Their first problem upon arrival was obtaining some clothes for Lettice. The dressmaker's eyebrows shot up when Lettice stepped into her store dressed as a man and accompanied by Charles. However, she quailed before Lettice's haughtiest expression and Charles's cold glance, and agreed to sew up two or three dresses without delay.

Lettice would have dearly loved to wear something soft and bright again, but Charles insisted on serviceable dark wool. It seemed to her that he took pleasure in dressing her as plainly as possible in blacks and browns, even insisting on purchasing aprons and mob caps.

"You are no longer going to be a lady of leisure," he warned her. "You'll have no need for frills or bows or hoops. All that will concern you is warmth and durability."

Lettice grimaced at her image in the mirror. She looked like a maid in this outfit! A large white cap covered her head, its only ornamentation a dainty frilled edge, completely concealing her glowing hair. The dress was a plain brown, with plenty of petticoats underneath, but no hoop to hold it out stiffly on the sides, and a high neckline and long sleeves to cover every inch of her skin. Warm shoes, laced up high, covered her feet, making any supposedly accidental showing of her shapely ankles impossible. It was the dullest clothing imaginable, Lettice thought, and she would have to be a witch to attract any man in it.

In truth, the cap framed her delicate face enchantingly, and the plain dress could not conceal her full bosom and trim waist. She was still lovely enough to turn the head of any man on the street, and Charles, who had hoped that the Puritan gown would alleviate some of his desire, found that her clothing merely made a man want to discover what lay underneath. He regretted the customary cap that hid the shining fall of her hair. It was all he could do to keep from untying the strings and whisking it off her head, so that he could delight in the silken silver-gilt beauty.

Once Lettice's clothes were taken care of, they set out for Boston. The roads were rough and rutted and the hired coach poorly sprung; Lettice felt as though her teeth would be jarred from her head before the journey was over—*if* it was ever over. It was a two-day trip to Boston, which meant a night spent in an inn. Lettice anxiously awaited the stopover, jolted as she was and stuffed into the coach with three men, all of whom studied her fixedly throughout the journey. One was a farmer who smelled strongly of manure; another puffed incessantly on a foul-smelling pipe. If it had not been for Charles's supercilious gaze on her, she would have given them all a piece of her mind concerning their rudeness to a lady. As it was, she did not want to give Charles the satisfaction of seeing how the crude conditions affected her.

When they at last reached the inn, the place turned out to be a severe disappointment. As the only female in the group, she was accorded a room to herself; she understood she should be thankful that she did not have to sleep in the large dormitory room with the men. The room she was given was tiny and dirty, however, and the bed lumpy. But despite the mysterious rustlings that sent her heart into her throat and the loud noises from men drinking downstairs, she soon went sound asleep.

The next morning she had to endure the curious stares and questions of everyone at the table, just as she had the night before. She was thankful that Charles had thought up a fairly plausible story to account for her being there. She had thought she could carry it off by employing her usual icy hauteur, but she could see now that this would have little effect on these rough, curious people, hungry for news. So she smiled calmly and said that she and her husband had sailed to the colony to settle, but that her poor husband had died of fever during the journey. Once on shore, a thief had stolen her purse, which contained all the money she had in the world.

Everyone seemed to accept her story without hesitation, and they fell to sympathizing on the lawlessness that was so prevalent these days. Fortunately, Charles managed to move the subject from her to the news of Boston, and so spared her any further questioning, which might have shown her strangely ignorant of important facts about her life.

After the communal breakfast, she was glad to escape to the relative quiet of the coach, even at the expense of another bone-jarring ride. Toward evening, they at last pulled into Boston. Lettice stared at the town in disappointment. She had thought Boston to be something of a city, but it seemed little more than a village compared to London. The churches were plain, as were all the other buildings, and everything seemed to be built of brown brick. To make it all worse, a mist hung over all, turning the landscape wetly drab. Lettice barely suppressed a sigh. How on earth was she ever to live here?

They left the coach and Charles set out briskly across the uneven cobblestones. Lettice was sure he was determined to make things as difficult for her as he could, so she set her jaw and followed him without complaint. She thought she would die before she would admit to the man that he had caused her any discomfort.

After what seemed an interminable walk, Murdock at last stopped before a plain brick structure, a graceful but hardly elegant two-story house with a dainty front yard and a small stoop reached by six steps.

"This is it," he said. "The Murdock home."

Lettice looked up at it nervously. Inside was his family, no doubt a bunch of suspicious, hard-minded sorts who would hate her on sight. She had a feeling that this morning's interview at breakfast had been nothing compared to what she would now face. Cold fear darted through her, but she ignored it. There was no time to be afraid; whatever lay inside she had to face and come out the winner. After all, she was, above everything, a survivor, wasn't she?

She straightened her shoulders and said firmly, "Let's go in."

Eight

*C*harles opened the front door and stepped inside. Lettice hung back for a moment, reluctant despite her bold words. Angrily she told herself not to be so foolish, and followed Murdock.

The foyer was small and modest, by her standards, but the wooden floor gleamed from careful waxing and was decorated with a bright red braided rug, and the walls were painted a smooth cream color, giving it a warm, cozy look despite its austerity.

Steps clattered on the stairway in front of them, and a boy in his early teens rounded the landing. "Charles!" he cried, his young face a picture of delight. "Charles! You're home!" He catapulted the rest of the way down the stairs as though he meant to fling himself at the older man as he had done as a child. Just before he reached Murdock, he remembered his age and dignity enough to come to a halt and merely clasp the other man's hand and shake it vigorously, while his face glowed with love and eagerness.

Now more sedate footsteps sounded on the stairs, and a woman came into view. She was older than Charles by a few years, but still firm and supple in her form, and the hair peeking out from under her white cap showed black. Her dress was a plain brown one, accented only by severe white cuffs and collar and a white apron, and her face was as unadorned as her dress, but she was not unattractive. Rather, her wide-boned face was handsome, and there was a certain sensuality about her firm mouth, now upturned in a smile. The dark eyes glowed warmly as she looked at Charles; then her gaze fell on Lettice standing behind him, and her eyes narrowed.

"Hello, Charles," she said smoothly as she came down the stairs, betraying not even a flicker of interest in his companion. "We are so glad to have you home."

Charles moved forward to take her hand. "Marian, it's good to see you again. You're looking well."

"Thank you." Her brown eyes slid curiously to Lettice and back to Charles.

Murdock started to speak, but he was interrupted by a young woman rushing headlong into the hall from the back of the house. She walked quickly, but with a curiously unrhythmical gait, and Lettice remembered that Charles had said his half-sister had a slight limp. Heedless of everyone else, she pitched herself into his arms, and he lifted her from the floor in a great hug and twirled her around.

"Oh, Charles, Charles, thank heavens you are home!" The girl began to chatter, her words tumbling out.

Charles laughed and cut through the verbal stream, saying, "Molly, Molly, please, we have a visitor. Allow me to make my introductions."

Now the girl blushed and for the first time turned to look at Lettice. Her eyes widened at the sight of the other woman, and she fell into a shy silence.

"Marian, may I present Mistress Lettice Holmes?" Charles said, using the name that they had made up for her disguise. "Mistress Holmes, my stepmother, Mistress Marian Murdock. And this impetuous girl is my sister, Margaret, and that young rascal is my brother, Bryan."

"How do you do, Mistress Holmes," Marian said, her voice cool, with a subtle hint of surprise, while her son made a creditable bow and her daughter bobbed a shy curtsey and murmured something so softly that Lettice could not understand her.

"Mistress Murdock." Lettice answered the woman with the same cold courtesy and then turned her radiant smile on the young people. "Master Bryan, Miss Margaret."

"I met Mistress Holmes in Salem. She and her husband recently traveled to Massachusetts but unfortunately her husband passed away on the trip over. Some brigands in Salem robbed her of all her valuables, so I offered Mistress Holmes the refuge of our home until she receives some help from her relatives in England."

Margaret looked at her with awe, obviously viewing her as a romantic victim of cruel fate, but Mrs. Murdock looked at her almost hostilely and said, "Indeed? I am most sorry to hear that, madame. However, Charles, you must know that this blockade of the port has plunged us into very grave times. We can hardly support an extra pair of idle hands, especially British ones."

Charles's eyes widened with surprise at his stepmother's rudeness, but before he could speak, Lettice cut through the silence with her clear, perfect tone. "But I would never think of being a burden to you, Mistress Murdock. Nor can I bear the thought of idleness. Your son asked me to be a companion to his sister, a sort of governess of the social arts, if you please, and I am more than happy to serve the family in that capacity."

Her little speech was a telling mixture of hauteur and blatantly false humility, and Murdock had to hide a smile at both the absurdity of what she said and the look of anger on his stepmother's face. The barb of calling him Marian's son had obviously penetrated; Marian hated the thought of aging and would never want anyone to think her older than Charles, let alone his mother.

"Charles is not my son," she said tightly.

"Oh, yes, of course, your stepson," Lettice said in her most severe drawing-room voice, her tone carrying the faintest trace of contempt, and the older woman flushed dully. Lettice did not know what it was in her words that touched the woman to the quick, but instinctively she had known how to pierce the other's protection. She had not spent the past few years of her life verbally sparring in the salons of London without learning how to wound.

Charles and the two adolescents, who had obviously never seen Marian bested, stared at her with amazement and a certain trace of glee. Lettice knew, with her well-trained instinct for social power struggles, that this family had long been dominated by Mrs. Murdock, especially the two younger ones, who were her children. Lettice suspected that Charles was blandly unaware of Marian's attempts to dominate him. She repressed a smile; there was something to be said for his sort of unawareness.

"Margaret, show Mistress Holmes to the blue guest room," Marian said coolly.

"But, Mother," Margaret protested faintly, and her mother sent her a quelling glance.

The girl subsided into silence. Charles opened his mouth as if to speak, then closed it. Lettice wondered what was the matter with the room.

She soon found out. Molly escorted her up the stairs and down the hall, not saying a word, her eyes kept shyly on her feet, and opened one of the doors. The tiny room she entered was barely large enough for the bed and wardrobe that stood within it, and there wasn't even a mirror to adorn the walls. One small window broke the cell-like atmosphere of the chamber. Lettice knew that this room had been given to her as an insult; it was little better than a servant's quarters, although it occupied the same floor as the family's rooms. Marian was trying to put her firmly in her place, and Charles's silence amounted to complicity in that insult; he, too, wanted her to remember that she was an employee in this house and here only on his sufferance. Anger and a strange, bitter hurt tore at her chest. She would show him; she would show both of them. If he thought he could defeat her with so little effort, he would soon find out differently.

"I—I am sorry the room is not ready," Molly said softly, her voice halting. She still did not raise her eyes to Lettice's face. "We did not expect guests. I will get some linens and make the bed."

She scurried from the room, and Lettice watched her retreating back thoughtfully. Poor little thing; she was painfully shy and obviously frightened of her mother. Her limp really was barely noticeable when she walked normally, rather than hurrying as she had when Charles arrived, and her small, triangular face held possibilities, with its great doelike brown eyes and sensitive mouth, framed as it was in soft brown curls. Many men liked that sort of soft fragility, although Molly was so retiring now that one could hardly get a glimpse of her face.

The girl returned and quickly began to make the bed, glancing now and then at Lettice from the corner of her eye. Lettice smiled at her once, and Molly blushed and looked back down at her work. Lettice felt something tighten and form in her chest. Poor thing; Lettice knew what it was like to be young and uncertain, scared and lonely. Perhaps she had never been this quiet or timid, but she had been abandoned and miserable before she learned how to fight back.

Margaret finished and stepped back from the bed, darted a look at Lettice and then back down at the floor. Then she blurted out suddenly, her voice so soft Lettice could barely understand the words, "You are the most beautiful lady I've ever seen, Mistress Holmes."

Lettice smiled and said, "Thank you," then reached out impulsively to take the girl's hand. "Don't be afraid of me, Margaret. I shan't bite you. May I call you Margaret?"

Margaret nodded dumbly, and Lettice went on, "Good. And you call me Lettice. I detest all these formalities. I hope that you and I shall be friends. Your brother very kindly offered to let me help you with some of the social amenities, probably as a sop to my conscience for throwing myself on his mercy. But I am not a teacher, and I hope you won't think of me as one. I had a horrid governess, and I detested her thoroughly. I promise you and I will have a merry time."

Molly looked at her squarely then and breathed, "I hope so, too. I'm sorry about your husband. It must have been dreadful for you."

It took Lettice a moment to realize what she was talking about; she had been so caught up in her words and feelings that she had forgotten she was playing a part. She smiled and patted the girl's hand. "It's been some time now; the heart heals quickly. Anyway, he and I were not exactly happy; it was, as they say, a marriage of convenience."

"Oh, how dreadful!" The girl's eyes were wide with sympathy, and Lettice felt an unaccustomed tug at her heart. She was such a kind, trusting little thing—how could Charles ever suspect Lettice of doing anything to harm the girl? Only a monster would . . . but then that was what Charles thought her: a heartless monster.

"You are very kind," Lettice said, her smile growing wider at the girl's embarrassed blush.

Awkwardly, Molly took her leave, and Lettice sat down on the bed with a sigh. Again she surveyed her room, the disdain now written on her face. There was not even a chair or a fireplace. No doubt it was bitterly cold in the winter. Well, she hoped she would not have to stay here long; she would accept as little as she had to of Murdock's grudging generosity. Somehow she would find a way out of this situation, even if she had to marry some colonial bumpkin. Anything would be better than staying in Marian Murdock's home, under Charles Murdock's scornful eyes.

Lettice did not see the Murdocks again until the evening meal. She spent the afternoon unpacking her little trunk of clothes, which a manservant had brought up, putting them away in the pine wardrobe, and trying to remove the ravages of travel from her appearance. She brushed out her hair, undressed, and washed her face and arms, then took a brief nap. When she awoke she brushed the dust from her gown and made herself as presentable as she could, considering her wretched somber garments.

Marian dominated the conversation at the dinner table. Molly was too timid to open her mouth, and Bryan was not much better, while Charles was his usual taciturn self, speaking only in answer to Marian Murdock's questions. Lettice listened to the conversation limping along, and felt no interest in trying to give it a little life. Let the selfish Marian struggle with it.

The woman's monologue was punctuated now and then by sharp comments to her children, particularly Margaret, to sit up straight or mind their manners or speak up more clearly. Lettice watched the poor girl wither under her mother's critical comments, and finally could contain her anger no longer.

"Margaret dear, I hope Mrs. Holmes can teach you the art of conversation," Marian was saying. "Any young man would find you as entertaining as a stick. I do think you could at least smile a little now and then. Everyone must imagine you are impossibly cold and full of airs, the way you go about without speaking to anyone," she finished sharply.

Lettice said, her voice smooth as honey, "Perhaps, Mrs. Murdock, Margaret might say more if she were given a chance to speak. I vow, I have sat here for almost thirty minutes, and I don't think there has been a minute in which I have heard anyone's voice but yours. I am amazed to find that Margaret has the power of speech at all."

Charles choked on his ale, and Bryan had to cover his

mouth with his hand to hide a smile, while Marian glared at Lettice. Lettice studiously ignored them all and returned her attention to her food.

The food, in fact, was the only thing in the colonies that she had found to her liking. It was very simple fare, meat and vegetables and a fruit pie, nothing to compare with the cuisine she had known at home. However, it was delicious and filling and a real treat after the bland shipboard menu of beans and salt pork. She had lost several pounds during the crossing, and now she attacked the food with relish, despite Mrs. Murdock's plain look of disapproval at her unladylike zeal.

After dinner, a young man named Jonathan Baker came to call, having heard that Charles had returned. Lettice thought him to be a rather sober sort, although his looks were pleasant and kindness shone from his eyes. When Murdock introduced him to his new house guest, the young man swallowed and flushed and stared at Lettice with admiration. After a moment, he recovered himself enough to remember his manners and make a presentable bow. But even after they sat down and began to talk, his eyes would stray now and then to Lettice, as if he could not quite believe she was real.

Lettice thought with amusement that she had made another conquest, and she pondered for a moment his possibilities as a means of escape from this household. He was a trifle young, of course, probably not more than twenty-four, and seemed to be a desperately earnest man. However, he was not bad-looking, and he was obviously smitten with her.

"Well, tell me, Jonathan, what has happened in my

absence? I will make my report tomorrow, but I might as well tell you now that I failed utterly," Charles said.

The other's eyes slid uncomfortably over to Lettice and back to Charles, a questioning look in them. Charles realized his concern about the woman's nationality and smiled wryly. "Don't worry, Jonathan, Mrs. Holmes could not care less about either side in this affair. I can promise you that she will not be visiting General Gage's house while she is in Boston."

"Heavens, no," Lettice said airily, stung by Murdock's dismissal of her. "Politics bore me to death, I fear."

"This is not just politics," Baker assured her gravely. "What concerns us here is our basic liberties."

"Mr. Murdock had told me something to that effect," she said drily. "Please go on."

"Some really wonderful things have come out of this, Charles," Baker began, needing little encouragement.

"What, pray tell?" Marian interrupted sharply. "I find little encouraging in starvation and penury, and that is what has descended on Boston."

"What I meant was, the people of the other colonies have rushed to support us," Baker said. "The Southern and Middle colonies seem to have stopped accusing us of being harebrained radicals."

"What about the King's ministers, though? I fear they would like to cut Boston off from the rest of the colonies, and break the back of our rebelliousness," Charles said.

"Well, they've not succeeded. Food has been pouring in from all over the colony and from other colonies as well. Why, Wilmington, North Carolina, alone raised two thousand pounds, and Christopher Gadsden in South

Carolina has sent us rice. Even Quebec has sent us ten thousand bushels of wheat."

"Yes, and tables have been set up to feed the poor of the city," Bryan chimed in.

Charles smiled, and his craggy countenance softened. "Good. Good."

"And all the colonies are sending delegates to a Continental Congress in Philadelphia," Baker said excitedly.

"That's what we need," Murdock said emphatically. "All the colonies must act together. Only through a congress can we put together our grievances and present a strong, united front."

"Exactly. Surely, then, King George will listen to us and replace his ministers."

Lettice did not know why she decided to join the discussion; she had no wish to converse with Charles and his friends. But she blurted out, "Then you do not know King George."

"What?" Baker turned to her, amazed.

She smiled. "I may not be politically inclined, sir, but I do know the King, and I can assure you that he is dead set against giving in to the colonies. If you think a change in ministers would alter your hopes, you are doomed to disappointment."

"Oh, no, I am sure that is not true," Baker said. "If he knew how things stood, if he were not so misinformed by his ministers—"

Lettice raised her eyebrows. "Indeed? I think not, Mr. Baker. I am sorry if I blight your hopes, but I think it is foolish indeed to hang your hopes on the King. He is an exceedingly stubborn man, and once he sets his mind one way, an avalanche could not stop it. And he *has* set his mind against the colonies. Believe me, I have met him and most of his ministers. You colonials have attacked Parliament, and Parliament is vital to his hold on the throne of England. It was Parliament that set him up in place of the rightful Stuart heir; he rules by right of Parliament. So when you say that Parliament is wrong, that Parliament has no right to tax you or to make laws against you, you are attacking the King's very foundation. He will give you no sympathy."

Baker frowned and swung toward Charles, his eyes asking for denial. Charles shrugged and said, "I don't know but that she is right, Jonathan. She is more familiar with the people involved. And when I was there, I found little sign that the King had any inclination even to listen to our cause. I know that the mainstay of our movement has been to get past the ministers to King George himself, who would be in sympathy with his people. But in England there were times when I gravely doubted that."

Baker's open face had grown troubled, but then he brightened. "The Worcester Resolutions—had you heard of them, Charles? They state that the people of Massachusetts owe no obedience to the English Parliament. Strong words, eh?"

"Strong, indeed. What did Gage have to say about that?" Charles asked.

"Why, nothing. He has done little since he came here that has been openly antagonistic. Dr. Warren is inclined to believe that the General is sympathetic to us, because his wife, you know, is a colonial, but I suspect Gage listens only to those abominable Tories, those loyalists who urge him against us. I fear we have little hope from Gage as long as those people surround him."

"Who is Dr. Warren?" Lettice inquired, interested in spite of herself.

"Oh, you should meet him, Mistress Holmes. You would find him an exceptional gentleman," Baker said enthusiastically.

"Yes, he is a well-set up man," Charles said drily. "The ladies are fond of him, especially since his wife died and he has become a single man again."

"I have little interest in men, single or otherwise," Lettice said coolly. She would have liked to have hit Murdock for the knowing glint in his eyes; no doubt he thought her nothing but an adventuress, who would pursue any man. "What relation does he have to your cause?"

"He is a leader, madame," Baker said. "He is not as famous as Mr. Adams or Mr. Hancock, but he is a real leader, a scholarly, kind gentleman, and he believes whole-heartedly in our efforts. He is a great friend of Mr. Revere."

"That silversmith," Marian sniffed. "A leader of riffraff and common malcontents."

"Don't discount Paul Revere or his 'riffraff,' Marian. They have done quite a bit for us."

"Quite a bit of brawling, you mean," Marian said scornfully. "How Joseph Warren, with his education and upbringing, can associate with low types like that—"

"It is very important, Marian, that the common people and the uneducated and the craftsmen be with us too. That is why Warren's friendship with Revere is so excellent a factor. It helps to weld some very disparate groups into a cohesive whole," Charles said.

"I thought it was a colonial idea that people were

equal. What I read of Mr. Paine's works indicated that class distinctions were frowned upon here," Lettice teased lazily.

"Thomas Paine!" Marian said disdainfully. "Why, that man is nothing but a radical and an atheist, just like that Virginian you are so fond of, Charles. If the people in England think we are all like Thomas Paine, no wonder they are so deaf to our pleas."

"Thomas Jefferson is a deist, not an atheist," Charles said, his voice wearily patient, and Lettice suspected that this subject was well-worn. "And the English people are so indifferent to us that they have no idea who Thomas Paine is, let alone possess firsthand knowledge of his works."

"But Mistress Holmes obviously has read him," Baker said and turned a warm smile on Lettice.

Lettice answered him with her dazzling smile, enrapturing the young man further. Stammering, he rose and said that he must go, but asked leave to call again soon. Charles looked at him grimly, thinking that the young fool was getting in way over his head, considering what the Englishwoman had done to him, a boy like Jonathan would be putty in her hands. Anger spurted in him at the thought of her using her wiles on Baker; he was a handsome lad—no doubt she would find it much less repulsive to bed him. On that bitter thought, he excused himself from the presence of the ladies and retired to his office to look over the correspondence and work that had accumulated in his absence.

As the men left the room, Lettice happened to glance in Molly's direction and saw her looking at Jonathan. Her young, shining face hid nothing of her feelings or thoughts; her brown eyes gazed at him with longing and pain. So, Lettice thought to herself, the girl is in love with young Baker. She glanced at Marian and wondered if the woman knew how her daughter felt. From what she had seen of the interaction between mother and daughter, Lettice doubted she had the slightest idea what Molly felt about anything. Marian was not the sort of mother in whom one would confide one's girlish dreams.

She was even more certain of it when Marian said, "That Jonathan Baker, I wish he would not come here so often. Charles really should not encourage him."

"Whatever do you mean?" Lettice asked, to draw the woman out; she wondered if Molly already knew her mother's opinion on the matter.

"He involves Charles in that Sons of Liberty nonsense. If he doesn't watch out, Charles will get himself hanged for his pains. And he really is not fit company for the children; after all, he is only a printer."

Lettice saw Molly's face turn white, and she felt a pang of sympathy for the girl. "Mama, printers are respected people. Besides, Mr. Baker publishes a newspaper."

Marian fixed her with a firm gaze. "He really is not of your class, my dear. Your father was one of the most respected merchants in this city, and my ancestors go back to the *Mayflower*. I hope your thoughts do not lie in his direction; you can do much better than Mr. Baker, even with that limp of yours."

Molly hastily lowered her eyes, and Lettice thought she saw a sparkle of tears on her lashes. She wondered how deliberate Marian Murdock's cruelty was; the woman sounded as though she thought the limp was something Molly affected to annoy her.

"The *Mayflower?*" Lettice said, to divert the older woman's fire. "What is that?"

Marian looked at her, brows lifting in astonishment. "The *Mayflower* was the ship that brought the original settlers of Massachusetts Bay from England."

"Oh, yes, those religious fanatics who had to flee England." Lettice yawned delicately. She stood and stretched a little, her gesture casually ending the conversation, and announced that she thought she would go up to her room now. "I am rather tired from my journey," she said and left the room.

All the way down the hall, she could feel the glare of Marian Murdock's eyes burning into her back; she had certainly made an enemy there. Well, Lettice Delaplaine had never been afraid to make enemies; she believed in playing her hand and living with the consequences.

So Mrs. Murdock did not like Jonathan Baker. That feeling certainly was not shared by her daughter, and Lettice thought that for once Molly ought to have her day. It was clear that Marian had kept the girl under her thumb all her life. Molly deserved her happiness if she could get it. Personally, Lettice doubted that any man could bring the happiness a young girl dreamed of, but she was determined that Molly should at least have the chance to find out. Jonathan Baker would come back, lured by her own looks, but she could make sure that he saw Molly at her best, that he talked with her, and that he realized Lettice was not the one for him.

She smiled to herself, savoring the unaccustomed role of matchmaker. It would be fun to teach the girl a few skills, to pretty up her appearance, to guide her through the shoals of courtship without having to endure that courtship herself. And it would not be so bad, she had to admit, to get back at Marian Murdock. Of course, that meant throwing away one of her chances of leaving this place, but there would be others; it would be too cruel to take away Molly's love.

"Mrs. Holmes." She heard Charles's voice and turned to see him standing in the doorway to his study. His face was cold and forbidding, and it made her cringe a little inside, as she used to when Philip looked at her thus.

"Yes?" Lettice kept a haughty expression on her face, determined not to show the faint stab of fears that went through her.

"I would like to see you for a moment."

"I am sorry, but I was just going up to retire."

"It will not take but a moment, I assure you."

His voice brooked no argument and so, with a shrug, Lettice followed him into his study. Murdock shut the door behind them and seated himself behind his desk; he felt the need to keep a barrier between them. Since he'd left the parlor, he had been brooding over Lettice and Baker. She had looked lovely tonight, despite the tiring travel, and he could understand why Jonathan wanted her. He wanted her himself, even as he cursed his weakness.

"I see you made another conquest tonight, Lady Lettice," he began, his voice sardonic.

Again Lettice shrugged, and her indifferent manner angered him. Tightly he went on, "I will not have you toying with Baker, do you understand?"

"Are you his father?" Lettice responded sarcastically, stung by his tone.

"No, but since I brought you here, I find myself responsible for the damage that you do."

"And why should I 'damage' Mr. Baker?"

"Simply because I doubt that you know how to do anything else!" he barked, and Lettice had to bend her head to hide the tears that sprang into her eyes. Charles went on relentlessly. "Just stay away from him, do you hear me? I will not let you break his heart." He clamped his mouth shut, holding back the word "too."

"You have no right," Lettice said fiercely. "You have no right to tell me what to do."

"Don't I? I have given you my protection, despite your treachery toward me."

"How long do I have to continue to pay for that? How long will you hold that over my head? What am I supposed to do—grovel before you in thanks? Let me repay you and be done with it!"

"I do not ask you for payment."

"Then what do you call it?"

Her words shook him, for he could not really deny them. He had no rights over her; he should not attach conditions to the refuge he had given her. It was just that he could not bear to think of her with another man.

"All right then, call it payment if you like. I don't care what label you put on it. But while you are under my roof, I will expect the same standards of you that I would of the women in my family."

Lettice's eyes narrowed dangerously. "You mean the women of your family are not allowed to attract men? No wonder Margaret is such a timid little mouse, growing up with such a selfish tyrant for a brother!"

Charles said nothing, but was forced to clench his

teeth against the rage that boiled within him. Everything about the woman tore at his control. He wanted to grab her by the shoulders and shake her, shake her until her prim cap fell off and the pale gold hair came tumbling to her shoulders, until she cried out to him to stop.

With a soft curse, he rose and turned away from her. Damn—around her he felt like an animal, his desire throttling all sense, all humanity.

Lettice watched him, her body tensed for flight. She could see the violence held back in him, and she had no intention of being the victim of his outburst. But then he turned back, his face again a careful mask, and she relaxed a little.

In a clipped tone, he said, "I will condone no immorality in this house, Lady Lettice. Is that clear?"

Her lovely face twisted in a mocking smile. "Perfectly. I am to restrain from whoring while I am here, although of course you doubt that that is possible." How she hated him for his low opinion of her. She would have loved to slap his sanctimonious face, send her nails slashing down his hard cheek, but she knew she dared not spark that powder keg of anger she had just glimpsed. "Now may I go? Or do you wish to humiliare me further?"

A muscle jumped in his jaw and was stilled. "I expect only one other thing of you, Lady Lettice, and that is to help Mrs. Murdock with the house. Here there are no platoons of servants to do everything for you. My stepmother and sister do much of the housework, especially since fear of the English blockade has sent one of our maids scurrying back to the country."

Lettice stood, her elegant body stiff and straight, almost quivering with rage. Did he really think that this physical humbling would wound her pride more than his insult to her character? Through lips white with fury, she said, "I understand, Mr. Murdock. Not only am I to be a governess for your sister, I am to pay for my keep by being a scrubwoman as well. Since I have no alternative, I accept your terms."

With those words, she turned and left, closing the door behind her with a soft click that was more final than any slam.

Nine

*T*he pale dawn light was barely seeping through her window the next morning when Lettice heard a soft tap at her door and Molly's gentle voice saying, "Mistress Holmes? I hate to disturb you, but it's almost time for breakfast, and Mother will not tell the cook to save you anything."

Lettice thanked her and groggily stumbled from her bed. The cold water that she poured into the washbowl and splashed on her face awakened her with a start, and she hurriedly began to dress in the early-morning chill. It made her shiver to think what this room would be like later in the year; it was barely September now. Her fingers fumbled with the multitudinous buttons and the starched white cuffs and collar. Even though her clothes were painfully simple and she did nothing to her hair but twist it up under its cap, she found it difficult to dress without a maid.

She thought with a grim smile of the hours she used to spend on her toilette, trying on and discarding dresses until she found just the one she wanted, having her maid lace her into her layers of clothing, hold the hoop and petticoats for her to step into, iron the ruffles, hang up her clothes. Then, of course, she would carefully apply her paint and powder, dwelling on decisions such as how many beauty marks to put on her face and what shapes to use—heart or diamond or square? Her maid would touch up her towering hairdo, smoothing and curling and powdering it, and twice a week Monsieur Jacquard, her falsely French hairdresser, would come to curl and shape her hair, stuff rolls into it to hold it in position, and add false pieces here and there, as well as bows or jewels or whatever struck his fancy, until he pronounced himself satisfied with his concoction. Many times her back had ached from the strain of sitting stiffly for hours while he worked. Lettice would change her attire two or three times a day, going from her relatively casual sacque dress in the early part of the day, while she breakfasted and prepared her face, to her day dress, and then to a formal dress in the evenings. Each change required a new selection of adornments, changing the ribbons and bows and jewels in her hair and rummaging anew through her casket of gems. Thinking about it now, she realized that she must have spent half her waking time on her wardrobe and toilette.

And now she could be ready within fifteen minutes. There was something to be said for this plainer style of dressing and coiffure—and she found she was pleasantly relieved of her headaches, now that she was free of the high, heavy mass of hair. Unfortunately, she had to pay the price of freedom with her diminished looks. With a sigh, she smoothed down her skirt and straightened her cuffs and wished she had a mirror in which to check her appearance before she ventured out. A quick peek in the hall mirror would have to do, she guessed.

As she slid into her place at the table, Charles barely glanced at her and did not address her at all during the simple meal. Lettice reminded herself that it really did not matter what she looked like, since there was no one here for her to enchant, anyway. Surprisingly, for she had always barely nibbled at breakfast, she found herself hungry and dug her fork eagerly into the mound of steaming eggs and helped herself liberally to the hot biscuits and salty bacon.

Later she was to feel that that had been her last enjoyable moment of the day. After breakfast, Mrs. Murdock set her to work. With a grim smile of enjoyment on her face, Marian gave her a list of tasks that set Lettice's head swimming. First she was to clean the ashes out of all the fireplaces and prepare the logs for the evening fire, and that pronouncement alone stunned Lettice so thoroughly that she took in little else of what the woman said. How on earth was one to clean out a fireplace?

When Marian left, Molly said gently, "Mistress Holmes, would you like me to help you?"

Lettice smiled at her gratefully. "Would you? I haven't the first idea how to begin."

Patiently Molly demonstrated the dirty task, saying innocently, "I cannot imagine why Mother gave this chore to you; it's far too hard for a lady. Usually one of the servants does it."

Lettice said nothing. She knew very well why Marian had assigned her this task: She disliked her thoroughly and hoped to harass her into leaving. And doubtless Charles had urged her to give Lettice the hardest, most humiliating tasks. Lettice did not know what his motives were—whether he simply wanted the satisfaction of seeing her brought low or if he hoped she would reduce herself to begging him to lighten her load. Well, whatever he wanted, she vowed grimly that she would not let on to him, no matter how much she suffered. He would never see a Delaplaine crawl.

By the end of the day, Lettice began to wonder if she would even be *able* to crawl. If it had not been for Molly's kind tutoring and assistance, she was sure she would never have gotten through the day. Cleaning the fireplaces was dirty, back-breaking work, and her clumsiness and ignorance only drew the task out. She could not seem to get the ashes out of the grate without spilling some on the floor or rug, and then she had to clean up the mess she had made. The dust got in her eyes and lungs, and grime clung to her clothes and skin, irritatingly imbedding itself underneath her long fingernails. She had barely begun the job when she broke one of her nails and almost cried with frustration; her fingernails had always been so well groomed and beautiful, and she had spent hours on their care.

Then she had stacked the logs and kindling; carefully following Molly's example, and discovered to her dismay that the logs were heavy and rough, scratching her hands. Almost every room had a fireplace, and Lettice could hardly straighten by the time she had finished. Never in her life had her back hurt so, even that time her horse had tried to run away with her on a hunt and she had had to battle him fiercely to pull him under control.

When she finished, Marian set her to cleaning the rugs, and only the glint of malicious satisfaction in the other woman's eyes kept Lettice from bursting into tears of exhaustion. Her pride forced her to march off to her new task with a rigid back.

Molly helped her carry out the heavy rugs and hang them up, then showed her how to pound the rug with a metal instrument made for that purpose, so that the accumulated dust went flying out. By the time she finished beating them and put the rugs back in their places, it was dusk, and Lettice's shoulders and arms trembled from the strain of wielding the rug beater. Tiredly she stumbled up to her room and stripped off her filthy clothes. She wanted to do nothing but collapse on the bed, but she could not bear to put her filthy face and arms against the clean sheets. So she took a bar of soap, filled the washbowl with water, and set about scrubbing her face and hands. It took several refillings of the bowl to wash herself clean, and she despaired of getting all the grit and blackness from under her fingernails. With only a faint sigh for her once-lovely nails, she ruthlessly cut them short to get rid of the grime and remove a future lodging place for it. When she held her hands in front of her for inspection, tears filled her eyes for the first time that awful day. Once her hands had been pale, slender, and delicate; more than one man had rhapsodized over their beauty. Now they looked strangely short and stubby with the long nails gone; they were red and chapped from the scrubbing she had just given them and covered with scrapes and scratches. A housemaid's hands.

She threw herself face down on the bed and gave way to sobs. Who would take her now, the way she looked? Who would ever guess she was a lady, descended from one of the oldest lines in England? If Philip could have seen her, he would have broken into gales of laughter.

Her crying bout spent, she crawled between the sheets and gave herself up to sleep. She was too tired to dress again and go downstairs to eat. Not even her pride could sustain her through a meal spent in the company of those two who despised her; she simply could not maintain a cool, composed front with them tonight. Let them think whatever they liked.

Molly slipped into her room about an hour later, awakening her to give her some meat and bread she had saved from dinner and hidden in a napkin. Lettice hugged the girl impulsively and thanked her for her kindness. As she wolfed down the food, she vowed to herself that she would see this through, that she would somehow overcome the Murdocks and get both herself and poor Molly away from this dismal house.

Her stubborn pride and persistence won Lettice no respect from Marian Murdock. In fact, her quiet, uncomplaining conquest of the tasks set for her seemed to increase the woman's spite. She gave the hardest jobs to Lettice, making her rise before everyone else and clean the kitchen fire for the day, as well as the other fireplaces. There seemed to be a never-ending supply of chores around the home; Marian was a meticulous housekeeper, and every woman in the household was constantly busy.

Once a week the wooden floors had to be scrubbed and waxed, another job that fell to Lettice, and they were swept every day. All the furniture was dusted every third day, and polished once a week. The silverware and a set of silver goblets also had to be polished. The mirrors and windows were washed spotless every week. Besides that, the dishes must be washed and the food cooked, as well as clothes and linen washed, hung to dry, and ironed.

Since it was fall, there was food to be pickled, or preserved, or dried and stored in the cellar for winter. There was the daily marketing to be done and the beds to be made, and the seemingly endless sewing and mending. And once a week the great feather mattresses had to be turned and plumped up, a task that took the strength of at least two women.

Lettice hung on grimly, cursing her clumsiness and her aching body, noting with horror the calluses that grew on her hands and the muscles hardening in her arms. Many times every day, she was on the verge of screaming aloud with vexation, throwing down her tools and simply walking out of the house. Only her tremendous will kept her at it—and Molly's kind sympathy.

For Molly's sake, despite her weariness, she seized every opportunity to talk to the girl, to teach her the paths to a man's heart—or, at least, to his groin, she thought drily, though she did not tell Molly her cynical thought. She taught her to flirt and talk to a man, how to smile and blush prettily, how to turn her head and use her hands gracefully. They carried on long imaginary conversations, with Lettice posing as a hopeful suitor and Margaret stumbling through the role of seductress.

Lettice was greatly relieved to discover that they did not always wear their drab clothes and caps, but only for their workaday world. On Sundays everyone dressed up, and there were even dinners and parties. Unfortunately, there was little ornamentation to work with, only a brooch or plain locket or lace cuffs and collar, but Lettice helped Molly sew up a sunny yellow dress that fitted the girl charmingly. And when Lettice pinned her brown locks into a charming mass of curls, even Molly had to stare at her reflection and blush with amazed admiration.

Lettice offered to teach her to dance, but the girl gasped, "Oh, no, I couldn't!"

"Why ever not? I can teach you all the dance steps, and I promise you will learn them in no time. Surely people do dance sometimes in Boston."

"Yes, we are not one of the strict old religionist families," Molly admitted. "But I would be too embarrassed. I would not be able to dance creditably, you see."

"Don't be a ninny," Lettice said, pushing a stray curl back under her cap and continuing with her scrubbing of the hallway.

"But Lettice," the girl whispered in a mortified voice, "I am lame."

"Oh, folderol," Lettice said bluntly. "We once had a stableboy who ran heedlessly out in front of my father's carriage, and his legs were crushed beneath the wheels. He could never walk again, only drag himself grotesquely around with his arms. Now, *that* is lame. You, my dear, have the slightest of limps, and I am sure it would not keep you from dancing. It is hardly noticeable when you walk, and if your mother would not go on and on about it, and make you so ashamed of it, I am sure that you and everyone else would not even think of it."

Molly stared at her, her eyes wide. "Do you mean it, Lettice? Do you really think I could? I have always wanted to dance, more than anything. It looks like such great fun."

"It is," Lettice assured her, "and I am certain that you can do it."

"All right, then, I'll try. When can we start?"

Lettice laughed at her eagerness. "How about tomorrow?"

"Oh, yes. And I promise that I will work very hard!"

"Margaret!" Marian's voice called. "Where are you? I thought I told you to make the bread."

"Coming, Mother," Molly called, and Lettice sighed with irritation at the way the animation drained from her face, leaving it dull and colorless.

A few moments after the girl left, while Lettice was still on her hands and knees scrubbing, the front door opened and she looked up in surprise. Charles Murdock came in and stood staring down at her. Lettice returned her eyes to her task, hoping he did not see the flush that mounted in her cheeks. He did not usually come home during the day, and never before had he caught her engaging in one of her menial chores. It galled her now that he should see her like this, on her hands and knees like a common scrubwoman. It must give him great satisfaction to see her brought so low, and the thought of her humiliation before him was almost too much for her to bear.

"Lettice, what in the world are you doing?" he asked, his voice startled.

"Haven't you eyes? I'm scrubbing the floor," she replied tartly, not looking up at him.

"Good God!" he breathed softly. "Get up off the floor."

"I am sorry," Lettice said sarcastically, angered by his commanding tone. Whatever he might like to think, she was not his slave. "I haven't got the time to converse with you. I have to earn my room and board, you know."

A hand like iron closed around one wrist and pulled

her to her feet. Lettice did not struggle, but stood stiffly, proudly, meeting his eyes. The blaze she saw there was enough to make her drop her gaze, but she swallowed and maintained her indifferent stare.

"What in the hell are you doing?" he asked, each word clipped and hard.

"Working, as you told me to. I also clean out the fireplaces, lay the fires, and once, when the maid was out ill, I emptied the chamberpots." She strove to keep her voice light, despite the grim look on his face. "Is that lowly enough to repay you for the hurt I did you?"

"I never meant this!" Charles said aghast, then lifted his voice in a roar. "Marian!"

Lettice was glad that she did not have to answer the look on his face when he turned to his stepmother. The woman halted uncertainly as she entered the door, her eyes sliding nervously to Lettice and then to Charles.

"What do you think you are doing?" Charles snapped at her. "Why is Lettice doing work that is usually given to the lowliest servant?"

"You said that she was to help me." Marian wet her lips nervously.

"My God!" Charles exploded. "I meant she was to help you with the light work, such as dusting, or maybe baking or sewing. She is a guest in our house, not a charmaid! Have I made myself clear this time?"

"Yes, quite," Marian said stiffly and shot Lettice a look of pure hatred; no doubt she blamed her for Charles's anger.

Charles turned back to Lettice, ignoring the other woman, and Marian swept angrily out of the room. "I apologize. No matter what you think, it was never my intent to humiliate or abuse you. I had noticed how silent you seemed at dinner, but I thought you were angry with me. I never thought it was fatigue—no, exhaustion. Please forgive me."

He reached out and took one of her hands in his, and Lettice thought with shame how callused her own was. She longed to snatch it from his grasp, but he retained hold of it and examined it, surprised at its roughness.

"My God, your poor hand," he kissed it, then turned it over to kiss the work-hardened palm.

At the gentle caress of his lips, a shiver darted through Lettice, different from anything she had ever felt before. She was aware of a childish desire to lean against his broad chest and cry; she wanted to go down on her knees before him and beg his forgiveness for all the things she had done to him, and for the fact that she had misjudged him so. For some reason, she remembered the feel of his hard, hot body against hers that night on the ship and his warm breath against her cheek. She blushed at the memory and pulled her hand away.

After that, Lettice's load lightened. Now she spent her time doing the lighter chores with Molly and Marian, polishing the silver, dusting, sweeping, and mending. Molly, shocked at her dismal ignorance of cooking, began to teach her.

Her weariness vanished, and she began to take an interest in the world around her. One day, not long after Charles's abrupt alteration of her life in his house, Lettice set out with Molly to explore the city she now lived in. She delighted in the chance to get outside, and only then realized how stifled she had felt.

Taking in a deep breath of the crisp fall air, Lettice looked around her at the neat, clean shops, the cobblestoned streets, the trees heavy with brilliant red and gold leaves. "How beautiful the trees are!"

Molly smiled at her words. "Yes, aren't they lovely? I love to walk in the city at this time of year, and even better, to drive into the countryside."

A young, matronly-looking woman, dressed in black wool, passed them on the sidewalk and smiled cheerily. "Miss Murdock," she said to Molly, and Molly greeted her pleasantly.

Lettice turned to stare after the woman in amazement. "That is the third woman I've seen walking alone since we came out! Yet they don't look common. Is it accepted that women walk alone here?"

"Why, of course." Molly turned to her with astonished eyes. "Don't they do so in London?"

Lettice laughed shortly. "No, not unless they are of the sort who welcome being accosted. I never went out unless I was with a male companion or at least my maid."

"How awful," Molly said upon reflection. "I couldn't stand never to be let out of the house unless I had a maid tagging along. Didn't you mind being so restricted?"

Lettice was thoughtful for a moment, then said, "Yes, I suppose I did. Certainly I chafed under the restrictions society imposed—and got myself into plenty of trouble. I wanted to go everywhere, and see things, and do what I wanted, as a man could."

"Well, here you can go for a walk alone," Molly assured her. "No one will think the worse of you for it. Oh, look, there is Admiral Graves's wife, getting into that carriage up there. That is the house where they live."

Lettice looked at the elegantly dressed woman whose footman was assisting her into her carriage. Her hair was piled high in an intricate, powdered style, the sort that used to give Lettice her blinding headaches. Thank heaven I no longer have to wear such things, she said to herself with relief, and then was stunned by her thoughts. Only a few months ago, she had mourned the loss of her brocades and satins and paints and hairdresser, and here she was being grateful for the loss!

Molly continued, her eyes dancing with amusement, "It is said that Mrs. Gage is absolutely furious with that woman. Mrs. Graves, it seems, has set herself up as the leader of society here, which, of course, should rightfully be the General's wife's position. There has been a feud going on between them ever since Mrs. Graves arrived."

Lettice laughed. "That sounds familiar. I can remember lifelong feuds being caused by some social slight or other. There was a coun—a woman that my mother refused to speak to for twenty years. If they saw each other on the street, they would snub each other." Lettice lifted her head in haughty imitation of her mother's snub, and Molly giggled.

"Why were they angry with each other?" Molly asked.

Lettice started to answer, then stopped, deciding that the cause of their feud was not for the ears of one such as Molly. "I don't know exactly," she replied smoothly. "It began before I was born."

They walked to the docks, and Lettice stared about her at the deserted area, empty of life. Ships moved gently at their anchors, their sails furled, and here and there sat barrels, waiting to be loaded, but no man moved on the docks in the normal hustle and bustle of loading and sailing. The only life was on the British naval vessels that floated farther out in the port.

"It's so deserted," Lettice breathed with awe, trying to imagine London's teeming wharfs so stilled.

"Yes," Molly said, her usually gentle voice hard with anger. "That's what Parliament has done to us."

"But how can a port city like this earn the money to pay the taxes that Parliament wants when no ships can come in or out?" Lettice asked.

"That's just it; of course we cannot. They hope to starve us into submission." Molly lifted her small chin proudly. "But that will never happen. They just don't know how stiff-necked we Bostonians are."

Lettice smiled at the girl's tone; she could readily understand the rebellious stubborness of these Bostonians. After all, hadn't she fought all her life against every attempt to turn her into a compliant, submissive woman?

They turned back into the city, Molly pointing out the sights as they went along: Faneuil Hall, the old North Church, Paul Revere's silversmith's shop, nestled in among the other craft shops. At last they turned into a chandler's shop, a cramped little room where candles hung in every conceivable place. While Molly made her purchases for the house, Lettice glanced around her with interest. Never in her life had she bought anything so mundane as candles, and the little shop seemed strangely fascinating to her.

A woman dressed in black, with a sparkling white mobcap on her hair, opened a small door at the back of the room and stepped out. She looked to be about thirty, with a plump, pleasant face. Her fingers were stained with ink, and in one hand she carried a quill pen. When she saw Molly, she smiled.

"Hello, Miss Margaret," she said, her voice hearty.

"Mistress Whitney," Molly replied. "I'd like you to meet our guest, Mistress Holmes."

"How do you do?" the woman politely inclined her head. "Would you care to take a cup of coffee in my office? I was just about to stop for a moment. I've never been talented with figures, and right now they are spinning around in my head."

With a laugh, Molly agreed. As they stepped behind the counter and into the minuscule office behind the front of the shop, Molly explained, "Mistress Whitney owns this store."

"She owns it?" Lettice's brows vaulted upwards.

"Yes," Mrs. Whitney answered, overhearing them. "I own it and operate it, too." She closed the door behind them and began to pour coffee from a pot that sat on the wide desk. "When my husband George died, the store passed to me. I've no choice but to keep it going, so that my children will have something to inherit when they grow up. The candlemaking I have no trouble with; I often helped George in the shop. But the books—" She shook her head with mock grimness. "Now that's a different story. I wish I had paid more attention to arithmetic in Dame School."

Lettice stared, her eyes wide with amazement. She could not imagine a woman owning and operating a store. "You mean that you are in charge of all the clerks? And you keep the books?"

Mrs. Whitney nodded. "Yes, and teach the apprentices how to make candles as well." She paused for a moment, looking at Lettice, then said shrewdly, "You aren't from the colonies, are you?"

"No, I'm from England," Lettice admitted.

"I thought so. Colonial women don't find it so strange for a woman to run a shop. There are quite a few women printers and other craftsmen, not to mention women merchants."

"I can hardly believe it," Lettice said. "Does no one object?"

Mrs. Whitney shrugged. "Who can object? We are an independent people here, Mistress Holmes. People can follow the trade of their choice; they can move on out of the towns and get new land just for the asking. That's why it's so hard to find labor; men do not need to work for someone else. Usually a man's wife and family must help him in the shop, and when he dies, who else is there to take over? Who else knows the business better? We have to work hard here to make our living, but I, for one, would not change matters for the world. Where else would I have such freedom? Certainly not in some tradition-bound society."

Lettice smiled. She liked the other woman's blunt manner of speech, her obvious independence and confidence. She suspected that not too many tradesmen were able to outwit Mrs. Whitney.

"I salute you, Mistress Whitney," she said, raising her cup. "I have never heard of such independence, but I must say I admire it."

The woman smiled back at her, as though recognizing a fellow spirit. "Thank you, Mistress Holmes. I'd hazard a guess that if your sympathies haven't already turned to us colonials, they will soon. You have the love of freedom in you. Speaking of which, have you heard the news from Worcester?"

"No, what?" Molly asked.

"The citizens of Worcester have forced their judges and court officials to recant that timid letter of loyalty to Gage they had signed. And not only that, they went on to reorganize their militia so that the people elect the officers."

"That hardly sounds like the way an army is run," Lettice commented.

"That may be," Mrs. Whitney said, "but it certainly is a way to oust all the loyalists from their offices, and put in patriots instead!"

"I see," Lettice said, sipping at her drink. She was beginning to find that these colonials were deadly serious, not the laughable yokels the people in England believed them to be. "You know, sometimes I think Parliament must be blind not to see their mistakes."

"Hear, hear," Molly applauded her friend's sentiments. "If only other English people thought as you do."

"Perhaps they would, if they saw what I have seen here."

When they had finished their coffee, Mrs. Whitney showed them the back room, where the candles were actually made. Lettice walked around it in fascination, examining the huge vats of wax, the long strings of wicks, the molds that lined the walls. When at last they left, Mrs. Whitney pressed an invitation upon Lettice to come again to visit, and Lettice promised that she would. It did not even occur to her to wonder at the thought of a Delaplaine making friends with a chandler's widow.

That evening at supper, Charles's face was grave, and

Molly asked him worriedly what was the matter. A small smile touched his mouth as he looked at his sister, and momentarily lightened his face.

"I am afraid that General Gage has made a decidedly martial move," he replied. "Up till now, I think he has been most circumspect. He's done his best to keep his soldiers in line and not allow any outbreaks of violence. I thought he was trying to keep a lid on the powder keg we are living in. But today he seized a munitions supply in Charlestown. A move like that is more like lighting the spark to ignite the powder."

"What will happen?" Lettice asked, fear suddenly clutching at her chest.

"I don't know," Charles replied and shook his head. "Perhaps nothing. Perhaps an outbreak of war. I don't know."

A loud knock on the door interrupted their meal, and when the maid answered it, Jonathan Baker rushed in, ignoring etiquette as he swept into the dining room, his face ablaze with excitement.

"Charles! You must come! The whole colony is in an uproar. When they heard about Gage's seizing the Charlestown munitions supply, twenty thousand men from Massachusetts and Connecticut rose up and are marching to Boston. If we're to avoid war, we must do something now!"

"What! Good Lord, what a coil! Why the devil did Gage have to do such a stupid thing?"

"I don't think he realized what effect it would have. You know the British don't take us seriously. Gage is reportedly amazed and appalled; he never expected such a spontaneous reaction. He wants to speak to you and Dr.

Warren; Joseph sent me to fetch you. He wants you to talk to the people who are massing across the Neck and convince them to go home."

Charles stood, tossing his napkin onto the table. "Then I must go. We cannot let this thing cause bloodshed. Excuse me, ladies."

"Why must Charles thrust himself into the middle of such things?" Marian said.

"Mama, everyone trusts him. Gage knows that those men will believe him if he assures them that everything is all right and Gage is not about to shoot us all. Charles has to go; he feels he has a duty to the people."

"The people!" Marian snorted. "Why should he have a duty to that rag-tag lot? A bunch of malcontents and rowdies, that's all they are."

"I think you are wrong, Mistress Murdock," Lettice said. "That is what people in Britain think, what I thought until I came here. But I've seen the people here, and I think they are strong and in earnest."

Marian looked at her scornfully. "And what, may I ask, does someone like you know of politics?"

"Not much," Lettice replied smoothly, "but I do know a lot about people, and I know there is something brewing here."

It was late the next afternoon before a weary Charles returned, his mission accomplished and the angry colonists dispersed to their farms. Seeing the sag of his shoulders and the tired droop of his eyes, Lettice was struck by a twinge of pity and sudden respect. Charles was a man of honor, one who followed his duty no matter what the cost. She could not remember ever knowing a man such as he. Hastily, she turned away from him so that he would not see the sudden flood of feeling in her eyes.

As Lettice's sympathy for the colonial cause grew, the only aspect of her treks through the city that made her uncomfortable was the presence of the red-coated British soldiers. She had seen them all her life, of course, but never before had she viewed them with the eyes of someone wanted in England for murder. She doubted that any of them had even heard of what she had done, or at least they certainly would not be on the lookout for her. Still, she was afraid she might meet an officer who knew her or get caught in the middle of one of the altercations that were always springing up between the soldiers and the citizens of Boston, and then they would question her, and it might all come out. For that reason, she studiously avoided every soldier that she saw.

One day, as she left a millinery store, where she had purchased a bundle of gaily colored ribbons to adorn Molly's hair, she had the misfortune to literally run right into a soldier. Hastily she backed off, murmuring an apology, but he would not let her go so easily.

"Here, now," he said cheerily, chucking her under the chin, "here's a pretty Puritan."

Lettice could smell the reek of whiskey on him and she frowned—drunk already, and it was only afternoon. She knew better than to tangle with a drunk; so she deftly moved away from his grasp and started to go past him. He fell in beside her, still talking.

"It's a crime to hide a figure like that in somber dresses," he leered. Lettice studiously ignored him, but he continued, "Now, I could dress you up real pretty, if you was to be nice to me."

"Thank you, I don't want anything. Please leave me alone," Lettice said, with as much severity as she could muster.

"Aw, now, don't be so cold," he whined and took her arm to pull her to a halt.

"How dare you!" Lettice swung on him instinctively, her bearing regal, her eyes flashing with contempt and outrage. "You common scum. Let go of me at once!"

"Oh, high and mighty, are you?" he said jocularly and jerked her to him.

Lettice began to struggle now, bringing her hand up for a ringing slap on his cheek, but he shoved her against the wall, knocking the air from her, and clamped his hands on her arms. She kicked and flailed at him vainly, and his loose, drunken mouth loomed nearer and nearer. In disgust she turned her head away, delaying even for a moment that awful contact with his mouth.

"Here! What is going on here?" a familiar voice barked out.

"Charles!" Lettice cried, and then suddenly her attacker was jerked from her, and she stumbled as the man went spinning to the ground.

Murdock loomed over him like an avenging angel, huge and thunderous.

"This young lady is under my protection," he said, his voice so cold it made Lettice herself shiver. "Should you ever touch her again, I will kill you. Do you understand?

The man nodded, his eyes glazed with fear, and quickly scrambled away. Murdock turned back to Lettice, the cold fury replaced with concern. "Are you all right?"

His arm went around her solicitously and, gratefully, Lettice leaned against his broad chest. "Yes, I think so. He had not really done anything yet. Oh, Charles, I am so terrified of those soldiers. What if—what if he should find out who I am?"

"I think there is little likelihood of that. I doubt if the news about Lord Philip Kenton has even reached Boston yet, and no one would think of your coming here, anyway," he replied reasonably. "Come, I'll walk you home."

Lettice straightened and moved away reluctantly; never before had she felt the comfort and security that the shelter of his arms had given her. "There is no need; I am sure that will not happen again."

"Nevertheless, I shall accompany you. I was returning home, anyway," Charles lied calmly. That moment of holding her in his arms had brought home to him how much he still wanted her and missed the friendly companionship of their days aboard ship. He could not resist the chance to spend a few minutes alone with her.

Awkwardly, Lettice fell in beside him; it had been a long time since Charles had been so warm toward her. Since their arrival in Boston, he had studiously avoided her, and she had supposed she was thoroughly repugnant to him. Lettice had to admit that she had been lonely and missed their talks, but now she hardly knew what to say to him. Everything was so different here.

"Has Marian been treating you well?" he asked, wanting to talk and yet unable to say any of the things uppermost in his mind.

"Yes. Thank you for speaking to her."

"Damn it, why didn't you tell me what was going on?" he burst out. "I had no idea."

Lettice blushed. "I thought you had encouraged it. I thought you wanted to see me humiliated."

Murdock stared at her. "Good God, why should I want to humiliate you?"

Her blush deepened, and she looked away from him as she said softly, "Because—of what I have done to you."

Charles, too, glanced away, and they were silent, both of them avoiding a subject too painful for discussion. "Lettice, I've been thinking," he said, to block the path their thoughts took. "I've seen how willingly you've thrown yourself into the housework, how uncomplaining you've been. Molly tells me you are kind to her and very helpful. She respects you tremendously."

Lettice said nothing, swallowing down the lump in her throat. What did it matter that Molly respected her? Suddenly she realized how much it had hurt that this man seemed to have lost all respect for her.

"It has occurred to me," Charles continued awkwardly, "that I have been unfair to you." Lettice's heart began to thud, and then dropped at his next words. "You deserve payment for what you do. I can hardly expect you to do all the work you do and receive no compensation."

Tears stung her eyes, and Lettice wanted to run away. A salary! He was offering her not renewed friendship, but money, dismissing her like a servant. That brief moment of comfort and tenderness when he had held her was gone, blasted by his cold remoteness. Obviously the only relationship he wanted between them was that of employer and employee; there would be no kindness, no gratitude, no companionship, just hard money.

As she had always done, Lettice masked her hurt with a stiffly haughty face. She would have liked to throw his offer in his face, but now more than ever she knew that she had to leave his house, and for that she needed money. So she inclined her head in a regal nod of assent.

They continued to the house in frigid silence, as distant as if they walked on different streets. Inside, Lettice felt she still carried within her that block of ice that had plagued her ever since she had refused his offer of marriage on the ship. It seemed to grow inside her, stifling her, cutting off her breath, and she cursed herself for letting him hurt her. After all, who was he, that his opinion should damage her, she reassured herself. For once, however, her proud words rang hollow in her ears.

Ten

$\mathcal{M}$olly twisted, craning her head to see her new-found glory from every angle in the short mirror above her dresser. Lettice watched her, smiling; the girl's naïve enjoyment was more pleasurable than any of her sophisticated amusements of the past.

"I can't believe it," Molly whispered, smoothing down her full yellow skirts. She swung to Lettice anxiously for reassurance. "Am I really pretty?"

"Pretty? You look absolutely beautiful," Lettice said stoutly.

Molly was dressed in the new yellow gown she and Lettice had created, and the fresh color brought sparkle to her face. Lettice had done her hair up in a charming cluster of curls, and here and there yellow ribbons peeked alluringly from her brown locks. As she looked at herself, her brown eyes wide with wonder, Lettice yielded to impulse and hugged the younger girl enthusiastically.

"Everyone will be enchanted," Lettice assured her. "Now, remember all the things I've told you."

Clowning, Molly went through a routine of alluring smiles and flirtatious pouts and mock frowns, until Lettice laughed and clapped her hands. "Bravo! Just don't panic and forget them. I will draw your mother's fire, and you can concentrate on Mr. Baker."

"Jonathan?" Molly said faintly, paling at the thought.

"Of course. You don't think all this is for the benefit of Bryan and Charles, do you? Surely you can't have forgotten that Mr. Baker is coming tonight."

"No, of course. But I didn't think—" the girl stumbled along, then blurted out, "Oh, Lettice, I haven't a prayer with Jonathan! He is mad about you, and I could never compete. You're so beautiful."

Lettice understood the girl's hesitation. Jonathan had taken to calling frequently since her arrival. Lettice had walked a thin line with him on every occasion, not wanting to discourage him so much that he quit calling before she prepared Molly for courtship, yet having to keep him at enough of a distance that he did not fall in love with her. She had flirted with him a trifle, but made sure they were never alone, and she was careful not to talk to him overmuch.

Much to her amusement, Marian had encouraged the suit, no doubt hoping to rid herself of her unwanted guest by marrying her off to Jonathan. She had even gone so far as to invite him to dinner this evening, despite her low opinion of his suitability. Lettice had seized the opportunity to present the transformed Molly. No doubt Marian would be aghast, but the thought of her discomfiture merely heightened Lettice's amusement.

"Oh, Molly, Mr. Baker and I would never suit," Lettice said offhandedly. "He is much too serious a man to remain long interested in me. He may suffer from a mild infatuation now, because I am someone new and different from other women he has known, but when it comes to love and marriage—then you may be sure that he will want a woman like you."

Molly stared at her, astonished. "But don't you want him, Lettice?"

Lettice laughed. Obviously Molly found it hard to believe that everyone did not love her Jonathan as she did. "No, Molly. Why, he is too young for me, and too serious. I would only make him miserable, as well as myself. No, I give you sole rights to the inestimable Mr. Baker."

The girl blushed and said, "Am I so obvious?"

"Not to the others, but I am more experienced in these matters. I saw the first night I came here that he held your heart."

"Oh, Lettice, you are the most wonderful person, to help me like this. Mother would be furious if she knew."

Lettice shrugged. "Believe me, Molly, I have cracked harder nuts than Mrs. Murdock. Don't worry about me."

Firmly she took the girl's arm and they went downstairs. Molly's appearance startled everyone, most of all Jonathan Baker. Lettice noted with satisfaction that he rose from his seat almost gaping with astonishment; it was clear that he was really seeing the girl for the first time.

Marian frowned and opened her mouth, but Lettice moved quickly to forestall any of the woman's critical attacks on her daughter's confidence. "Mistress Murdock," she said in a voice so sweet that it roused the other woman's suspicion and gained all her attention. "I am quite looking forward to this evening's meal. I'm sure it will be a vast improvement over your usual colonial fare."

"We find nothing wrong with plain food," Marian replied primly, locking horns with the enemy.

"No doubt that is because you have had nothing else," Lettice said haughtily and launched into an imperious account of the food and entertainment she was used to, a performance guaranteed to enrage Marian Murdock and to disillusion her erstwhile admirer.

They quickly removed to the dining room, where Lettice kept up her bombardment of Marian. She could feel Charles glowering at her from the other end of the table, clearly disgusted by her sudden relapse into aristocratic vanity and shallowness. However, across the table, she saw his sister deep in conversation with Jonathan, unimpeded by any attention from the others, and the glow on the girl's face was worth ten times the measure of Charles's disapproval. After all, his opinion meant nothing to her; she had long since determined that.

Following the meal, they removed to the drawing room, where Lettice proceeded to put the second part of her plan into action. "Molly tells me how beautifully you play the harpsichord, Mistress Murdock," she said in a bright, clear voice. "Do play something for us."

Marian looked suspicious at her request, but when the others chorused their agreement, she could do little but give in and sit down at the instrument.

After the woman played a song or two, Lettice said, "I declare, I feel like dancing! Play a minuet, do, Mistress Murdock. Mr. Murdock, won't you dance with me?" She moved quickly to cut off an invitation from Baker.

Murdock frowned at her and she cried, "Oh, please, do! It would be such fun. Molly, wouldn't you like to dance?"

"Lettice!" Charles's frown deepened at her tactlessness and he whispered, "You know Molly does not dance."

Defiantly she threw back her head and met his thunderous face with a mocking smile. "That proves that you, sir, like all men, are quite unaware of us females and our accomplishments. Mr. Baker, dance with Molly, and show Mr. Murdock how mistaken he is."

Molly blushed shyly as Baker rose, stammering in confusion and dismay. Charles took Lettice's arm and dug his fingers in painfully, until tears sprang to her eyes.

"Damn it, Lettice," he murmured, "stop this outrage at once, or I swear to God I'll break every bone in your heartless body."

Lettice merely laughed, not even protesting his steely grip. She was utterly involved in the excitement and fear and eagerness that afflicted her pupil as she rose to face her first test.

Molly held out her hand, unconsciously imitating Lettice as she said, "Come, Jonathan, I promise I shan't disgrace you or tread on your toes."

Baker went to take her hand, astonished and yet lured by her manner and the sparkle in her eyes. Angrily Marian began to pound out the notes of a minuet, and Baker led the girl into the intricate steps. Lettice watched proudly as Molly walked through the graceful dance without mishap. She scarcely felt Murdock's grasp on her arm slacken and fall away as he watched his sister dance.

"Lettice, what is going on?" Charles grasped her by the shoulders and turned her to face him.

Lettice looked up at his broad, rough face, which was a strange mixture of puzzlement, joy, and the blazing remnants of his fury. "Why, a dance, Mr. Murdock. I trust you don't object to your sister dancing," Lettice said, seized with a wicked impulse to tease him. He had been a brute to hurt her arm like that and to think her capable of making fun of Molly; he deserved a little needling. Besides, there was something exciting about the flare of emotion in him, and she felt a perverse longing to goad him until he boiled forth, unleashed and wild.

"Damn you," he breathed, looking down at her lovely, mocking face. Her green eyes glittered with unholy mirth, and the cool set of her mouth challenged him to conquer it. He felt shaken by passion and a matching anger.

"Do you refuse to dance with me?" Lettice mocked, and angrily he held out his hand to her.

His lips tight, seething with unspent emotion, he stumbled through the steps of the dance. He had never been a good dancer, always feeling awkward and shy at the social graces. Now he felt ten times a fool, exposing his ineptitude in the presence of Lettice's elegant, skilled grace, and his embarrassment increased his clumsiness.

When the dance ended, Molly and Lettice clapped their hands and cried for another one, and Marian reluctantly started up again. With an angry twist of his mouth, Charles took a firm hold on his partner's wrist and pulled her out of the room and into the sitting room next to it. He closed the door with a final click and turned to face her. It was all he could do to keep from flinging her across the room.

"I demand an explanation," he said in clipped tones. "What is the meaning of this performance tonight?"

"I don't know what you mean," Lettice said airily, turning away from him.

Goaded beyond endurance, he spun her around to face him. "Tell me what game you are playing at now! What are you doing to Molly? Tell me!"

"Or else what?" Lettice faced him, feeling the excitement rise in her. She did not stop to inspect her reasons; she knew only that she wanted to prod him to the breaking point. "Will you hit me? Beat me? Take a crop to my back as Philip did? Or will you rape me? Tear my dress and pin me to the floor?"

Her luscious mouth lingered over her words, and Charles could not take his eyes away from her pink lips. The blood was pounding thunderously in his head, and he could not think, could not breathe. All he knew was that he trembled and ached, that he suddenly wanted this woman past all reason, past bearing.

"Lettice, stop." His voice was choked.

"Stop what?" Daring him, she stepped closer until less than a foot separated them. She felt possessed by emotion, in the grip of some power stronger than she, stronger than her fear.

"Your lies. Your deceit," he whispered desperately.

"I would not lie to you. I am your faithful servant now, am I not? How could I do aught but your bidding? You are my master." Her green eyes taunted him, and her voice was as soft and seductive as velvet.

Suddenly his hands dug into her shoulders and he pulled her against his hard body, molding her to him, and his full mouth came down, possessing hers. She responded to his strength, his mastery, and her arms went round his neck, holding on to security in her rocking world. For the first time in her life, delight seared through her at a man's touch. His hot, hard kiss sent a thousand tingling shivers all over her body, and she wanted suddenly to have him take her, to use her body for his pleasure, to be the source of his fulfillment.

This strange new feeling terrified her, shook the very foundation of her life, and in fear she wrenched herself from his arms, stumbling backward.

He faced her, panting, his eyes heavy-lidded with passion, his face a mask of desire. He took a step toward her, and Lettice retreated from his naked hunger.

"No, please, Charles," she whispered. "I beg of you, don't."

With visible effort, he stopped and drew a deep breath, fighting his desire, until finally his will won over his driving physical need, and he turned from her, white and shaken.

"God, Lettice," he groaned, "why must you torment me? Does it give you satisfaction to see me driven to my knees by lust?"

"No!" Lettice cried out, her eyes swimming with tears. "Oh, no, I am sorry, Charles. Sometimes I think I am possessed by devils. I did not mean to, I did not want to hurt you. I was excited by Molly's success, and silly and careless in my joy. I am sorry. I should not have teased you."

Charles passed his hand shakily across his face. He did not know how much longer he could stand this. She drove him wild, even when she did not try to entice him, as she had done tonight. Just the sight of her, the faint scent of lavender that clung to her clothes and hair, the musical sound of her voice, sparked his passion. He had tried to settle down to his former life, had worked hours on end to save his father's business, now struggling and dying under the embargo, as well as picking up his law practice again. He had been elected to the illegal assembly that Massachusetts had formed in defiance of the Crown, and he spent every spare moment of his time on it and the colonial struggle. But no matter how he weighed himself down with work, he could not seem to drive Lettice from his mind. He lay awake in bed at night, no matter how tired, torturing himself with the memory of her naked body and the one tumultuous time he had possessed it. Sometimes he wished he had married her despite her deceit, just to have that sweet body in his bed. There were even times he thought of using his knowledge of her husband's death to force her to yield to him, though he hated himself for the unworthy idea.

And now, tonight, all she had done was tease him a bit, prod at his anger, and his control had snapped. Almost, almost he had forced her again.

"I'm sorry," he mumbled, "about your arm. Did I hurt you?"

Lettice shrugged, and her voice strove for lightness. "I've known worse. I'm sorry too; I should not have taunted you like that. I suppose I wanted to pay you back. I know I am a wretch."

With a sigh, he walked to the window and stared out at the black night; even now he could not bear to look at her for fear he would lose control again. "Will you tell me now about Molly?"

"Yes. I taught her to dance; I knew she could do it. Everyone emphasizes her limp too much; it is barely noticeable. She is a sweet and pretty girl, and I've been trying to teach her a few ways to attract men, how to flirt and how to dress her hair. She sewed up a new gown with a little assistance from me in designing it, and I got yellow ribbons for her hair, and tonight we were trying out the new Molly."

"Why did you persist in that ridiculous, obnoxious manner this evening? What did that have to do with Molly? Why not tell us straight out what you were doing?"

"She wanted to surprise you, Charles. She didn't want you to expect too much and then perhaps see her fail. And I acted that way to draw her mother's fire. There's nothing wrong with Molly that couldn't be cured by getting her away from that woman for a while. She undercuts her confidence horribly. I'm sorry, I know she is your stepmother, but all of you cater to her too much. She is a bully, especially with her own daughter. And I knew that if she started in about Molly's new dress and hair style, Molly would absolutely wilt and lose all her joy. So I acted in such a way that she would be too absorbed in battling me to spare a barb for her child."

Murdock smiled thinly. "You need not apologize to me. I know she intimidates Molly, but I have no right to interfere. I cannot take Molly away from her mother. But I thank you for what you have done for her."

"It was nothing. I enjoyed it. Molly is a sweet girl," Lettice demurred.

"Sometimes I think you are fond of her," Charles said.

Lettice laughed, a little bitterly. "I am. Did you think that I was capable of liking no one but myself?"

Charles flushed. "No, of course not." He paused, then burst out, "Well, frankly, yes. I have seen little from you except that done out of selfish interest."

Lettice flared angrily. "Just because I don't wish to fling myself into your bed does not mean I am selfish! My God, is a woman entitled to no self-respect, no dignity? Can I not even choose to sleep alone?"

"I was not referring to your disgust for me," Charles

said flatly. "I was thinking more of your plan to trick me into marriage when you had no feeling for me—or worse, feelings of dislike."

Lettice's green eyes darkened stormily and she muttered, "What else was I to do? I faced starvation when we landed. I was penniless and friendless."

"I have taken care of you, have I not? Without your marrying me."

"How was I to know you would do that?"

"What manner of man do you think I am? Did you imagine I would actually turn you loose to starve in a foreign land?" Charles asked, offended. "You think I would abandon you to your fate; you think I set you noisome tasks in the household to humiliate you. Good Lord, woman, I've had my heart in my hand for you ever since I saw you; you know that. How could I hurt you? I'd sooner hurt myself."

He turned away, embarrassed at what he had revealed about himself. Lettice stared at him, amazed at his honesty and feeling. He was so kind, so different from any other man she had ever known. She felt something warm stir in her, a cracking of the ice that resided within. What did it matter, really, that he was plain and unfashionably dressed or that he did not speak elegantly? It occurred to her suddenly that he was ten times the man of any other gentleman she had known.

"I wish," she said softly, "that things had been different, that I had been different. I am truly sorry for what I did to you, Charles. I can offer no adequate excuse. I should have stood up to Philip; I was a coward not to. Please, believe me, I did not deceive you to hurt you; I did it selfishly, true, to protect myself, but I had no desire to hurt you."

"Why didn't you simply refuse to do it for your husband?" he asked, the old hurt still lurking in his eyes.

"Oh, Charles, I am not brave; I am not good. I didn't want to do it, but when he threatened me, I could not stand up to him."

"He threatened you?"

"Yes." Lettice could not bear to meet his eyes and see her humiliation mirrored there, but she felt she had to make him understand her treachery. So she looked steadily at an embroidered footstool as her story poured forth. "Philip wanted to fleece you at cards, and he had forced me to before, but I refused. I hated doing his filthy work, but then he said he would give me to Lord Harold if I did not, and I could not bear that."

"He said what!"

"That he would give me to Sir Harold. Harold always wanted me and was forever chasing me, but I despised him. He is like Philip; he enjoys my pain as much as his own pleasure. You would not understand; even when you took me by force, you did not wish to hurt me. But Harold—"

Charles went rigid and pale. "You mean your husband would have sent you to the bed of a man you hated?"

"Yes, he knew no other punishment I feared as much. I hated it; I hated him. You have slept with me; you know that I am unable to respond."

"Lettice, no," he protested gently, taking both her hands in his. "I raped you; how could I expect you to feel desire? I was repulsive to you."

"No more so than any other man."

"You have had other men?" His voice was thick; he had to ask, though his mind shrieked that it did not want to know of the other men who had caressed her body. Were the rumors about her in London true then?

"Yes, two besides Philip and you," Lettice admitted, past caring now, lost in her past pain. "Philip made me sleep with Lord Danby to get out of a debt he owed him: He was an old man, wrinkled and horrid. And then once I slept with a young man, one who could get Philip a government post that would give him money."

"Lettice," Charles said haltingly, unable to think of anything adequate to say. "I had no idea. No wonder you did not trust me. No wonder the prospect of marrying me repelled you so."

"On the night we were married," Lettice said, as though she could bear to hold it in no longer, "I was a virgin and quite frightened. I did not love Philip; I was too smart for that. I begged him not to hurt me, to go slowly, but he laughed at me. I didn't know then that his pleasure came from pain. It was a dreadful experience, and even worse was the way Philip mocked me and told me what a cold unsatisfactory woman I was. It was awful, and I hated it. Every time it got worse." Her voice cracked, and at long last dry, wracking sobs began to pour forth from her, and she raised trembling hands to her face.

"Lettice," Charles said, his voice filled with anguish, and he pulled her to his chest gently, his arms encircling her lovingly. She cried against his chest, weeping for all the pain and degradation of the past. Finally, when at last she stopped, drained of all emotion, Murdock said gently, "Don't worry, Lettice; you will never have to face that again. Philip is dead, and I will take care of you. Always. Do you understand? You don't have to marry anyone unless you want to. You have a home here as long as you want. And no man will take you to his bed, I promise you, unless you desire it. That includes me. I swear it; I'd cut off my hand before I'd hurt you again."

With a sigh, Lettice buried her face in his chest, feeling at last secure here, at last at home.

Eleven

$\mathcal{A}$s the weeks passed, Lettice found that her days settled into a comfortable pattern. There were even times, much to her amazement, when she actually felt happy. She grew daily more skilled in the household work, and began to take pride in what she did. There was a certain sense of satisfaction, she discovered, in looking around a gleaming house, or sitting down to a solid, delicious meal, and knowing that one's own efforts had produced it. Never before had she achieved anything tangible, or done a task that she could point to with pride.

Molly had undertaken to teach her to bake and cook, and her pride was almost unequaled one night when Charles ate two pieces of her cake and pronounced it absolutely delicious.

Her friendship with Molly deepened. They gossiped together merrily, and Molly confided deep secrets about her love for Jonathan Baker while Lettice amused her with some of the less risqué stories from her life in London. Under Lettice's tutelage, Molly grew daily in confidence and poise.

After that evening, when Lettice revealed to him the

painful facts of her marriage, Charles fell into an easier relationship with Lettice. Although there was still a certain reserve in his manner toward her, he no longer avoided her. Instead of withdrawing to his study most evenings, he spent them in the company of the women, Lettice included, and most of his conversation was directed toward her. Lettice suspected that he pitied her for Philip's cruelty and her deficiency as a woman, but she enjoyed their companionable conversations too much to stand on her pride.

Usually their conversation centered on the increasingly warlike hostilities between the British and the colonials. One evening Charles announced, "General Gage has started fortifying the approaches to Boston."

"What?" Marian asked in amazement.

"Well, you know that for some time soldiers have been guarding the Neck." He looked toward Lettice and added, "That's the thin strip of land connecting the peninsula of Boston to the mainland."

"I am not entirely ignorant," Lettice retorted tartly. "I know that the city of Boston is almost an island."

"Jonathan says," Molly began, then stopped, blushing, and continued haltingly, "that is, Mr. Baker told us the other evening that General Gage is bringing in more troops."

"That's true," Charles responded. "He's scouring the colonies, trying to bring in every soldier he can get his hands on. He has already brought the number of his men in the city up to thirty-five hundred."

"It's terrible," Marian said, turning a sharp gaze on Lettice, as if she were responsible for the actions of the soldiers. "Our own countrymen treating us like an occupied country! They'll stir up a fight, if they don't watch out."

Although Lettice had little sympathy with British soldiers, she felt compelled to come hotly to their defense at the woman's words. "You can hardly expect them not to employ martial measures, considering the way the colonials are smuggling out ammunition. Why, I heard that the other day a farmer's cart was stopped, and when they searched beneath the hay, they found nineteen thousand musket balls! Wouldn't you call that a warlike gesture? And what about the way the 'liberty boys' roam the streets at night, picking fights with the soldiers? I think Gage ought to be praised for the way he restrains his men. Why, a soldier who breaks the law is punished more severely than Boston's laws require of its citizens."

"That is true," Murdock agreed and smiled at Lettice; he enjoyed flexing his intellectual muscles against her. "However, you cannot ignore the fact that the British have used measures against us that they would never think of using on an English city. Putting an embargo on us, changing our judicial and legislative systems, quartering soldiers on us—those are the actions of a conquering country."

Evening after evening passed in this way, broken only by Jonathan's visits or the time Charles spent at secret political meetings. The days grew colder, and soon winter was upon them.

Despite the increasingly harsh weather, Lettice still slipped out every week or so to visit her new friend Ruth Whitney. The woman always had something interesting to talk about, whether it was her business or the state of the depressed Boston economy or the political situation with England, and Lettice never grew bored with her, as she often had with her friends in the past.

One day in early December, she walked to the chandlery, contentedly breathing in the crisp winter air. Lettice smiled at the clerk behind the counter, then made her way to the private office. Ruth opened the door at her knock and at the sight of Lettice, her face was instantly wreathed in smiles.

"My," she said, "don't you look pretty today? This Boston air agrees with you."

"I think you may be right," Lettice said with a laugh, and sat down.

"How about some hot chocolate? I'll ask Mary to make us some." Lettice nodded and the woman bustled off to call to her servant. In a few minutes she was back and plopped down in her chair. "Whew! What a life this is! When I was a girl, I never dreamed I would spend my days this way."

"I admire you for it," Lettice said honestly. "Before I came to Boston, I had never done a smidgin of work—but, you know, I find it strangely invigorating. And your work, in which you actually create something—that must be satisfying indeed."

A small smile touched Ruth's lips. "Yes, it is, in a way. But the problems are multiplying now until I sometimes wonder how we shall ever make it. There is no commerce, therefore no money, and who is going to buy candles when they haven't the money to purchase food? I sell more now to the soldiers—blast their hides—than I do to the citizens of Boston!"

Mary, a skinny servant girl about fourteen years old, brought in a tray containing two cups and a steaming pot of chocolate. Awkwardly, she laid the tray on her mistress's desk, bobbing a deep curtsey at Lettice and Ruth, then backed out of the room. When she had gone, Ruth laughed.

"The girl is awed by your looks. She's a poor country lass who's never before been off the farm, and no doubt you are the most beautiful woman she has seen in her life. The other day, after you left, she sidled up to me and said in a breathless little voice, 'Oh, mum, who was that lady? She looks like a princess!'"

Lettice smiled and sipped her cup of chocolate. It was deliciously warm and sweet and melted away the cold that the December weather had put in her bones. She and Ruth continued to talk until suddenly a distant crash interrupted their conversation.

"What in the world?" Ruth began, standing up and setting down her cup.

"I don't know . . ." Lettice murmured. "It sounded like glass breaking."

Ruth opened the door and peered out into the store. "What was that, Samuel?"

"I don't know, Mistress Whitney. Sounds like it's coming from down the street."

Ruth crossed the store to the front door, Lettice quickly at her heels. As she opened the door, another crash sounded, followed by the tinkling of broken glass and the sound of harsh jeers and catcalls. Ruth stuck her head out the door and looked up and down the street.

"Well!" she exclaimed angrily. "Of all the—they're breaking up Daniel Potter's shop!"

Lettice pushed out after her and turned to look down the street. In the next block stood four Redcoat officers, weaving slightly, hallooing in front of a store. As she watched, one of the men picked up a rock and sent it sailing against the front door. Splinters of wood flew from the door, although it held. The window of the shop had already been shattered, and shards of glass lay in the street.

Like many of the shopowners and craftsmen, Potter lived above his shop, and now on the second story a set of shutters flew open and a middle-aged man thrust his head out. His face was flushed with anger.

"Begone, you jackasses!" he yelled. "What right have you to plunder an honest tradesman?"

One of the officers hooted with laughter. "Honest tradesman is it? More like a lying, dirty whoreson of liberty! Come on, Potter, come out and face a real Englishman face to face!"

"Vandals!" the man returned, shaking his fist. "Filthy lobster backs!"

Almost involuntarily, Lettice felt herself drawn toward the conflict. She and Ruth trailed down the street, their eyes wide with astonishment and fright. All around them, other store owners and customers also moved slowly toward the store, and Lettice could hear their angry muttered comments.

"They're drunk!" Lettice said to her companion. "What on earth are they doing?"

"Oh, I've seen it before," Ruth said, bitterness tinging her normally placid voice. "Daniel Potter is a patriot, and last week he refused to sell a cask of ale to a Redcoat. This is their revenge."

"But I thought Gage had commanded his men not to harass the citizens."

"Oh, yes, he commanded it; Gage is not a bad sort—at least he has a colonial wife. But his officers are not prone to follow orders. More than once I've seen them engage in drunken mockery of our leaders or vandalize an honest citizen's property, like Daniel's here."

The crowd around them grew as they neared the scene and came to a grumbling halt. Only a few feet away from the officers, they halted and slowly swelled as more and more citizens came to see what was happening. The officers ignored the people, continuing to jeer at the man in the window above, who hurled helpless imprecations down upon them. Finally one of the soldiers picked up a stone and flung it at the man; it struck heavily against the wooden shutter beside Potter's head. Potter ducked back inside, and the four soldiers howled with laughter. An angry murmur ran through the crowd.

"That's right, Red-bellies!" a man's voice cried. "Only it's more like yellow-bellies, ain't it?"

"Yeah!" several voices called out, and one man cried, "What brave men are the King's soldiers, to throw rocks at a defenseless old man!"

The soldiers turned, for the first time aware of the growing, restless crowd of people that had gathered at the perimeter of their conflict.

"Scum!" one of the officers sneered heedlessly. "Boston rabble! There's not a man among you fit to be in the King's Army!"

Lettice looked around her and saw hatred etched on the faces of the people. With horror, she realized that the spontaneous gathering was quickly turning into a mob. The crowd surged suddenly toward the soldiers and helplessly she was shoved along with them.

The soldiers suddenly became aware of their danger, and they stepped back quickly, pulling their pistols from their belts with one hand while the other went to the hilts of their swords.

"Stand back!" one of the officers shouted, but slowly, inexorably the people moved forward.

Lettice's heart began to thud wildly in her chest as she was pulled along. For a moment the soldiers stood firm against the angry crowd, then suddenly broke and ran. Hoots and laughter followed them, and one or two boys picked up rocks and hurled them after the retreating Redcoats.

Lettice relaxed, and her breath came more normally again. The awful threat of bloodshed was over. But the event was not, for now a man seized the moment and the crowd to jump up on a watering trough and wave his hat wildly in the air.

"Hurrah for liberty!" he shouted, and the crowd shouted back. "Hurrah for Sam Adams! Hurrah for John Hancock!" Again and again the crowd thundered its approval.

Now the first man jumped down and another took his place, a burly fellow dressed in the rough clothes of a workman. "Did you see those Redcoats run?" He was silenced by cheers, then began again. "That's the way we'll make them run again! We are a peaceful people, but how long can we stand by and watch these foreign devils occupy our city? We are British subjects, but we are denied the liberties given to every Englishman! We are being crushed under the heel of King George. And how long do they think we will take that without answering back?"

All around her, people cheered and applauded, calling out words of approval. Even Lettice felt something warm swell in her chest, something proud and angry. Intently she listened as the speaker began to recount the wrongs done to Boston, until she felt an urgent tug at her elbow.

Turning, she saw the anxious face of Jonathan Baker. "Mistress Holmes!" he exclaimed. "Whatever are you doing here? This is no place for a lady like yourself."

Baker took her arm and firmly pulled her from the crowd, battling his way back to the periphery. "These rallies can become a bit violent at times," he told Lettice sternly. "You mustn't put yourself into such a situation."

"But I was interested in what that man was saying!" Lettice protested his high-handed treatment.

"Mistress Holmes, I've seen a rally turn into a tar-and-feathering, and that is no sight for a lady's eyes."

Lettice started to protest, but remembered her panicky fear when the crowd had moved against the soldiers, and she had been swept along helplessly with it. Certainly she had no desire to see any violence done to anyone.

"Well, I didn't come to it purposely," Lettice said and pulled her arm from his hand. "It just happened. Four soldiers were wrecking this poor man's property, smashing his windows and throwing rocks against the building. Everyone came out to see what was going on. I just happened to be here, visiting with Ruth Whitney."

"Of course, Mistress Holmes," Baker said, set down by the flash of anger in his companion's eyes. "I am sorry if I spoke roughly to you. I was frightened when I saw you there in that mob."

Lettice unbent enough to favor him with a smile. "I will

forgive you, Mr. Baker, if you promise that you will not wait again so long to visit us."

An almost embarrassed smile crept across his sober face. "The truth is, Mistress Holmes, I was beginning to feel somewhat of an intruder. I have visited the Murdock house so often of late . . ."

Lettice laughed. "But you're always most welcome, I can assure you of that."

"Miss Molly is very young," Baker said, following his own train of thought.

"In age, perhaps," Lettice agreed. "However, I find her to be a very mature girl—and one who knows her own mind."

"No, she would not be inconstant," Baker agreed quickly, the lines around his mouth lifting. He was silent for a moment, then began to speak, staring intently in front of him. "Mistress Holmes, would it be presumptuous of me to ask—that is, do you think that Miss Murdock has a, well any fondness for . . ." He paused, clearing his throat in an agony of embarrassment.

"Does she have a fondness for you?" Lettice finished for him. "Of course, I cannot reveal a young woman's secrets, entrusted as they might have been to me. However, I feel quite secure in giving you hope where Molly is concerned," Lettice hinted, trying to relieve his mind and yet spark his interest at the same time.

Baker's face cleared with relief. "Truly? You don't know how that eases my mind, Mistress Holmes. I must confess that lately I've formed a deep attachment to the girl, but she is so young, and I know that her mother would not welcome my suit."

Lettice airily waved away the problem of Marian Murdock. "Charles likes you, I know that. And he, after all, is the head of the family."

"I know, but I fear that Mistress Murdock will try to influence Miss Molly against me."

Lettice laughed. "Molly may appear a frail little thing, but I can assure you there is stubbornness in her as well. I think it would take more than her mother's warnings to move her affections from the man she has set them upon."

"Oh, look," Baker said suddenly, looking down the street. "There is Dr. Warren. Would you like to meet him?"

"Why, yes," Lettice answered, following his gaze. "I have heard so much about him."

Lettice studied the man as he came toward them. He was a good-looking man, as Charles had said, with a clean, honest face and bright, intelligent eyes. For a Bostonian, his clothes bordered on the elegant; they were better cut, more expensive, and lighter-hued than were usually seen in the city.

He tipped his tri-cornered hat to Jonathan. "Mr. Baker. Nice to see you."

"Dr. Warren," Jonathan responded. "May I have the pleasure of introducing you to Mistress Holmes? She is a houseguest with Charles Murdock and his family."

A smile spread across the other man's features. "Ah, yes, I had heard that Mr. Murdock had a beautiful visitor. I had no idea how very lovely, however. I have been remiss in not calling on Charles earlier." He made an elegant bow over her hand.

"I had heard you were a patriot, sir," Lettice returned merrily, "but no one told me how gallant you are as well."

"I hope you're enjoying your visit here. It is a sad time to be in Boston, I'm afraid."

"But most interesting."

"Yes," he said. "I do believe that we are at this moment living a wonderful piece of history."

"Really? And is it the beginning or the end of an era?"

"Both, I think," he replied soberly. "Now, if you will excuse me, I must be going. I have a very sick patient waiting for me. Good day, Mistress Holmes, Mr. Baker." With a tip of his hat, he left them, hurrying on to his destination.

Lettice looked after him, her eyes narrowing. "He seems a most intelligent man."

"Oh, yes, he is, one of the finest. He would make an able statesman. There are those who laud Sam Adams, but he is an instigator, a man who causes things to happen, pricks people to action. Joseph Warren is one who accomplishes things; he is a true leader."

Lettice sighed. "Mr. Baker, sometimes it frightens me, the situation here. What is to become of men like you and Dr. Warren and Charles? Where is all this going to stop?"

Baker frowned. "I don't know, Mistress Holmes, but we must act."

"I fear that soon there will no longer be any turning back."

Baker fixed his level gaze upon her. "There are those of us who hope that moment comes quickly."

"But what will you do? What can this one city do against the might of the British Army?"

"Not one city, we hope, but a whole continent."

"Even all thirteen colonies—what could they do against the mightiest empire in the world?" Lettice cried.

"Strength is not always the answer," Baker replied solemnly. "Tell me, Mistress Holmes, if it came to that, which side would you choose?"

"I doubt that my preference would have much influence," Lettice said, then added with a sparkling smile, "But, I must confess, I've always been a rebel."

Winter continued, and Christmas came and went, with little of the pomp and pageantry that Lettice had been accustomed to in England. But her reduced fund of money made it more challenging and enjoyable to buy presents for everyone. For Molly, she made a set of beautifully embroidered cuffs and a collar, and for Charles, she sat up many nights, straining her eyes in the dim candlelight, to sew an elegant linen shirt. She knew when he opened the gift that it was too personal a thing for her to give him, for Marian's quick, disapproving frown told her so. However, his smile and the warmth in his eyes as he took out the delicately monogrammed shirt, with lace ruffles cascading down the front, made the work and Marian's disapproval worthwhile.

Charles's gift to her was a rich maroon leatherbound book with gilt-edged leaves, a collection of poetry that was lovely, expensive, and thoroughly appropriate. For some reason, however, Lettice felt a faint stab of disappointment that the present had not been something more personal.

After Christmas, winter deepened into the snow and ice-bound days of January. Lettice rarely went out into the frozen white world, and she began to feel restless, penned in. To make matters worse, Marian had become even more antagonistic since Christmas, constantly sniping at her and making pointed comments about her over-long stay.

One day, as the three women sat together by the fire-place, doing their needlework, Marian said, thin-lipped, "I hate to mention such gossip to you, Mistress Holmes, but I think that you should know what people are say-ing."

Lettice quirked an eyebrow at her. The woman's prefa-tory comment was one she had heard many times before, and she had learned that it usually preceded something decidedly hurtful, which the speaker took great glee in transmitting.

"There's been quite a bit of talk about town concern-ing you and Charles, what with the months you have been here, living under the same roof with him."

"Talk?" Lettice repeated frostily, sending both her eye-brows up haughtily.

"Yes, indeed. An attractive woman like you, who turns up out of nowhere, living in the same house with a single man. After a time, people begin to wonder," Marian went on, with a dismal shake of her head.

"When there are a stepmother and a brother and sister to chaperone?" Lettice replied coolly.

"If one lives in the same house, who is to say what happens when the others are asleep?" Marian said in-sinuatingly.

"Why, one could say the same about you," Lettice suggested. "After all, you and Charles are not flesh and blood, yet you live together in the same house."

Lettice was surprised and somewhat taken aback by the flash of straight hatred in the other woman's eyes. Marian had never liked her, but Lettice could not fathom why she should have such an intense dislike for her. Then suddenly it came to her, and she almost laughed. She had been an idiot not to see it before: Marian wanted Charles for herself. It was not that outlandish an idea; she was only a few years older than Charles and still an attractive woman, even if she was a shrew. No doubt she had hoped that over the years their living in such close quarters would lead him to seek her bed, and perhaps her hand in marriage. Would marrying one's stepmother be banned as incestuous? Perhaps—the thought stopped Lettice with a thud—perhaps her plan had worked. Was it not possible that Charles was a frequent visitor in Marian's bedchamber, or had been in the past? He was a man of great sensual appetite, as Lettice well knew, no matter how morally upright he might be. It was not at all unlikely that years of proximity to a willing female would have their effect on him. Lettice felt a sudden fiery ripple of jealousy run through her. She was more attractive than Marian; why would he not seek her bed?

Surprisingly, the timid Molly leaped to her defense. "Mother, how can you say such things? No one would think that; it is perfectly proper with all of us living here."

Marian stared at her daughter with such astonishment that Lettice had to stifle a giggle. Obviously, Marian had never expected her daughter to stand up to her on anything. However, the woman recovered quickly, and her face darkened ominously.

Lettice knew that Marian was about to unleash her fury on Molly to bring her back in line, so she stood, saying, "Well, I shall speak to Mr. Murdock about it. He will know what is best to do, I'm sure. Molly, I thought I would try my hand at rolls today. Would you come supervise me?"

Molly followed her to the kitchen with grateful alacrity, and when they reached their refuge, she squeezed Lettice's hand. "Thank you for warding her off; I literally tremble when Mother gets angry with me."

Lettice smiled, and began to gather up ingredients. Molly helped her, frowning a little, and Lettice knew she was still worried about her mother's words.

"Lettice," she began at last, "I wouldn't worry about what Mother said. I'm sure it isn't true; no one would think anything wrong was going on between you and Charles. It's common knowledge, anyway, that Charles has a—a woman he sees, you know."

Lettice felt her heart skip a beat and said with a determinedly casual air, "You mean he has been calling on a lady regularly?"

Molly blushed up to her hairline. "No, not a lady. I mean, the sort of woman men go to when—when they have carnal needs."

"A mistress?" Lettice turned to stare at her, heedless of her reaction now. "You mean that Charles has a mistress in town?"

Molly gulped and nodded. "No one speaks of it, but such things are not that uncommon, even here in Boston, particularly for an unmarried man. I am sure that people are aware of it. Even I know about it, and I am no sophisticate. Her name is Anne Lindon."

Lettice turned back to her bowl, her stomach fluttering and jumping wildly. So Charles had a mistress, someone to satisfy his "carnal" needs, as Molly so primly put it. God knows, he certainly had his carnal needs; she thought of that evening in the sitting room, when he had kissed and caressed her so hungrily. She wondered if he had visited his mistress later, and if she had assuaged his lust.

"What does she look like?" Lettice asked quietly, her eyes intent on her work.

"Why, I don't know. I've never seen her," Molly replied, taken aback. "Why?"

Lettice shrugged. What business was it of hers if he kept a mistress? He was a friend to her, nothing more. Certainly she wanted none of the sexual favors he bestowed on Anne Lindon. She ought to be grateful that he had a mistress, or else he might force himself upon her some night, as he had on the ship.

"Oh, nothing," she replied airily. "It just surprises me. Charles doesn't seem the sort to keep a mistress."

Lettice dropped the topic and returned to her work, but over the next few days she had trouble keeping Anne Lindon out of her thoughts. She found herself wondering what the woman looked like and where she lived. Was she a ravishing beauty or a common slut of the streets? Was her hair black or red or blond, and what color were her eyes? Was she as attractive as Lettice herself? She wondered if Charles lavished presents on her, if he visited her frequently, if he held her tenderly and comforted her when she was frightened.

It was ridiculous, Lettice told herself, to have such curiosity about Charles Murdock's private life. It was no concern of hers and displayed a deplorable lack of dignity on her part. The way she was acting one would think she was some naïve country girl, not a London sophisticate who had been raised in a world of wealthy, aristocratic gentlemen who kept mistresses as a matter of course. Why, Philip had had any number of mistresses all through their married life, and she had never been curious about any of them.

But no matter how much she resolved to cease her foolish thoughts, Lettice could not seem to stop them. She could hardly look at Charles anymore in the evenings as they talked without thinking of him lying naked in his mistress's bed.

"Mr. Jonathan Baker, Mistress Murdock, come to call," said the maid, bobbing a curtsey.

"Yes, send him in," Marian said in a falsely pleasant voice, beginning to put away her mending in her bag.

Lettice hid a smile. All winter long Baker had continued his visits and Marian welcomed them, mistakenly assuming that it was still Lettice the young man's hopes were set on. She nearly always excused herself soon after he came, leaving Molly as a token chaperone. The irony of it, to Lettice, was that ever since that night when Molly had blossomed forth, Baker's attention had turned more and more to the young girl, until it became obvious that it was Molly he came to court, not Lettice.

"Jonathan," Charles said, rising to shake his hand, his affable expression of a moment before now marred with a slight frown. "Good to see you."

"Charles. Mistress Murdock." He made a polite bow in the older woman's direction, then took the languid hand that Lettice offered him in greeting. "Mistress Holmes."

He turned away from the rest of the group to greet

Molly, and only Lettice saw the fierce light that shone in his eyes when they rested on the girl.

He took the empty seat on the couch beside Lettice, and Charles shifted uncomfortably in his chair. Damn the man, he thought, as he searched his mind for some excuse to leave. He could not bear to stay and watch Lettice flirt with him; it made his insides coil with jealousy.

"How is your paper, Jonathan?" he asked civilly, reminding himself that this man had long been his friend and that he should be happy for Lettice that such a fine man as Baker wanted her. Jonathan could fix her affections as he never could; he could awaken her to the delights of love. Charles knew he was a selfish beast to wish the man to hell every time he appeared.

"Fine, Charles. At least the British have not stopped our newspapers."

A thin sheen of sweat broke out across Charles's forehead as he looked at Baker and Lettice side by side on the couch: What a fine-looking couple they made, not incongruous as he and Lettice were. Stiffly Charles kept up the light, superficial talk for a few moments more, then rose.

"I—I must attend to some of my papers, if you will excuse me."

Again Lettice smothered a smile. Charles's excuses for leaving when Jonathan came were becoming weaker and weaker; he was not a man adept at lying. It was dear of him to leave to try to further his sister's interests with Baker, but Lettice often wished that he would remain so that she could have someone to talk to. It was deadly dull watching two lovebirds coo.

"I must go also," Marian said soon after Charles's

departure. "I will leave you young people by yourselves."

The other three in the room smiled politely, relaxing with a sigh once Marian's steps sounded on the stairs. Casually Lettice rose and sat down in the chair the other woman had vacated. Jonathan immediately turned his entire attention to Molly, and they began to speak softly to each other, oblivious to the rest of the world. Lettice yawned. She had little liking for the role of chaperone. After a few moments, it occurred to her that it would be a kindness to the couple for her to slip away for a few minutes, at least. An opportunity for some kisses and lovers' confidences might spur their romance, which, though obviously sound, seemed a trifle dull to Lettice. Certainly there could be no harm in leaving the girl alone with Baker; Lettice could not imagine a more trustworthy soul.

"Please excuse me for a moment; I want to fetch a sampler I've been working on," Lettice said, quickly leaving the room before the all-too-proper Jonathan could protest the unseemliness of it.

Making her way down the hall, Lettice stopped at Charles's open study door and looked in. "Hello. Care for some company?" she asked gaily.

Charles looked up, startled. "Lettice! Did Jonathan leave?"

"No, but I left him and Molly alone for a while. I hope that doesn't shock you."

"Hardly. There is no one I would trust more with my sister. But why did you leave?"

"Oh, I thought it would encourage them," Lettice said airily and sat down in the chair across from him. "There is nothing like privacy to make love bloom."

"What?" Charles looked at her, thunderstruck. "Are you saying that you hope Jonathan and Molly will fall in love?"

Now it was Lettice who looked surprised. "Of course. Why, I thought you guessed long ago. That's why Mr. Baker comes here, to see Molly. I hope you have nothing against it."

"No, no, of course not. Baker is a fine young man. I couldn't hope for better for Molly. But I thought—it's you he loves, Lettice, not Molly."

Lettice giggled. "Oh, at first he thought I was rather alluring, but I knew Molly was in love with him, so I encouraged a change of direction in his attentions. All it took was getting him to really look at her as a woman, and a little bit of silliness on my part to make him realize that Molly was what he wanted, not me."

A smile burst across Charles's face. Doubtless it was wrong of him to be glad that Lettice had not found love at last, but a sweet happiness exploded in him at her words. Thank God, she would not be leaving him to marry Baker; at least he would still be able to see her and talk to her. He would not have to writhe under imaginings of her pale naked body being caressed by Baker's strong hands.

"You have been very kind to Molly," he said, to hide his real reasons for happiness. "Thank you. I never expected you to do so much for her."

Lettice shrugged, embarrassed. "She is a lovely child; it isn't hard to be kind to her."

"Don't discount your own goodness, Lettice. You have turned out to be a—well, quite different from what I thought you to be," Charles said and looked away. He remembered the pain and bitterness he had felt about her, the angry judgments he had made. It had been his own disappointment that had spoken then; he had not really seen her or made any attempt to understand her actions. The black picture he had painted had not been accurate—look at her kindness to Molly, the uncomplaining way she had tackled the housework, no matter how strange and demeaning it was to her. It was no wonder she had sometimes acted selfishly, considering the society she grew up in, the cold inattention of her parents, the loneliness, the agony of her marriage to Philip. And he had not tried to help, had only condemned her.

He could see now how frightened and unhappy she was, how trapped in frozen isolation. If only someone could bring her heart to life again—but, he reminded himself, wryly, that someone would not be Charles Murdock. No, he was too plain, too ugly, too ordinary to warm her heart; he had raped her and hurt her further; he had scorned and reviled her. He knew with a great empty longing that Lettice could never love him.

She saw the bleak look that flittered across his face, but could not guess the reason for it. To try to dispel it, she said, "Jonathan told us about the children's delegation to General Haldimand. Have you heard the story?"

Charles smiled at her, a smile that did not reach his sad blue eyes. "No. What happened?"

"Well, the General's orderly, it seems, threw ashes from the fire onto the hill outside his quarters. A group of children went to Haldimand and complained that the ashes had ruined their sleigh riding; they said that they and their fathers before them had coasted on the hill

since the colony began and demanded that he repair it."
She laughed. "Even the children here demand their
rights from the Crown."

Charles joined in her laughter, and they began to talk
easily of recent events. So effortless was their conversation, so friendly and warm the atmosphere, that Lettice
found herself suddenly blurting out the subject that had
been so much on her mind recently. "Charles, is it true
that you keep a mistress?"

Murdock blinked at her in surprise. "What?"

"Molly told me that you had a mistress here in Boston,
that that was the rumor. Is it true?"

"How in the devil does Molly know about such
things?" he exclaimed, his brows contracting thunderously.

Lettice laughed, although there was a curious tightening in her throat. "Women know far more than men give
them credit for." She paused, and looked at her hands.
"So it is true."

"Yes, it's true," he admitted. "Surely that does not
shock you."

"Oh, no," Lettice said lightly and smiled. "My husband kept many mistresses. I suppose it surprised me a
little; you and Boston seem so moral somehow."

"I am not married; I would not keep a mistress if I
were." He smiled thinly. "I have the same needs as other
men; you well know that. And considering my face, I've
far more luck hiring a woman than marrying one."

Lettice looked up at him and said, "What do you mean,
considering your face?"

He flushed a little. "Please, don't try to flatter me. I
know I am an ugly man, a lumbering ox."

"No, you are not!" Lettice cried in protest, then realized with astonishment that she no longer considered him ugly. She could remember her opinion of him when they met; she would have described him much as he himself had. But now his height and heavy chest appeared to her not hulking, but solid and safe, and his square, heavy-featured face not homely, but kind and oddly attractive. She remembered that brief moment when he had kissed her, and she had felt a passionate response; she blushed a little. Confused and disturbed, she mumbled, "At least, that is, you do not seem so to me."

He looked at her, his heartbeat skittering wildly, wondering what she meant. She was merely being polite; he must not think that her words indicated any strong feeling toward him. And yet, he waited on tenterhooks for her next words, praying for some hint that she would not be averse to his suit.

Under his steady gaze, Lettice's eyes fell. She wondered what had possessed her to say that and what he thought of her behind that inscrutable face. To cover her embarrassment, she changed the conversation abruptly. "Do you still go to those interminable meetings?"

"What? Oh, those—yes, of course." He told himself he was a fool for the way his heart plummeted at her words. "In fact, next week we shall meet here."

"Isn't that dangerous? I have heard that Gage is trying to flush out the leaders, to catch them in a seditious meeting and arrest them."

"I have heard that too, but so far he has not succeeded," Charles said with a wry smile and a shrug. "What else can we do? We must move forward. If we stop, if we let the protest die, than we will sanction what the Parliament has done to us. We cannot acquiesce in our own defeat."

"But what do you plan to do?" Lettice asked, frowning with worry. Not for the first time, she was aware of the danger of what Murdock was engaged in. "What can you accomplish against the British Army? Surely you cannot be contemplating out and out treason?"

"Does that idea bring out the Britisher in you?"

"I don't know what you mean. It frightens me, for your sake—and Mr. Baker's and all the others like you. Are you actually considering rebellion? Pitting yourself against the mightiest army in the world? They would squash you like an insect!"

"The whole continent? What if the colonies united against the army?"

Lettice stared at him, appalled, her eyes round and big. "Charles, you cannot mean it. You would be hanged!"

He laughed shortly. "No, I do not really mean it. We still hope for reconciliation; we hope the King will recognize the justice of what we say. But I think that is a vain hope. Once everyone realizes that, what is left to us except to knuckle under? Lettice, we are too proud a people to do that."

"Better to lose your pride than your life!" Lettice retorted hotly.

"Is one's life worth more than freedom, though?" Charles responded. "Have you ever seen a people more free, more in control of their own destinies than here? A man can make of himself anything he wants. He is not bound by the rigid rules and classes and mores of England."

"A woman, too," Lettice murmured thoughtfully.

"What?"

"I said, 'A woman, too.' I have never seen females so free to do as they please as the women here. I have met women shopkeepers, bakers, printers, all manner of things. They manage their own money; they walk the street alone safely. Why, I have even heard their opinions listened to and respected."

"That's exactly what I mean," Charles said earnestly. "This is a new place, a new era. We are free here. But how long do you think that will last, if we allow Parliament to impose its will on us? We have fought the Members every time they sought to, and that is what has led to the independent spirit you see here. Such people cannot be asked to give up their freedom."

"I—I know the feeling you talk about, the pride, the self-respect. I see it here all around me. Sometimes I have even felt it too." Lettice halted, frowning. "I've always wanted to be free, Charles. And when I saw those officers attacking Mr. Potter's shop, I loathed them; I hated my country. I wish—I wish you could succeed. But, is it worth giving up your life?"

Charles's blue eyes flashed with fire. "Yes," he said firmly, and repeated, "yes. Whatever I love that dearly is worth dying for."

Twelve

*L*ettice was seized by restlessness in the week following her talk with Charles. The long, bleak February days often made her feel trapped. Charles was out almost every evening, and Lettice, a reluctant chaperone, was left alone with Jonathan and Molly. She could not rid her mind of the thoughts Charles had planted there, heady, exciting visions of freedom, nor could she keep herself from speculating about Charles's mistress. She had thought his admission or denial of the woman's existence would end her curiosity, but instead she now longed to see Anne Lindon, and wondered where she lived, how she dressed, and how she spoke.

Some evenings when Jonathan did not come, the women suspected he was accompanying Charles in one of his seditious activities, and Lettice and Molly were left to while away the evening by themselves. At these times, Molly's conversation turned almost exclusively to Jonathan and her feelings for him, and Lettice, much to her surprise, began to feel an intense annoyance with the girl.

"Do you think he loves me?" she would ask over and over again, never completely reassured by Lettice's answer, until Lettice would have liked to take her by the shoulders and shake her till her teeth rattled.

Once when the girl reiterated her constant question, Lettice ripped out an oath her father often used and added, "For mercy's sake, Molly, let it be. How can I say whether the man loves you or not? All I know is what I see: Jonathan comes here almost every day, and it certainly is not to see me or Charles or your mother. Obviously he must have some interest in you. Do you think he is so frivolous as to play with your affections? Would he have so little honor as to shower you with his attention, if he felt nothing for you?"

Molly stared at her, blushing at Lettice's language and shamed by the rebuke in her words. "I'm sorry," she said softly, ducking her head. "I'm a trial, I know, always rattling on about Jonathan. I'm just so scared that what I wanted so long is not really happening; I can't quite believe my good fortune."

Lettice heaved a sigh and said, "Oh, I'm sorry, too, Molly. I should not have said that. I've been nervous and jumpy lately. This constant cold makes me feel like a prisoner; sometimes I think I shall explode if I can't get out of the house soon. You have every right to talk of Mr. Baker if you want to, and I am a nasty old bear to begrudge you your lover's chatter. Will you forgive me?"

"Of course," Molly answered quickly.

It was jealousy, Lettice thought to herself, that made her tongue so sharp. Not that she cared for Jonathan, of course; he meant nothing to her, and she was very happy for Molly to get him. It was the girl's youthful rush of emotions that she envied, her ability to love and desire. Lettice felt a wistful pang, realizing that she had never experienced the feeling Molly was so radiant with. Other men, other women loved. Was she the only person so stunted in the growth of her heart? Was she the only one who felt encased by ice, imprisoned by her own lack of feelings?

Quick, hot tears sprang into Lettice's eyes, and she bent her head over her sewing to hide them. A few moments later she stood up, laying her mending aside.

"I think I will go for a walk," she said.

"Bundle up," Molly said, not offering to accompany her. She knew intuitively that Lettice wanted to be alone.

Lettice smiled and went to the coat closet to wrap herself up in boots and woolen cloak, muffler and hat, with heavy mittens on her hands. She trudged along the streets of Boston aimlessly, breathing in the stinging air and reveling in her escape from the house. Who would have thought, she asked herself, mere months ago, that this vain, porcelain London beauty would be wading along the streets of Boston, tramping through snow and slush and ice—and loving it?

As so often, her steps turned toward Ruth Whitney's shop. There was a woman whom she could talk to, one who would understand her strange, conflicting emotions as the shy, immature Molly never could.

When she knocked at Ruth's office door and stepped inside, the other woman smiled and cheerfully set aside her books. "Thank heavens," she laughed. "You've come to help me evade this boredom. Sit down and tell me what you are doing out in this foul weather."

"Oh, the weather isn't bad. Cold perhaps, but at least it isn't snowing any longer. Besides, I had to get out."

"I know exactly what you mean," Ruth commiserated.

"Do you know, I had the most peculiar thought when I was coming over here."

"What?"

Lettice paused, then said almost wonderingly, "I think that I have come to love this city!"

"Bravo!" Ruth applauded, laughing.

"This dour, cold, brown city of Puritans and patriots! Can you imagine that?"

"Easily," Ruth rejoined. "I've loved it for years. It may not have the glitter and the sights of London, but there is something in the air here, something very special."

"Do you know, I think if someone came to me right now and offered to magically transport me back to London, make everything the way it was before—I don't believe I would take him up on it."

"I should hope not," Ruth replied stoutly. "We would miss you far too much here."

"There are none of the amusements here that I loved so: the parties, the card games, the theater. But somehow I don't miss them. It's as if all those things were just something I used to fill up an empty life, a way I could avoid realizing what an utter vacuum it was."

"Here you work hard every day," Ruth said, nodding her head, "but you have something to show for it at the end of the day. You have something to keep you interested, something to accomplish."

"Yet I don't create things as you do," Lettice said.

"You do create things: a delicious pie or roast, or silverware that gleams, or a mended shirt, a winter bouquet of dried flowers."

"That's certainly more than I ever managed before," Lettice agreed with a laugh. "And when I think of the headaches I used to endure because of that pile of powdered hair on my head! And the hours I spent tending to my face and dress."

"You don't need any artifices," Ruth assured her friend. "You are beautiful without them."

A shadow crossed Lettice's face. "I thought about that too. I was wondering this morning, what good has my beauty ever done me? All my life I've been able to attract men like bees to honey, and I never felt anything myself. What good is that?"

"I don't know what you mean." A puzzled frown touched Ruth's forehead.

"Of course not. Because you are a woman who knows how to feel, to love. I am not."

"Oh, Lettice!"

"No, it's true. I've never loved any man. And, oh, Ruth, I wish I had! I wish I could feel something, instead of just this cold deadness inside. I can love a city, my life here, my freedom. But I cannot love a man!"

"You were married. Did you feel nothing for your husband?"

"Only loathing," Lettice replied shortly, then sighed. "Oh, Ruth, I hope you will not think too badly of me. But I never had any love for my husband, or any man."

"Not even Charles Murdock?" Ruth asked shrewdly.

"Charles!" Lettice exclaimed. "Of course not! Mr. Murdock is my friend, nothing more."

"I think he could be. It seems to me your conversation is always smattered with quite a few 'Charles this' and 'Charles that' for you to be so entirely indifferent to him."

"I live in the same house with him and see him often, that's all."

"Is it? Well, if you say so. But it seems to me I never hear Miss Molly or Master Bryan mentioned so often. Or your constant visitor, Jonathan Baker."

"That is only because their conversation is not as interesting or bright as Charles' is."

"You respect the man, then?"

"Yes," Lettice nodded. "I do. I think he is a fine, intelligent, honorable man."

Ruth shrugged. "I've heard of worse foundations for love to grow on."

"Oh!" Lettice exclaimed in amused exasperation, and Ruth burst out laughing.

"All right, I promise, no more of Mr. Murdock. I'll send for something hot to drink, and we'll discuss the latest gossip."

Despite the cold, Lettice continued her walks every afternoon. With much wheedling and trickery, she obtained from Bryan the address of Anne Lindon, Charles's mistress. She wanted to see where the woman lived, that was all, Lettice told herself. But every walk she took found her steps going past the woman's small, inoffensive gray frame house, and Lettice had to admit that she wanted something more than just to see the dwelling.

She hoped to see the door open and Anne Lindon herself come out. Lettice could not understand it exactly, but she knew she had a burning desire to know what the woman looked like who was the object of Charles' affection.

Finally, one day, Lettice threw caution to the winds,

and, with her heart thudding wildly in her ribcage, she walked up to the front door and knocked. The woman who answered the door was not beautiful or flamboyant. She was dressed plainly in a trim blue dress, and her features were even but unremarkable; only her hair, uncovered and the red-gold color of burnished copper, was unusual.

"Yes?" She made it a question, her eyebrows vaulting up.

Lettice realized that she had absolutely no reason for being there, and she almost turned and fled. Then the other woman's eyes narrowed and she said harshly, "Are you Lettice?"

"Why, yes," she replied, startled that the woman should know her and taken aback by the flare of hatred in the woman's eyes. "How did you know?"

Anne smiled sourly. "Charles has mentioned you." She did not see fit to add that he often came to her hot with passion for Lettice, not for her, or that he moaned Lettice's name in the fire of lovemaking, or that he more than once poured his troubled, futile longings into his mistress's supposedly indifferent ears. He was not unkind, only self-deprecatingly unaware that his words made Anne Lindon ache with jealousy. To him theirs was a business relationship, nothing more, and it never occurred to him that Anne might love him.

"Has he?" Lettice took refuge as she had in the past in a cold, haughty, attitude, and her tone sparked the other woman's anger even further.

"What are you doing here?" Anne snapped, her brown eyes blazing now.

"Just curiosity," Lettice said truthfully, but her mouth curled in such a way that it seemed an insult.

Angrily the woman flung the door open and stepped aside, letting Lettice enter, then slammed the door behind her. Viciously she said, "How dare you come here? I hate the very sight of you. Do you think that because you are an aristocrat you can simply barge into anyone's home whenever you feel like it? What did you come here for?"

"Charles told me that you are his mistress."

"Yes," the woman said, her voice and stance full of pride. "I am, and I give him more comfort than he will ever find in your cold clutches."

"I have no desire to take him away from you," Lettice replied distantly.

"No? Then why are you staying at his house? Why do you cling there, dangling yourself in front of him all the time? A decent woman would have left by now, found herself a home and work, not lived on Charles's charity and thrown herself in his path at every opportunity."

Lettice laughed, looking every inch her old self, a haughty noble among plebeians. "As if I wanted Charles Murdock. Don't you think that I could catch a much bigger fish than he?"

Anne Lindon snorted and moved away. "What did you really come here for?"

Almost as surprised as the other woman by the words that tumbled from her mouth, Lettice said, "Is Charles—I mean, when he comes to you, what does he—"

Anne laughed scornfully at her blushing confusion. "Are you trying to ask me if Charles is a good lover? Well,

I will tell you: Yes, he is; he is the best lover I ever had. He knows how to give a woman pleasure, and he uses his knowledge to the fullest. Why, if he tried, he could probably make even a cold bitch like you respond. But don't bother asking him to, if that's what you want. He told me what you did to him, how you tricked and deceived him. Believe me, he will always resent you for that; his desire turned to hate long ago, and he will not get over that. Besides, why should he bother with you? You probably could not give him even the barest taste of pleasure."

Lettice swallowed hard, appalled at the woman's words and at her own forwardness in coming here. What did she care what Charles Murdock and Anne Lindon did in the privacy of this little house? Was she becoming voyeuristic as well as frigid? It had been insane of her to come, to meet this woman face to face.

Blindly she stumbled to the door and rushed outside, not pausing until the house was far behind her. Finally she stopped, her breathing labored, and leaned against a fence for support. Looking around her, she realized that she did not even know where she was. Aimlessly she began to walk, wandering until she came to a familiar area, and then she turned slowly toward home. Her mind shied away from her visit; she could not bear to examine her reasons for going there. Yet she could not put Anne's words out of her head.

Anne Lindon had said Charles resented her for what she had done to him; certainly he had every right to. Life in Boston was difficult enough, with the embargo strangling the prosperity of the city, without his having to clothe, feed, and house her too. Lettice knew she ought to leave, take her pitiful hoard of money and set up residence somewhere else, another city even. She could find something to do to keep herself fed; surely she could succeed as a dressmaker, with her knowledge of fashions and her flair and style. It would be better for all concerned if she did.

Yet the thought of leaving made Lettice want to cry. She remembered Charles's proposal and wondered what would have happened if she had not refused him. Perhaps she would have liked sharing his life, his dreams, his thoughts. If only she were capable of love.

Hot tears sprang into her eyes. Why could she not feel anything? Once, she remembered, she had felt a brief spurt of passion—that time when Charles dragged her from the drawing room, furious about the dancing, and then kissed her. Something hot and starving had leaped in her, frightening in its intensity.

Could Charles take her to bed and awaken the fire in her? The thought was exciting and yet frightening. Anne had said that he no longer desired Lettice. But once he had trembled with passion for her; had the desire truly died in him? Or did it burn on, even without love?

Jonathan came over that evening, but not to visit Molly. He disappeared with Charles into his study, along with Sam Adams, Dr. Warren, and half a dozen other men. It unnerved Lettice to think of the danger of what they did, but she forced herself to sit in the sitting room with Molly and sew on a sampler she was making, pretending that nothing was unusual and that she wasn't frightened.

But her heart leaped into her throat and the blood pounded in her ears when they heard voices outside and then a thunderous knock on the door. Molly flew to the front window and peeked out, then turned back to Lettice, her face as white as the snow outside.

"It's soldiers. British soldiers," she whispered.

For a moment Lettice was paralyzed. Then with a start she recovered her wits and hissed, "Hurry, run back to Charles and tell them. Get them out the side door. I'll hold the soldiers off here."

"How?"

"Never mind! I'll think of something. Just get all of them out as quickly as you can!"

Molly raced down the hall, and Lettice approached the front door at a calmer pace, smoothing her skirts and patting her hair, gestures more necessary to soothe her nerves than to improve her looks. She paused before the door and drew in a shaky breath. Soldiers. She must somehow fend off a group of soldiers, even though she was terrified of them.

Lettice swung open the door just as the officer raised his hand to knock again. She gasped a little and stepped back, then burst into a bubbling laugh.

"No, please, sir, do not strike me," she said gaily and flashed him her brilliant smile.

The officer, who had looked thunderous, relaxed a little at her coquettish air and her British accent. He bowed gravely. "Madame. This is the home of Charles Murdock, is it not?"

"Why, yes, it is," Lettice said, turning the full radiance of her green eyes on him, but not giving an inch of space. She kept the door close beside her, so that any vision down the hall was blocked. Behind her, she could hear the soft shuffle of feet as the men left the study. "Why—

oh, my voice gave you pause. Well, I am a fellow country-man. I am just a guest at present in the Murdock home."

"I see," the man said and drew breath to speak, but Lettice interrupted him.

"It is ever so pleasant to hear a familiar voice. I have grown so dreadfully weary of these nasal accents. Can you tell me why these Bostonians insist on speaking through their noses?" The man smiled, and she chattered on, "But, there, I am keeping you from your business. You must forgive me; it is just that it has been so long since I've been home. No doubt you wish to see Mr. Murdock? Do come in and sit down, and I will go get him."

"Well, it is not precisely that, madame. We have re-ceived reports that there is a meeting here tonight of some of these patriot leaders, and I have been ordered to search the house."

"Search the house!" Lettice gasped and let her hand fly gracefully to her throat. "But they couldn't! I mean, how—Mr. Murdock has been in his study all evening, I am sure." Pale and dithering, she stepped back from the door and allowed them to enter. "I cannot believe that the Murdocks would be involved in any such activity."

"No doubt they would keep it hidden from you," the officer assured her as he and his men pushed in around her.

"Shall I show you about the house?" she asked and then blushed. "No, how silly of me. I suppose you do not need me."

"What is the meaning of this? What is going on here?" Charles's crisp voice demanded as he strode down the hall toward them, and Lettice barely kept from sagging against the door in relief. His visitors must be all gone, then. "Are you intimidating Mistress Holmes? She is a guest in my house, and I will not have it."

"Oh, no, Mr. Murdock," Lettice laughed. "Why, I quite enjoyed talking with the Major."

"*Captain*, Mistress Holmes," he corrected, a little embarrassed in front of his men.

"Oh, yes, of course, how stupid of me," Lettice fluttered. "But I'm sure Mr. Murdock can explain to you how mistaken you are. If you gentlemen will excuse me . . ."

She slipped into the sitting room and joined Molly, rigid and as white as paper. Lettice pinched the girl sharply and whispered, "Act more normally, girl, if you don't want to give the game away."

"What can I do?" Molly whispered back.

"Pinch some color into your cheeks for one thing, and for another, don't sit straight as a board. Let's chatter about something totally inane."

"All right." Molly forced herself to settle more comfortably in her chair and pinched her cheeks hard to bring color to her face.

Neither of the women could later remember a single word of what they said to each other. They forced themselves to talk of shoes and dresses while all their attention was focused on the sound of the soldiers' booted feet thundering through the house. Lettice felt as though her nerves would crack under the strain. She hoped that the men had been clever enough to remove any traces of their presence from the study, and she prayed that the soldiers would not chance upon footprints leading from the side door. Finally, when Lettice felt that she might burst into nervous tears at any moment, the British officer entered the sitting room, his face grim.

"I beg your pardon for disturbing you, Mistress Holmes. It seems our informant was wrong," he said and bowed gracefully.

Lettice smiled at him, hoping that he did not see how the corners of her mouth trembled. "There, Captain, I told you, didn't I? I knew that the Murdocks could not be involved. But," she added archly, flashing her eyes at him, "I hope your visit was not a complete loss."

He rose to the bait and complimented her extravagantly, assuring her that their meeting was worth any amount of effort. Then, politely, he took his leave of the ladies and left, his men clomping out behind him.

"Phew!" Molly sighed, dropping in her chair. "I have never in my life been so petrified. Oh, Lettice, how did you manage?"

Lettice shook her head wordlessly and stood. Her knees were trembling now with delayed reaction, and she felt unbelievably weak. "I am going to go to bed," she said huskily. "If I don't, I think I shall faint right here."

Holding tightly to the banister, Lettice pulled herself upstairs. In her room, she stripped down to her petticoats and washed her face, then sat down and began to brush her hair, hoping the rhythmical movement would soothe her tattered nerves. She felt as if she had faced death that night. What would have happened if they had found the men there? What would they have done to Charles? Just the thought of it made her mouth go as dry as cotton.

Thirteen

There was a soft tap at her door. Lettice rose and quickly flung her dressing gown around her and tied it, wondering what could be the problem now. She opened the door, expecting to see Molly or Marian; she stepped back in surprise when she saw Charles on her threshold.

"Is there something wrong?" she asked quietly and he shook his head, then stepped inside, softly shutting the door after him.

Charles had not really thought about the lateness of the hour when he decided to thank Lettice for what she had done, and he had not expected her already to be undressed. Now, seeing her clad in her dressing gown, her pale hair loose on her shoulders, a wave of desire washed through him. Dear God, if only he had the right to touch her, to kiss her, to try to thaw the ice that encased her heart . . .

The course of his thoughts shook him and he swallowed, fighting for control. Never before had he let his thoughts run riot like this in her presence; it was dangerous for both of them. The animal in him was too likely to overcome all reason.

Lettice watched him curiously, wondering what had brought him to her room so late at night. There was a glint of something in his eyes, and it occurred to her that passion had spurred him to take her again; the thought made her stomach leap in a strange way. Did he still want her that much? She was suddenly very aware of the fact that he had removed his coat and his shirt was unfastened halfway down. She could see the firm flesh of his chest, the curling red-brown hairs that showed above the white cloth of his shirt, and her breath seemed to stick in her throat.

"I wanted to thank you for what you did tonight," Charles began, willing himself to normality despite his leaping emotions. "I know how frightened you are of the soldiers discovering your identity; it must have cost you a great deal to hold them off that way, revealing to them that you are an English lady."

Lettice's smile was a little lopsided. "I could hardly let them capture you, could I?"

"Has—has our cause come to mean anything to you?" he asked, though the question he longed to ask was whether *he* had come to mean anything to her.

"Perhaps. I had not really thought about it. But I know how much I treasure freedom, how wonderful it is to be free of the ties that once bound me . . ." She smiled up at him, tears sparkling in her green eyes. Free—of all except the chains that bound her heart and body to her fear of the past.

Charles, sensing her distress though he did not know the cause of it, reached out and took her hand in his warm clasp, and it seemed to Lettice as though it burned her and yet was strangely comforting. His sleeves were rolled up, and Lettice felt that same wild leap in her stomach when she looked down at his arm, the heavy muscles corded beneath the skin, the skin brown and hard. How would it feel to have those arms like iron around her? To feel those blunt, square hands upon her body . . .

Hastily she pulled away, and Charles watched her, puzzled. Something in her manner, in the way she glanced at his body, made his blood race in his veins. He longed to reach out and pull her back.

"Charles, do some women—find pleasure—in bed, I mean, with a man?" Her voice was halting and so soft he could barely hear it.

"I believe so," he replied, straining to keep his voice steady, though her words stirred him.

"With you? I mean. I hope you will not be angry with me, but I sought out Anne Lindon."

"Anne! What the devil?"

"No, please, don't be angry. I did not go there to harm either one of you. I was curious. You see, I want so much to know!"

"Know what?"

"I'm not sure. About what happens between men and women . . . about you . . . All my knowledge of such pleasure is second hand, based only on gossip . . ." Her voice trailed off, and she flushed under his steady gaze. "Charles, pray, don't be angry with me. I am so confused. I've changed so, I hardly feel as if I know myself anymore. I think back to what I used to do and say, and I despise myself for it. I hate what I did to you. I was such a calculating bitch!"

"Lettice, please. You have always been the woman you

are, deep inside you. It only took the freedom you love for your true self to come out." Gently he took her chin in his hand and turned her face up until she was forced to gaze into his eyes. "Now, tell me: What is all this really about? Why did you go to Anne?"

Nervously Lettice wet her lips; she felt embarrassed and a little frightened before his kind, honest blue eyes. "Don't. I feel as though you look into my soul when you look at me like that."

"Tell me," he said relentlessly.

"I'm not sure exactly why I went. I think I wanted to see the woman who—who shared your bed; I wanted to know what she looked like, how she acted. Do you love her?"

"Love?" His voice was harsh. "Love has nothing to do with it. She eases my body, and I pay for her keep, pay her well enough to endure my face."

"I think she loves you," Lettice said solemnly. "I don't think you would have to pay any woman."

His eyes darkened as he gazed down into her face, and he went on as if she had not spoken. "God knows, I have had need of her these months you have been in the house."

Something painful and exciting darted through her at his words, and she wanted to hear more. "Why?"

"Why?" His laugh was short and strained. "Lettice, please, you push me too far. Surely you must know what you do to me; just to stand this close to you and talk about such things makes me—" He broke off suddenly and moved away from her.

"Then why do you do nothing about it? Why have you not come to me instead of to your mistress?"

"Come to you? What are you talking about? Do you actually think that I would force myself on you again? I gave you my solemn oath that I would not take you again."

"Not even if I asked you to?" she said, her voice striving for lightness.

"Don't tease me, Lettice."

"I am not teasing. I am deadly serious. Your mistress said you are a gentle, persuasive lover; she said you gave a woman pleasure. Is that true?"

"I try," he said, his voice thick.

"I want to be a whole woman, Charles. I don't want to be cold anymore. Please, I want you to make love to me."

Charles stared at her, incredulous. It was beyond his wildest dreams that Lettice should ask him to come to her bed. A wild tremor shook him; her words had set him on fire, and he could hardly think for the wild pounding of his blood.

"Lettice," he managed to say, "you don't know what you're saying. You can't mean it."

"I do," she replied, looking straight into his eyes. "If you want me, I would like to have sex with you. I want to feel; I want you to teach me how to make love. Please, tell me you will do it; tell me it can be done. I don't want to be lonely the rest of my life."

Charles felt as though he were drowning in her gaze; his body trembled from the strain of holding back. Yet he had been deceived by her too often simply to let go and believe. The small, cold voice of reason inside him told him that she was acting on one of her wild whims, which would doubtless pass quickly, while he would fall more deeply in love with her, be even more tied to her.

"Lettice, think," he said, making one last stab at dissuading her. "I am not the one to awaken you. I am a big, clumsy, unsophisticated man. You deserve a man worthy of you, someone who could stir your blood, who could arouse your passion."

"I want you," Lettice said stubbornly. "I know you; I trust you. You would be gentle with me, wouldn't you? You would be patient and kind; I know you. You would not laugh at me or ridicule me or hurt me."

"I cannot think when you look at me like that," he said shakily.

"How should I look at you?"

His breath came out, half sigh, half laugh. "Like that; just like that . . . forever."

His hand slid from her chin along her neck and across the delicate structure of her collarbone, then down the smooth fabric of her dressing gown to the tie that fastened it. Charles untied the sash and pushed the robe back off her shoulders, and it slipped with a silken swish to the floor, leaving her standing in only her shift. Slowly, almost leisurely, Charles untied the strings of her chemise, and it too dropped to the floor, followed the next moment by her petticoat and undergarments, and Lettice stood naked before him. With his eyes he explored her, his breath uneven, drinking in the beauty of her body.

Lettice blushed beneath his regard, and he smiled. "You are beautiful. Lovely." He reached out and lightly touched her breasts with his fingertips; the peaks hardened under his fingers, and Lettice felt a strange ripple across her abdomen. He walked around her, like a buyer observing a horse; Lettice thought she should feel humiliated, but she did not. Rather, his gaze warmed her, made her feel unbearably beautiful, and when his hands caressed her rounded buttocks, she felt a shiver of fire dart through her.

Charles picked her up, cradling her in his arms like a child, and carried her to her bed. He sat beside her and his hand began to roam her body, caressing her everywhere, touching her so lightly that she could not be frightened. All the while, he spoke to her, a quiet, rhythmic monologue extolling the beauty of her body, words so passionate and hungry that, said in his desire-hoarse voice, they stirred her blood.

"What is that you are saying?" she murmured, taking his hand and softly kissing the palm.

"The Song of Solomon," he replied, his words choked, and Lettice looked up to see hunger stamped upon his face: his full, sensuous mouth; his hot, dark blue eyes.

"From the Bible?" Lettice asked, amazed, and he chuckled at her surprise.

"Yes. You can see why we Puritans are not so completely passionless after all." He stood and unfastened his shirt, and Lettice watched in fascination as he undressed. Her eyes followed his movements greedily, exploring the breadth of his chest, the hard strength of his arms, the ripple of his muscles as he moved. For the first time that she could remember, she wanted to see, wanted to know a man's body. Only when he stripped off his breeches, revealing his stiff, enlarged manhood, did she feel fear clutch at her vitals.

He saw her start and her eyes glance away, and he said, "Don't be afraid. I won't hurt you. If something causes you pain, tell me and I will stop. You know I will not force you."

"I know," she said and summoned up a smile for him.

Once more his smooth, light caresses began, and he began to talk of his first, virginal gropings until she had to laugh and relax. He smiled back, his eyes heavy-lidded with passion, and she realized how much control he was exercising over himself in order to relax her and bring her along slowly. "Do you remember the first time I saw you?" he said huskily, and she nodded. "This is what I wanted to do at that moment. You had on a gold dress, cut very low, so that I could see much of your breasts, and I was throbbing with wanting you. Did you know that? Did you know that I stripped you with my eyes and laid you in my bed and touched you like this?"

A small moan escaped Lettice under his expert hands, and the sound almost broke his control. For a moment he paused, his teeth biting into his lip, and then he began his slow, lazy caresses again. Charles leaned forward, his face looming closer and closer, and then his lips were upon hers; she could taste the blood where he had bitten his lip. Gently he played with her lips, teasing her mouth open and exploring it with his tongue. Then the pressure increased, and his lips dug into hers, searching, demanding, hot and greedy, until at last he tore his mouth away and she was left gasping at the loss. His searing lips trailed across her face and neck, nibbling at her earlobes, sending quivers of delight through her.

Again and again he kissed her, making her dizzy and tingling with passion, while his hands continued to stroke her body. His hands cupped her breasts, and his mouth moved down her skin to take the soft pink circle of her nipple and played with it, gently sucking and teasing. She felt hot and trembling all over, a great aching void inside her, and she wanted him to possess her.

"Oh, Charles," she moaned. "Now, oh, please, take me. Love me."

A tremor shook his body at her words, and then suddenly his heavy weight was upon her, pinning her down, pressing her back into the bed, but she felt none of her old fear, only pleasure at his demanding weight, and an overwhelming satisfaction as he entered her and began to thrust. Lettice clung to his heaving body, delighting in the feel and scent and sound of him as he rode out his passion. It seemed to her that she must die, that she had gone too far into the outer realms of pleasure ever to return, but she did not die, even when he cried out hoarsely and crushed her to him, then relaxed against her, trembling.

Lettice kissed his cheek and whispered, "Thank you. Thank you, Charles."

His words were muffled against her skin. "Lettice. Lettice, my love."

Lettice moaned and stirred as the first pale glow of dawn came through the window. Something was different, she thought sleepily, coming slowly awake; the sheets felt so cool, so soft against her body; she felt so . . . Suddenly her eyes flew open, and she was fully awake. Charles! Charles had been here last night and had made love to her. A smile curved her soft lips; she closed her eyes and remembered the evening before, from Charles's soft knock to the sweet pleasure of his hard male body on hers. No wonder the sheets felt different; never before had she lain between them naked. Lettice decided that she rather liked the feel, the light touch on her sensitive flesh, faintly reminiscent of his hands upon her. She giggled to herself, feeling her nipples harden at the memory of his fingers.

Charles. Lettice turned on her side, burrowing into the pillow, where the faint scent of him still clung, wishing he were here by her side. No doubt after she had fallen asleep last night, he had stolen from the room to protect her reputation. All his thoughts had been of her; she knew he had held back at the expense of his own pleasure, just to bring her to desire. How gentle, how knowledgeable, how tender.

Raising her arms high above her head, she stretched. So this was passion, this was what men felt, what other women had felt, what she had never known before. Well, now she knew, and she hoped never to lose it again. Quickly she flung back the covers and hopped out of bed, hurrying to wash and dress and run downstairs to see Charles. But in the middle of her toilette, she stopped, brought up short by the thought of him. Did he want to see her? What did he feel? Thoughtfully, she continued to pin her hair, her green eyes darkly troubled.

He was, after all, a proud, high-minded Yankee, no matter how intoxicatingly sensual he was. It might very well be that her boldness last night had lessened her in his eyes. Who was to say her asking him to her bed had not made him think her a slut?

When she went downstairs, her heart was in her throat. How should she act? Lettice did not know what he expected of her, even if he wanted to continue the relationship. She supposed that she must try to act as if all was normal—and yet how was she to keep from blushing or to stop her face from lighting up in pleasure when she saw him?

It was rather disconcerting, after all her worry, to find that Charles was not even at the breakfast table. Molly explained that he had left for the office early, just grabbing a warm roll as he left. Numbed, Lettice sank into her chair and began mechanically to eat.

What did his leaving mean? Did he want to avoid seeing her again? Should she know that she should discreetly pack her bags and leave? Oh, but she could not; she simply could not!

The day passed slowly, and Lettice could have screamed as the minutes inched along. She did her chores with only half of her attention, and had to go back over nearly every room she had dusted, because she had skipped so many pieces of furniture in her mental fog. Molly wanted to talk about last night, finding release in speaking of their mutual fear and effort. Lettice tried to smile and make appropriate answers, although she was so preoccupied that she heard little of what the girl said.

Had Charles known of her fears and doubts, he would have been stunned. He had left before breakfast this morning because he could not bear to meet her in front of his family, afraid that he would go to her and take her in his arms right there, so insanely did he want her. After he left her bed the night before, he had slept little. He lay staring into the dark and recalling their lovemaking, examining and caressing the memories like precious jewels. Never in his life had he felt anything like that, never had he known that sweet, wild joy of surging to ecstasy in the arms of the woman he loved.

He was caught, just as he had feared, and he thought his face would reveal as soon as he saw her exactly what had happened between them. His work suffered that day, and he went home that night torn between excited anticipation and worry that she would spurn him.

They met at the dinner table, and both of them quickly looked away from the other, then spent the rest of the meal glancing at each other with brief, furtive looks, anxious and yet clamoring with desire. Lettice, more experienced than he at concealing her emotions, kept her face a careful blank, waiting to discover his mood before she committed herself. Throughout the evening he seemed ill at ease, but he made no gesture toward her that indicated desire or love or anything at all; in fact, he seemed to try to avoid her. When he at last retired to his study, Lettice excused herself and went up to her room, claiming a headache as an excuse.

Once in her room, she flung herself upon her bed and glared gloomily at the ceiling. Obviously last night had been a great inconvenience for him, she told herself. He could not bear today to be in the same room with her, he was so embarrassed. She gave way to a flood of tears, then undressed and miserably crept into bed.

Charles spent the evening pacing his study until the rest of the family went up to bed. Finally, he snuffed out the candles and went softly up the stairs, intending to go straight to his room. She did not want him—that was clear from her cool expression tonight. And now he was worse off than before.

But as he reached her door, he stopped, unable to pass her by. Desire pounded in his loins, pulsing through his veins, and he knew he had to see her. If nothing else, he had to know for certain that she refused him. He could not go on supposition.

Softly he opened her door and slipped inside. Lettice sat up in her bed and peered through the dark, her chest shaking from the bludgeoning of her heart.

"Charles?" Her voice caught with hope.

"Lettice." He crossed the room in two quick strides and stood looming above her.

Moonlight poured through her small window, bright from the reflecting snow, and lit her face palely. She looked up at him, her eyes great pools of darkness, the bones of her delicate face stark.

"Lettice," he said again and his voice shook. "I want you."

"Oh, Charles," she breathed and held up her arms to him.

With a groan, he sank down on the bed and enfolded her in his arms.

"I was afraid you did not want me again," he breathed against her silky hair, his hands caressing her back.

A half laugh, half sob escaped her throat, and Lettice said, "I do, I do. I thought you were ashamed of me, that you hated me for my wickedness."

He drew back and put his hands on either side of her face, and stared down into her eyes. "I could never hate you. God knows, I have tried hard enough in the past. But I cannot."

Like a hawk his mouth came down upon hers, and Lettice met him, kiss for kiss, caress for caress, eager to learn, to experience the sweet passion of the night before. They broke apart only once, to quickly remove their inhibiting clothing, then melted back together in a trembling embrace. Deeply they kissed, his mouth leaving hers only to trail hot kisses over her face and down her neck. He nibbled tenderly at the sensitive cord of her throat, then back up to her earlobes, working the soft flesh between his teeth until a moan rose from deep within her.

His hands strayed down over her body, cupping her breasts and stroking the rosy nipples to diamonds of hardness. Softly, searchingly his hand slid across the flat plane of her abdomen to the mound of her womanhood and in between her legs, seeking the soft inner recesses of her being.

Lettice shuddered with pleasure at his knowledgeable touch, and restlessly began to move her hands over his body, feeling the hard muscles of his arms and back, the solid bone of his furry chest, even sliding down to explore his legs. The hot rasping of his breath excited her, and suddenly she yearned to feel him inside her, ached for the glory of his pounding maleness.

"Please," she whispered, and instinctively he knew what she wanted. Charles covered her with the full, tough length of his body, weighing her down deliciously, and smoothly entered her. Rhythmically he moved within her, and Lettice wrapped her legs and arms around him, matching his every movement, delighting in the searing, damp feel of his skin beneath her hands. His face contorted with passion, and her inexperienced hands brought a groan from his lips.

Lettice felt lost in a glorious haze of pleasure, her senses at once dazed and sharply alive. Then something churned within her, a wild feeling that swirled and built and grew into an irresistible force that demanded release. Never had she felt anything like this. And then at last it came, a great cataclysm of ecstasy, the force exploding inside her and sending shock waves all over her body. Wordlessly she cried out, and above her, Charles held her close, sharing her passion.

Spent, they lay together in a warm, satiated tangle of arms and legs. Lettice, numbed by the new piercing sweetness of lovemaking and shaken by its power, could say nothing nor make any move; silently the tears rolled down her cheeks.

"Lettice," Charles said anxiously, his hand tenderly brushing the wetness from her cheeks.

She shook her head, unable to form her inchoate feelings into words. Somehow all the pains and fears of the past, the pent-up longings and frustrations and guilt boiled up in her and, relaxed and unguarded as she was now, they poured forth. She began to cry in great shuddering sobs, blindly reaching out for the comfort of Charles's arms. He gathered her against his chest and held her gently, stroking her hair and back, rocking her, while she cried away the grief of the past.

Fourteen

*L*ettice moved through the following day bathed in the warm glow of love. No longer was she a woman made of glass; she had felt passion and fulfillment.

She knew now that she loved Charles. Only he had been able to move her, pull her from her lonely isolation; only he had awakened her senses; only he had stirred her emotions. Charles had touched a chord in her that no one handsomer or more powerful had ever been able to do. He was so different that he had been able to slip past her defenses and reach her heart. Smiling secretly, she moved through her daily chores, marking time until he returned home. She found that she could hardly wait to see his face again, and it seemed almost unbearable not to be able to throw herself in his arms as soon as he entered the door. Now and then a little piercing doubt would creep into her happy thoughts to worry and annoy her: She knew how she felt about him, but what did Charles feel for her? He desired her, of course, but once, she knew, he had loved her. What if her tricks and deceit had effectively killed that love? What if he merely wanted her as he wanted Anne Lindon?

When such thoughts crossed her mind, she shivered a little with a thrill of fear. It was quite likely that her rejection had smothered his deeper feelings for her. Certainly he had not mentioned love or marriage, just come to her in his need and shared her bed. What was she to do if he did not return her feeling?

His attitude when he returned home gave nothing away. From his grave greeting and the polite conversation he made with her through dinner, one would have thought that nothing but friendship lay between them. Lettice felt as though her stomach had dropped to her feet, but once she looked up from her plate and found Charles's gaze upon her. A blue fire flashed forth from beneath his drooping lids, and she felt a leap of hope.

Whatever the outcome, she knew she could not go on like this without knowing. Anything was better than this uncertainty. Besides, Lettice felt that she would burst if she had to contain her love for him; she wanted desperately to let it pour out unrestrained. She could not hold such a glorious new feeling to herself.

So, after dinner, when Charles excused himself and went to his study, she followed him and tapped timidly at the door. He called out to enter, and she drew a deep breath and whisked inside, shutting the door after her.

"Lettice!" He was on his feet in an instant and around his desk, sweeping her into his arms. He kissed her thoroughly, his arms tight around her as if she were a lifeline. "I thought I would die at dinner, I wanted so badly to do that. I wondered how much of a stir it would cause if I seized you right there and took you, as I longed to do."

Lettice laughed lightly at the thought of his stepmother's shock and indignation at such a scene. "I think it is just as well that you did not."

He smiled down at her, and Lettice wondered with amazement how she could ever have thought his rough, strong face to be ugly; it seemed to her now the handsomest face in the world.

"I came to tell you something," she said breathlessly, "and I must tell you quickly, or I'm afraid I shall never get it out."

"What?" His face grew suddenly shuttered and wary.

"I love you."

"What?" he repeated, stunned.

Lettice gave a nervous giggle. "Surely you heard me. I love you."

Charles stared at her, torn between excitement and a horrible fear that she was joking with him. "Lettice, do you mean it? I beg you, don't tease me about this."

Lettice pulled away indignantly. "Mean it? Of course I mean it! I would not tease about something like this. It took me a world of courage to say it!"

He stood uncertainly, hardly able to believe that what he heard was real. For so long he had loved her, wanted her, and known it was hopeless, that now it was difficult to take in the fact that his hopes had materialized. Something in him cried out that it would all vanish like a dream, a mist; she had lied to him time after time. And yet—he knew he had to believe her; it was unbearable not to.

"Lettice," his word came out a sigh of surrender. "Oh, Lettice, my love!"

He bent, his mouth seeking hers, taking possession of it, and Lettice responded, glorying in his ownership. "I've waited so long, so hopelessly for that," he said shakily when at last he raised his head from hers. "I love you, I never stopped loving you all these months. Lettice, will you marry me?"

Lettice pulled away a little and looked up at him, delight mingling with concern on her face. "Oh, Charles, I—no. That is, I want to; but no, it would not be wise. It is enough for me to be able to love for the first time in my life; it is enough to know that you return it."

"But why?" Charles felt as though he had been punched in the stomach; so it was a game she was playing, not real at all.

Lettice frowned. "Charles, I am not good like you. I might hurt you, even destroy you. I've been bad all my life; all the Delaplaines are. What if I changed, went back to the way I was? What if I woke up some morning and realized I no longer liked this life, that I wanted the gaiety of London again, wanted to drink and play cards and dance the night away? Charles, I am not good, and if I hurt you again, I could not bear that. You know what I was like; you despised what I did. Other men have known me. I married for wealth, I duped innocents into losing their money to Philip—"

"Lettice, no!" he cried, his voice hoarse with desperation. "I don't give a damn about your past. That is all over and done with; you can't live the rest of your life dreading a return to it. Why should you change? Why should you revert? It was just your way of life that made you act that way, what other choice did you have but to fall in with Philip's plans? He hurt you, abused you; no one was there to love or rescue you. I cannot blame you for what you did in those circumstances. I love you now and that is all that matters. Please, if you love me, don't deny me. Please, Lettice, I beg of you. If you meant what you said, marry me."

For one long, agonized moment, Lettice looked at him, torn by her love, and then she threw herself against his chest. "Yes, oh, yes, I will marry you. I love you, Charles; I love you."

With a shudder of relief, his stiff body melted against hers, and he kissed her as if he would never again let her go.

There was a touch of spring in the air, and Lettice dawdled along, luxuriating in it. She had an ultimate goal; she needed to buy ribbon for a sash for her wedding dress. But it was early March, and the winter was melting away around her, and a faint, fresh smell of spring hung in the air. On such a day, she was in no rush to complete her errand; it was much too pleasant to saunter along, examining the store windows and letting her mind drift on the pleasant thoughts of her wedding plans.

When Charles had announced their engagement to the family, Bryan and Molly had laughed and hugged them and poured forth their congratulations and happiness. Predictably, Marian had frowned and offered her congratulations in a stiff voice that belied the words; Lettice had almost had to laugh at the obvious disappointment and disapproval on her face. But Marian could not spoil her happiness, and Molly's and Bryan's responses had warmed her heart. With some amazement, she realized that they truly wanted her in the family.

For the past week, she and Molly had been deep in preparations for the wedding. It was to be a small ceremony, and Charles was impatient for it to take place as soon as possible. Marian said slyly that such haste was unseemly and likely to cause talk about its reason, but Charles cut her off with an oath and a growl that he did not care what others thought of it; then he looked at Lettice with such desire that it set her insides to trembling.

Their passion for each other seemed to grow daily, and though Charles said he should not visit her bed until the wedding, in order to keep her reputation pure, he could not stop his nightly visits. On the one night he managed to restrain himself, Lettice crept to his room and crawled into his bed, and immediately his defenses crumbled. Again and again their desire flared; the slightest look or movement could set them afire. The secrecy of their lovemaking grew almost unendurable; it was no longer enough to make love after the others had gone to sleep. They wanted to belong to each other openly, to be able to sleep the night beside each other and wake to their lover's face in the morning.

Thank heaven, Lettice thought, in less than a week it would all be over; in only four days, they would stand together in the parlor with the Murdock family around them and say their vows. And then, with deep satisfaction, Lettice would take her place beside Charles as his wife. Her eyes sparkling at the thought, she peered into a window full of pots and pans, hardly noticing what she saw.

Then a voice sounded at her ear, and her delicious dreams fled with it. "Lettice! Sweet Jesus, I never thought to find you here, of all places!"

Lettice began to tremble violently. Slowly, fearfully,

she turned and stared at the slender, elegant man before her, and knew that all her happiness had vanished into the air. "Philip!"

A smile touched Philip Kenton's sharp, handsome features, but did nothing to warm the chill of his gray eyes. "My dear wife," he said mockingly, "you don't seem happy to see me. Come, isn't a husband returned from the grave a cause for rejoicing?"

"How—I thought—" Lettice gasped, her brain whirling. "What the devil are you doing here?"

"My dear girl, did you really believe you had killed me?" he asked and laughed a short, ugly laugh. "You have always been far too impulsive, haven't I told you that? You should have checked more closely before you ran from the house. I had quite a concussion, of course, but I was still breathing. The servants found me and sent for a doctor; I was unconscious for a while, but I awoke— and, I might add, found myself in quite a predicament. Without you, I could expect no help from Sir Harold. I had to sneak out of the country like a thief in the night. Thank God I was able to fool a fisherman with those glass jewels of ours and get a boat ride across the Channel."

Lettice sagged against the building, clinging to the wall for support. Her knees felt as though they had turned to water, and she feared that she might slide ignominiously to the ground. Weakly, despairingly, she said, "Why, oh, why did you have to come here?"

"Well, this is a fine turn of events. Here I tell you the happy news that you are not after all a murderer, and you act as though you wish you had not seen me. Are you afraid that I shall punish you?" His eyes glinted danger- ously. "Well, no need to be. God knows I would love to wring that slender neck of yours for trying to kill me, but need must take precedence over pleasure. I make a living now, of a sort, by playing cards with the soldiers. You would be quite a drawing card, yes, quite an addition to my humble rooms. So—I forgive you, Lettice; I will take you back with open arms. The prodigal wife, so to speak."

"No!" Lettice cried, aghast at the thought of returning to him. "God, no, Philip, I will never return to you! You are right; I wish I *had* killed you that night. It would be no sin to kill a serpent like you."

"Lord," he said in a bored voice, "don't tell me you've gone Puritan on me. I realize that dress makes a splendid disguise; you look positively plain in it. But surely you are not taking on the morality of a Puritan as well. But wait—of course, why did I not realize it at once? You ran away with that colonial—what's his name, the one with the face like a hound. No doubt he was overwhelmed by the honor, but you can't seriously expect me to believe that you enjoy living here! You must be bored stiff in this backwater. Of course, that dull colonial no doubt respects your reluctance to share his bed—they hold such things in honor here, I understand. But surely that can't make up for the life you knew. My God, Lettice, we were at the pinnacle of London society. We knew everyone!"

"You know nothing about me!" Lettice spat out, blind with rage at the aspersions he cast on Charles. "That colonial, however dull you think him, is ten times the man you are. He has taught me how to love and be loved. I am not cold with him. It was you, your clumsiness and cruelty, the way you hurt and abused me, that made me dread my marital duty. With Charles, it is no duty at all, but wonderful pleasure!"

A dull flush spread over Philip's features, and Lettice knew that her remarks had hit home. No doubt it pierced his pride to hear that a man like Charles had succeeded where he had failed time and again.

His voice was a sneer as he said, "And what would this paragon of yours think if he knew that your husband was alive? What would the city of Boston think of him if they knew he was an adulterer?"

Lettice froze with fear. Unsteadily, she said, "Philip, please, just go away. Let us pretend we never met again. We will both be far happier without each other. Please, leave me alone. Let me continue my life in peace."

His smile was vicious. "I think not, Lettice. I have found that my schemes have little success without you as bait; you are quite useful to me, and I don't intend to give you up. I am your husband, after all, whatever your feelings on the subject. You are bound to me for life, you know, and I insist that you return to me."

"No! Never! I could not bear it. Just the thought of you makes my skin crawl," Lettice cried angrily, throwing caution to the winds in her revulsion. Let him tell Charles; she would rather live the rest of her life without marrying him than submit to Philip again. She would simply remain as his mistress, living as Anne Lindon did.

"Indeed?" he drawled. "And what if I told the soldiers about my adulterous wife and her lover? What if I told Gage about the way you and your precious colonial tried to kill me, fortunately failing, and then ran away to the colonies?"

"That's not true!" Lettice exclaimed. "Charles had nothing to do with it!"

"Oh? Do you really expect anyone to believe that,

when everyone saw you leave my house with him? Then I am mysteriously struck over the head and left to die, while you escape to Massachusetts with your lover? Only a naïve fool would believe your story. And even if he were not arrested and tried—though wouldn't it be nice for Gage to have an excuse to get rid of one of these 'sons of liberty'?—the whole town of Boston would hear the rumors. And in this Puritan community, the slightest breath of scandal would ruin a man. Surely you can't want that to happen to him."

Tears sprang into Lettice's eyes. Her defiance was gone, for she knew Philip to be right. Gage would be happy to find an excuse to arrest Charles and jail him; they would take him back to England and try him and no doubt hang him. At best, the scandal would ruin his stature in Boston and hurt his cause. Philip, as always, had her under his thumb.

Wearily she said, "All right, Philip, what do you want?"

"Nothing much, my love. Just your return to your proper place as my wife. Everything will be just as it was, no questions, no rebukes. Just cooperate with me."

Lettice felt drained, numbed. She should have known something would happen to spoil her happiness. She was not meant to have the peace and joy of marriage to Charles. It had been ridiculous of her ever to think she could find such loving simplicity.

Dully she said, "All right. Tell me where your rooms are, and I shall come there this evening."

"No need to go home and pack, my dear. Those clothes are a dead loss anyway; we shall have to find you something pretty to wear, though God knows where in a city like this. Just come with me right now."

"No! I must say good-bye to Charles. I cannot leave like this."

"But I insist. You don't think I'm about to give you another chance to run away, do you? No, I'm keeping you in my sight."

Even as she thought of seeing Charles again, Lettice knew that she could not bear it, could not stand to see the hurt in his eyes. It would be better for them both if she did not return, for there was nothing either one of them could do. She would send him a note explaining what had happened; that would be cleaner, quicker.

With a sigh, she agreed, and Philip gave her a thin smile. Triumphantly he took her arm, and they began to walk back to his quarters. Lettice moved along beside him, encased in her sorrow; it seemed as though with every step she took her heart was being cut, bit by bit, from her body. By the time they reached her husband's room, she knew her heart was gone, and that she would never feel anything again. Even Philip was almost frightened by the cold, dead look in her green eyes.

Charles paced the sitting room impatiently. "Where could she be? When did you say she left, Molly?"

"Earlier this afternoon," his sister said, frowning. She, too, was distressed by Lettice's absence. "She said she had several errands and that she might be gone much of the afternoon, but I can't imagine any of them taking her this long. It's well past the time when we usually eat. Surely she would have let us know if—" She broke off miserable, unable to think of any reasonable excuse to have kept her friend away this long.

Murdock thought of that afternoon months ago when

he had rescued her from the unwelcome advances of a British soldier, and in his mind's eye he pictured her being accosted by a soldier, drunk or vicious, and struggling helplessly in his arms. He started at once for the hall to get his hat and coat. He could not stand around here any longer, waiting and worrying; he had to go out and look for her, no matter how unlikely it was that he would find her.

But just as he was about to open the door to leave, a knock sounded, and he whipped the door open to find a young boy, obviously frightened by the suddenness of his action and the black expression on his face.

"Ch—Charles Murdock?" he stammered.

"Yes?"

Wordlessly the boy extended a sealed note, and Charles grabbed it, recognizing Lettice's spidery writing. "Who gave you this?" he barked.

"Lady, sir," the lad said, gulping. "A beautiful English lady."

"Where?"

"The inn where I am serving boy, sir. She was in the English lord's room."

At his words, Charles's heart seemed to hang suspended for a moment, then began to thud in quick, heavy beats. Tossing the boy a coin, he went back into the house, ripping open the seal on the note. Tauntingly Lettice's perfume drifted up at him as he raced through her note.

Dear Charles,
    I cannot think of a way to break this to you except as suddenly and shockingly as it happened

to me. Philip is not dead. Far from it: He is very much alive and in Boston, making his living cheating soldiers. I bitterly regret that I was so frightened in London and ran from him so quickly. I should have checked more closely and finished the job.

However, I am no murderess, and I know no way to get out of this tangle. I cannot marry you. Philip is my husband and he wished me to be with him, no doubt to better lure the soldiers to his table. Well, I care not what I do now; I knew when I saw Philip that my chance for a life with you was gone.

I am sorry for the misery I have caused you. Please believe that I love you. God keep you safe.

Lettice

A pain stabbed through his chest, and in disbelief, Charles read through the letter again, this time more slowly. Dear God, it could not be true; it could not have happened. Philip alive and Lettice gone back to him!

Slowly he crushed the delicate paper into a ball, rage pounding in his chest. It was the most damnable of fates for the man to show up now! And why had she gone back to him? It was impossible for them to marry now, of course, for neither Charles nor Lettice was capable of murdering her husband in cold blood. But if she loved him as she said, would she have been able to go straight back to her husband? Would she not at least live in separation from Philip? Shaken, Charles could not help but wonder if she had ever really loved him, or whether she had simply used him as her most likely means of support, then when she discovered that her husband was not dead, rushed back eagerly to the life she had known before. Until Philip showed up alive, she had had no hope of ever returning to that way of life again, but now she could. Maybe that was what she really wanted.

Or maybe—was it possible that everything she had told him, including her struggle with her husband, had been a lie? Perhaps that had been a ruse they cooked up to get her quickly and safely away, while Philip fled in another direction, so that they could escape their debt, then rejoin each other later. Dear God, if that were true, if she had been toying with him all along . . .

"Charles?" Molly's worried voice cut into his thoughts. "Charles, what is it? Was that note from Lettice? What's the matter?"

Murdock looked up at her, his face bleak. "Yes, it is from Lettice. She will not be returning here, and there will be no wedding. It seems her husband has turned up alive. Lettice is gone; we will not see her again."

Slowly, heavily Charles walked past her down the hall to his study, his face like stone. He stepped inside his sanctuary, and the door closed behind him with a solid, final click.

Fifteen

*L*ettice walked beside Philip, hardly noticing where they went, until at last he pulled to a stop before a narrow three-storied house painted a light shade of tan.

"Your future home, my dear," he said with a flourish and bow.

Lettice brushed past him and went up the steps, not even deigning to wait for him to open the door for her. Once inside, she glanced without interest around the foyer.

"Where is my room?" she asked abruptly.

"But, come, let me give you a tour of our new abode," Philip said mockingly, offering her his arm. "Not quite the match of Grenwil, of course, or even of our little townhouse in London, but seemingly as decent as one can find here. I was fortunate to find it so soon after you were miraculously restored to me."

Lettice swept her cool gaze over him, pointedly ignoring his proffered arm. "Philip, I have no desire to see this house. I only want to know where my rooms are; I would like to rest."

Philip's face tightened, and a slow, thin smile touched

his lips. "How blunt you have become, living here among these bumpkins. Really, Lettice, you will have to mend your manners."

His wife's voice was icy as she replied, "Philip, I am in no mood for your tasteless jests and senseless raillery. You have forced me to return to you; I will appear at your treacherous little card games and smile poor young boys to their ruin, since you threaten Charles. However, I refuse to fall in with you and become like you. I want nothing to do with you, now or ever. I have not agreed to talk with you or listen to your jokes or put up with your sarcasm. Have I made myself clear?"

"Perfectly," he replied drily, his eyes narrowed as he watched her. "What a shrew you've turned into. Of course, you always had that capability in you. All right, Lettice, I agree: I will not expect any camaraderie between us. God knows, you were ever a dull companion, anyway. My room is at the head of the stairs; you may have any one of the others that pleases you. I will send a maid up to you to prepare the room."

"Thank you." Lettice swept past him with icy disdain and climbed the stairs.

It did not take her long to choose which room she wanted for her own. Quickly she walked down the hall to the room farthest from her husband. It was smaller than the other two she had passed and too dark for her taste, but that did not matter.

Lettice sank down in a chair by the window and propped her head in her hands, letting the awful reality of her situation wash over her. Charles was lost to her forever, and her only prospect was a life of misery with

Philip. Tears slid between her lids and fell with fat plops onto her skirt.

It was a little later when a maid appeared, her arms full of bed linens. The girl bobbed a curtsey to her.

"Good afternoon, milady. My name is Becky, milady."

Lettice summoned up a small smile for the girl. She had been called Mistress Holmes for so long that her proper title sounded strange to her ears.

Becky worked quickly and when she had finished Lettice said, "Thank you for preparing the room. Now, if you will excuse me, Becky, I think I shall take a little nap."

"Yes, mum. If you should need me, just ring."

"I will. Oh, Becky, I think that I shall have my supper on a tray in my room tonight. You may tell Lord Philip that I am feeling rather ill."

After Becky left, Lettice lay down, but she could not sleep. All she could think of was Charles and his reaction to the letter she had sent him last night. Would he believe her? Or would he think the worst, believe that she had tricked him yet again? With a sob, she turned her face into her pillow, stifling the anguished cries that rose in her throat. Oh, dear God, do not let him hate me, she moaned. Anything but that!

Philip did not disturb her that evening. She ate her meal in solitude and retired to bed early to toss and turn alone. But the next morning there was a loud knock on her door and Philip unceremoniously entered.

Lettice, already dressed and sitting by her window, staring out, turned to him, her brows arching haughtily. "I never thought to see you up at this hour."

Philip laughed. "Ah, the colonies have corrupted me.

I find myself rising damnably early. There is nothing to do here in the evenings after I've finished with my games. For the first time in my life, I have been going to bed before the dawn."

"I really am supremely uninterested in your nocturnal habits," Lettice replied and returned her gaze to the street below.

Philip grimaced and said, "Sorry to bore you, my dear. However, that was not the purpose of my visit. I came to fetch you; we are going to visit a dressmaker. I can't have you running around in those somber rags."

Lettice shrugged and rose. It really made no difference to her what she did. Dresses interested her no more than staring out her window. Had any of her old friends in London heard her utter that thought, they would have roared with laughter.

The dressmaker was a middle-aged woman who gleefully began pulling out her brocades and satins and laces at the sight of the elegant lord and his lady. Lettice shrugged and glanced over the materials with indifference. Once she would have oohed and ahed over the emerald brocade that would enhance the bright green of her eyes; she would have stroked the black velvet and fingered the ivory lace and declared that she must have a dress from the cherry red satin. Today there was no room in her sad heart for the delight of clothes.

"You choose them," she said to Philip. "You are the one who wants them."

Philip, who had never known a visit to the modiste to fail to lighten his wife's nastiest mood, raised his eyebrows at her statement. "Gad, Lettice, what have you turned into?" He ran his eyes over the materials the dressmaker held. "She will need everything, from skin to dress; nothing she has is suitable. Let's have a day dress in that ivory silk, with a touch of lace around the throat and cuffs. An evening gown from the emerald brocade, of course. And one from the red satin and the velvet as well. A couple of sacque dresses, oh, from the blue and pink silk, I suppose. And the sea-green silk, another day dress from it. And what about that black-and-white diamond-patterned evening gown in your window?"

"Oh, sir," the woman breathed in awe. "That is promised to a Colonel's wife. I cannot sell it."

Philip smiled suavely. "Oh, I think you can, for the right price, don't you?" He unfolded a roll of bills before the woman's dazzled eyes. "You see, I must have a dress for my wife this evening, and that one is already completed. It will require only a little alteration to fit Lettice, who, as you can see, will show it off much better than the dumpy Colonel's wife."

The dressmaker melted before his charm and money. "Of course, sir, I'll fit it right away and have it ready by this evening."

Numbly Lettice submitted to the fitting, letting the woman take her measurements, putting on the cumbersome petticoats and stiff hoops that she must buy for her new clothes, even carelessly picking out the styles for her gowns from a book the dressmaker proudly displayed. Lettice refrained from telling her that no doubt the styles in her precious book were already hopelessly out of date, considering the time it had taken it to cross the sea.

By the time the woman was finished, Lettice was exhausted from standing, and she wondered why she had once found it such pleasure to buy new clothes.

At home, she found that the maid Becky had been sent out to purchase powder and rouge and paint for her. Lettice sat down before her vanity, where the porcelain pots were lined up. Slowly she lifted off each lid and looked down on the contents: a pot of red rouge; a tiny jar of green tint for her eyes. Beside the pots lay charcoal pencils she would use to line her eyes, and next to them a tiny brush and the pot of black to darken her eyebrows and eyelashes. A small silver case held beauty patches, and beside it sat a silver-backed set of brushes. A profusion of ribbons met her eyes when she opened one drawer, and in another lay combs to hold up her stiff, wired coiffures. Vials of perfumes lined the vanity, and Lettice picked one up and sniffed it. The fragrance was one she had often used in London, and the smell transported her back to the life she had known. If she closed her eyes, she could almost imagine the noise and laughter, the tinkling of crystal, the heat of bodies packed together, the crush of skirts, the ache of her head and the feel of champagne in her mouth.

Queasily, Lettice turned away from the table. Something awful was rising in her, something more than a memory—a time, a being experienced again. Shakily she sat down in her chair, fighting the memory, willing the picture of Charles to rise in her mind. Then the past receded, leaving her cold and shaken with fear. Dear God, she could not become that person again.

Slowly the afternoon passed. Lettice ate a cold, light supper in her room, so that she would not have to see Philip again. After her meal, the maid Becky came in excitedly, holding out the black-and-white diamond-patterned ballgown.

"Oh, look, milady, isn't it beautiful? You will look like a vision in this. It just came from the dressmaker, and I ironed it for you. And see, the master gave me this for you. Won't it look mysterious with this dress?"

The girl held out a half mask, in a black-and-white harlequin pattern to match the dress. Lettice glanced at it and the gown, sweeping them both with an indifferent eye. She knew how the mask would look on her, how cunningly it would accentuate the beauty of her delicate face, hiding her alluring eyes yet hinting at their beauty. Philip had chosen it to beckon the men more surely than her natural beauty would.

Lettice sat down at her vanity, and Becky rushed to help her with her hair. Without a skilled hairdresser, she could not hope to attain one of the fantastical styles she had once worn. Instead she pulled her hair to one side of her head, puffing it out with wads of padding; then she fastened it at the side and curled the remainder into long thick curls. She pulled out the powder box and liberally powdered her hair until every vestige of the glimmering gold was gone. Finally she pushed a curved comb into her hair at the back and adorned the fastening of the curls with a winking false diamond.

Next she turned her attention to her face, painting it as carefully as an artist might touch a canvas. She touched her lids with emerald-green and outlined her eyes with black pencil. She rouged her cheeks, then covered her whole face with the dead-white powder. She drew in her lips and colored them red, and blackened her lashes. The finishing touches were two beauty marks, one triangular and one heart-shaped, which she placed high on one cheek and close to the corner of her seductive mouth.

Lettice stood and Becky helped her into her clothes, tying the multitude of petticoats and the stiff hoop about her waist and cinching her into the stays that made her waist seem minuscule. Silk stockings clung sleekly to her legs, and she slipped her feet into narrow black velvet high-heeled slippers. Finally, her maid carefully lowered the dress over her head, fastening the buttons and smoothing the heavy skirt down over the froth of petticoats.

Lettice turned slowly and looked at herself in the mirror. The bodice of the dress clung to her tightly, her firm breasts swelling over the square-cut neckline, and she felt a cowardly desire to cover up her nakedness. Her feet hurt in the pinching shoes, and the stays seemed to cut off her lungs. She had been too long without these imprisonments of fashion to feel comfortable in them now.

Looking at herself, seeing the cold, perfect, pale beauty, Lettice felt as though she was gazing on a statue or picture, not herself at all. Yet this was the face and form she had seen so many times in the past, that had seemed so natural to her then. She felt once more the shaking fear, the boiling in her stomach that had accompanied her throughout her career in London. Only the huge green eyes that stared out of her face did not fit; they seemed to belong to another person. The new Lettice stared out from the old one's face, and her emerald eyes were wide and frightened. Tears welled suddenly.

Becky spoke, breaking the spell, and Lettice blinked her tears away rapidly. "Oh, milady, you look absolutely beautiful!" the girl enthused, handing her the mask and fan. "I've never seen anyone who looked as lovely as you."

Lettice took the objects and smiled brittlely at the girl. "Thank you, Becky. Would you tie on my mask?"

The mask in place, she looked even more remote and mysterious, and Lettice could bear to see herself more easily; it could have been some other person beneath that mask. With a snap, she unfurled her fan. It was time for her to perform.

Downstairs, Lettice swept into the gaming room, where several officers idled about, sipping at drinks and casually talking. A few sat at a table with Philip, absorbed in their cards. Lettice noted with amusement that Philip's games were not exactly well attended. No doubt he truly did need her.

She paused for a moment in the doorway, letting the full effect of her entrance soak in, then swayed into the room, her fan plying daintily. Immediately half the men in the room were beside her, offering to seat her or bring her a glass of refreshment or a bite from the buffet table.

"What a vision you are," one soldier declared, his eyes gleaming avidly. "Tell us, what is your name?"

Lettice laughed a tinkling laugh, searching her memory for the proper response. How long it had been since she had had to lie and posture thus! "Visions have no names," she replied in mocking rebuke. "We are mere phantasms in the air."

Another officer insinuated his hand beneath her elbow and sought to lead her away from the others. "Indeed, madam, I think such a form can only be flesh and blood and thus must have a name."

She moved her arm out of his grasp by reaching up to

pat back a nonexistent tendril of hair. "Cannot you guess who I am?" she countered, struggling to hold her own in the arena that had once been hers.

"There is no lady in Boston half so beautiful!" declared one of the men, who had a lilting Irish accent. "I think you must be an angel who has appeared to ease our plight."

"An angel?" Lettice repeated and laughed. "Thrown down in this den of iniquity? Come, come."

"Perhaps she is a lovely Puritan maid, escaping the cold Bostonians to find men who can appreciate her beauty," someone suggested laughingly.

Another took up his theme. "Aye, that's it. She has grown tired of men who have nothing on their minds but liberty and taxes."

Lettice had to bite her lip to keep from snapping back a sharp retort. It galled her to hear them jest at the colonials she had come to love. Thinly, she smiled and said, "It is not fair that I should have to give my name, when I am fully as ignorant of who you are."

"Captain William Evelyn, ma'am," said the Irish fellow, sweeping her an elegant bow, "at your service."

Quickly the others followed suit, chiming in with their names and fighting to outdo the others in courtesy. Lettice tilted her head to one side, studying them with her bright emerald eyes, which could not be fully hidden by the mask.

"Then it is only proper that I should respond in kind," Lettice said and swept them a graceful, low curtsey that was sure to give them a good look down the front of her brimming dress. Even as she moved, she felt chilled with self-disgust, realizing that all her old ways of flirtation had been little short of whoring. She pulled herself back up proudly and thrust her chin out, promising herself inwardly that she would not sink back into that morass. "I am Lady Lettice Kenton. And now, if one of you kind gentlemen would be so good as to bring me a little something to drink—my throat is parched from all this chatter."

Immediately they fell to bickering over who should be the man so honored as to fetch her glass, and languidly Lettice worked her fan, bored with their silly posturing.

The rest of the evening Lettice moved about mechanically, talking to the men who were there, responding to their overblown compliments with vague smiles and warding off their eager advances. By the time the group began to break up and leave the house, she felt as if she had been stretched on the rack. Her head ached from the wine she had consumed; her feet were pinched and sore from standing in the dainty slippers; and her lungs felt crushed. Lettice wondered wearily how she had ever stood such a life.

When the last man had left, Philip turned from the door to her, his face cold and tight-lipped. "Well, that was certainly a meager performance tonight. Hardly up to your usual standard, my dear."

"Don't call me that!" Lettice snapped, bending down to take off her shoes. "I am in no mood for your jests, Philip. I am tired and I am going to bed. Good night."

She moved to pass him, but his arm lashed out and seized her by the wrist. "Not so fast, milady. I was not jesting. I was registering a complaint. You wouldn't have lasted five minutes in London with that wilted look and half-hearted conversation. I saw you, Lettice. I made it a point to watch you tonight. You were hardly convincing."

"I am not the same person I used to be!" Lettice cried. "How can I act the same? I loathe what you make me do; I cannot stand listening to their stupid *bon mots* or seeing their leering faces! All evening I've been pawed and slobbered over by a bunch of buffoons, and I despise it."

His grip on her arm tightened painfully. "That is your job, Lettice. You are supposed to lure those men to come back, time and again, and bring their friends with them. And that isn't done with the tight smile I saw you wearing this evening, nor with the way you shrank from their touch. Give them a little taste of your delights, Lettice, so that they return for more. You used to know that most elemental rule."

"I don't want to!" Lettice pulled desperately at her arm, trying to get out of his grasp, but she could not.

He grinned and twisted her arm behind her back, bending it cruelly until at last she cried out in pain. The other hand he put around her throat lightly, almost caressingly.

"Do you defy me, Lettice? Haven't you yet learned that that is not wise? Will it take a visit to your bed to remind you of it?"

A dark passion touched his eyes, and with horror Lettice saw his face draw nearer to hers. His hold on her arm slackened, and furiously, spurred by fear and anger, Lettice wrenched painfully from him.

"Don't touch me!" she shouted, her eyes blazing. "Don't you ever touch me again. Because of your threats, because of the things you could do to the man I love, I have agreed to come here to live; I have consented to be at your nasty little parties, to smirk and flirt with your vile soldiers. But I have agreed to nothing else, Philip. And if you ever again so much as lay a hand on me, I swear to God I will kill you!"

For a moment the two of them stared at each other in shocked silence, then Lettice whirled and ran up the stairs to her room, locking the door behind her. Philip looked after her, his face closed, his eyes icy. Damn her; he was not going to let her get away with that. Somehow, at the suitable moment, he would repay her—in double.

Lettice went numbly through the following days, her heart heavy with despair. At night she smiled and pretended to be sparkling and happy, and her enticements lured men in ever-increasing numbers to Philip's table. However, hardly a moment passed that she did not think of Charles and long to return to him and the life she had known so briefly and loved so well.

One day, lonely and desperate, she dressed in her "Puritan" clothes and slipped out of the house to walk. The crisp air of early spring picked up her spirits somewhat, and she felt almost normal again, walking as she once had. Her steps turned almost automatically toward the row of shops where Ruth Whitney resided. Lettice did not realize where she was going until suddenly she found herself standing across the street from Ruth's shop, gazing at her front window.

She wondered if Ruth had heard what happened to her. Did she know that Lettice had returned to her English husband and cavorted merrily every evening with the British officers? For a moment Lettice considered entering the shop and trying to speak to her, so hungry was she for companionship and consolation, but her fear of rejection held her back.

A few minutes later, the door to the shop opened, and Ruth herself stepped out. Lettice stiffened; the moment had been thrust upon her, whether she liked it or not. Swallowing, she looked across at the other woman, a tentative smile forming on her face. Ruth Whitney glanced across the street, then straightened, her eyes narrowing. No welcoming smile spread across her face. Instead, her lips dipped down disapprovingly, and she swung her gaze away from Lettice, walking straight ahead as though she had not seen her.

Bright tears flooded Lettice's eyes, and with a half-smothered sob, she turned away. She had no friend left in this world, no one! Almost running, she retraced her steps, hurrying back to the dubious comfort of her home. Racing upstairs, she ran into her room and flung herself across her bed, sobbing uncontrollably.

Dear God, she was lost! Utterly, utterly lost!

Sixteen

$\mathcal{L}$ettice sat by the window, her
fingers drumming a bored tattoo on the windowsill as she
stared out at the city of Boston. In a few more minutes,
she would have to make her appearance downstairs at
Philip's gaming room; by now it was no doubt already
filling up, and Philip would be up here to pull her down
if she did not appear soon. Ever since her appearance at
his table, business had boomed, and he was not about to
let her spoil his profits by her reluctance.

With a sigh, she stood and took one last look at herself
in the mirror to make sure she presented the proper
image. It had been two weeks now since she had returned
to Philip, and she had learned to get through the evening
by distancing herself from her role. She would posture
and pretend as though she were an actress and not think
about what she was doing. That was the only way it was
endurable. Otherwise, she thought she would crack right
down the middle, as a mirror would crack if she hit it, and
simply shatter into nothingness.

She had no choice, really, Lettice told herself, as she
left her room and started down the stairs. What else was
she to do? Kill herself? No, she had found out once

before, on the *Sally Blue*, that she was not meant for suicide. But she could not go back to Charles. Sometimes she thought of running away, but to what? Where? Without Charles, what awaited her anywhere that was any better? At least here, she could walk past his house and hope for a glimpse of him; she could perhaps run into him on the street. Lettice felt that without that faint hope, she would surely die.

Lettice straightened her shoulders and fixed a false smile on her face, then stepped into the gaming room which was already crowded with soldiers. She paused for effect at the door, and as every eye turned toward her, she carelessly swept the room with her gaze, noting who was there and locating the men she had not met and must make sure to greet before they left. Captain Evelyn was there, as usual holding forth about the cowardice of the colonials. Evelyn had all the devilish charm of the Irish, but his contempt for the colonials set Lettice's teeth on edge, until she found it difficult to force herself even to chat with him. And Lord Rawdon was there, another Irishman; he wasn't as handsome as William Evelyn, but he was every inch a rigid, athletic officer. And there was George Hunter, a puppyish Lieutenant, as naïve as a child and silly in his adoration of her. As soon as she stepped in the room, he was hurrying to her side. He was one whom Philip complained about; he was so enamored of Lettice that he spent every moment with her and no time at all at the card tables.

Mechanically Lettice moved around the room, flirting expertly and convincing everyone that she was having the time of her life. She was careful to float, to join every conversational group briefly, offending no one but never staying long enough anywhere to arouse another's jealousy.

"There are colonial spies everywhere," Jack Martin was saying earnestly to Captain Evelyn, and Lettice let out her tinkling laugh and put one slender white hand on his arm.

"Careful, Major Martin," she said playfully, "I might be a spy, you know."

Evelyn snorted. "Egad, Jack, what if they are all over the place? They haven't the wit to get any information nor the nerve to risk getting caught."

Martin shook his head ponderously. "You can laugh if you like, William, but I tell you it is a situation that should not be ignored. All our officers talk to anyone and everyone about all they know. And the colonials somehow know everything Gage does. How else do you explain it? Think of all those damn loyal colonials Gage listens to all the time, instead of to his own officers. How many of them are really secret sympathizers with the radicals, feeding information back to their compatriots and guiding Thomas Gage in the wrong directions?"

"Is it really that serious?" Lettice asked, letting her eyes widen innocently, and the Major waxed eloquent, citing all the times that soldiers had gone to a house where it was known the radical leaders were meeting, only to find the leaders gone. And then there were the times when Gage's men had marched on munitions stores, only to find the supplies spirited away.

"They must have prior knowledge!" he exclaimed.

Evelyn shrugged and said, "I think you overestimate the importance of spies, Martin. You know that Gage is a blundering idiot sometimes and, I suspect, a colonial sympathizer, what with having a colonial wife. His informers are a pathetically stupid lot, and I am sure they give him incorrect information half the time. It is no wonder to me that so many of his efforts fail. He has never really tried wholeheartedly to squelch these upstarts."

Lettice smiled at both men and made a light comment to block an argument between them, but even as she talked and smiled, her brain was whirling excitedly. Spies! Why had she not thought of it before? She probably was privy to more officers' secrets than anyone in the city; they thought her a Britisher like themselves and said things they would never say to a colonial, even one they thought was a Tory and therefore loyal. She was the confidante of their drunken or lovesick ramblings; she overheard many conversations between the men that they no doubt thought were private. Indeed there was no one in the whole town of Boston in a better position to spy for the colonials.

She could help Charles and his cause and get back at Philip at the same time. It would alleviate some of the deadly boredom she felt these days, with nothing to do but dress herself for the evening card parties. And if she was caught—well, what worse could happen than that there would be a scandal and Philip would be disgraced, as well as she! No doubt they would make him leave Boston. And Philip's disgrace would bring her more glee than sorrow; she did not care about herself. Her safety and reputation seemed of little importance now; nothing could hurt her more than she had already been hurt. It would be exciting, and a blow for the freedom she had come to love so dearly, a slap in the face for the rigid English structure that had confined her life for so long.

Her eyes dancing with wicked excitement, Lettice moved on to another conversation. Tomorrow she would sneak out of the house and go to see—whom? Not Charles. No, she could not bear the pain of facing Charles; she could not stand the hurt and disillusion that would be in his eyes nor the knifelike pain that would pierce her own chest at being so near him and yet so locked away from him. It would have to be someone else. Dr. Warren? Samuel Adams? No, they were too much suspected by the British; no doubt she would be quickly caught if she went to see them often. It must be someone less obtrusive, less famous, yet still a party to the radical cause. But, of course—Jonathan Baker. There was no one better. He was entirely loyal to the cause of liberty, as Lettice knew, yet he was not one whose name was well known by the British officers. And she knew him better than any of them, except Charles. She could convince him of the honesty of her actions, she was sure. Tomorrow, then, it would be to his house that she would make her secretive way.

When his housekeeper informed him of a visitor, disapprovingly announcing her to be a painted English lady, Jonathan Baker frowned at the woman in disbelief.

"What?" he exclaimed. "Who? I know no English lady."

A familiar musical laugh sounded in the hall behind the housekeeper, and Lettice pushed past the woman into the room. "Why, Jonathan, it is I. Surely you cannot have forgotten."

With a dark glance at Lettice and her employer, the housekeeper stalked with great dignity from the room, leaving Jonathan staring in amazement at his caller. It could not be! And yet it was—there was no mistaking that perfection of face and form, even disguised as it was by powdered hair and painted face and stiffly hooped dress.

"Mistress Holmes!" he exclaimed, shocked.

Lettice laughed again and carefully closed the door behind her. "Yes, it is I, although I am forced to admit that my name is Lady Lettice Kenton, not Holmes."

"I don't understand. Why—" He broke off, confused and embarrassed and angry.

Molly had been hurt and bewildered by this woman's sudden disappearance, but had known little of the truth of her leaving, and Charles had glowered and refused to speak of it at all. So Baker had been completely in the dark; he wanted to barrage Lettice with questions to satisfy his curiosity, but his loyalty to his friends stopped him. He did not even want to give her an opportunity to excuse herself for what she had done to those who loved and helped her.

"What do you want from me?" he said coldly.

Lettice sighed. It was going to be harder than she had thought; obviously Baker disliked her for the hurt Charles had suffered. Making her voice matter-of-fact, she said, "Nothing. I came to offer you something."

"What could you possibly offer that I would accept?"

"Help. A spy in the heart of the British camp." A disbelieving sneer began to form on his lips, and Lettice went on hurriedly, "Oh, I realize that you dislike and distrust me, Mr. Baker. I don't know what Charles or Molly told you about me, but it is obvious that you think I am guilty of some heinous breach of trust." She shrugged, her face and tone cynical, and then dropped gracefully into a chair facing him. "But, really, do you have the luxury of turning down such an offer out of personal dislike?"

"It is not just personal dislike, Mistress . . . that is, Lady Kenton. Molly and Charles have told me little, but it is obvious that you lied and deceived us. How can I place any confidence in you?"

Lettice turned her clear green gaze on him. "It is no business of yours, but I shall tell you what transpired between Charles and me, so that you will see it was an entirely personal matter and does not touch upon my honesty in more political matters." Quickly, colorlessly, she sketched for him the details of her life since she had met Charles: the fight and her presumed murder of her husband, her escape with Charles's aid, the masquerade she had had to play to avoid discovery, her love for Murdock, and then the untimely resurrection of Philip.

When her story was ended, Baker blinked a little in shock and glanced away from her, then back again. "But, if all this is true, how can I place any trust in a woman who nearly kills her husband or who acts as the bait for his schemes of cheating at cards, who lies whenever it suits her purpose?"

Again Lettice shrugged. "I cannot answer that. I can only swear that I hold Charles Murdock in great affection; I would never be part of a scheme to harm him. I do what I have to, that is true. I am not an angel of virtue; I don't claim to be. However, what you need is not an angel of virtue, but a spy, and I think that I will prove quite competent at that. Surely you must see the advantages that my position gives me. The very flirting and deception that my husband forces me to perform will also open up quite a few army secrets to me. I have the opportunity, the skill, and the nerve to make an effective spy. I fail to see how you can pass up that combination."

Baker sighed. When she had looked at him with those huge eyes and told him of her life, he found that he pitied her and wanted very much to believe her. She *would* make a good spy; men would tell her anything. And he knew well enough that any person who made a good spy must have untrustworthy aspects as well; an entirely honest person would be caught immediately. It was a profession that required deviousness. He really could not reject her because she was not a perfectly upright character.

Lettice could see the struggle going on in the man, but she leaned back in her chair, waiting for his decision and making no effort to persuade him. He would have to come to accept her for himself, without her blandishments and persuasions; otherwise, he would never fully believe in her, and that would make her task more difficult.

"All right," he said at last, and the words seemed torn from him grudgingly. "All right, bring me your reports, and I will listen to them. Beyond that I promise nothing."

Lettice shrugged. "That is no concern of mine. All I can do is offer them to you; what you do with the knowledge I give you is your responsibility."

"Whenever you have information for me, come to this side door and knock. It leads into my study, and I can open it to you without your having to pass my housekeeper every time. The less anyone knows of your visits, the better."

"I agree," Lettice said. "I will keep my visits secret

when I leave my home as well, you can count on that."

Stiffly, awkwardly they stood and parted, on a new standing now and uncertain of it. Lettice left his house quickly and started back toward her new home, but she found her steps turning first in the direction of the Murdock house. And as she had so many times in the past weeks of loneliness, she walked slowly down the street across from the house, searching the door and windows and yard for some sight of Charles. She knew that the sight of him would be painful to her, would cut her to the core, but stronger than that was her longing to see him. Somehow, she could not keep away.

Today, as always, he was not in sight, even though she loitered several minutes on the corner, watching the house. Just as she was about to turn to leave, the door opened and a man stepped out. Lettice's breath caught in her throat: Charles. It had been so long, and his absence was a never-ending desolate ache within her. She wanted now to run down the street to him and throw herself into his arms, to beg him to forgive her and take her away from Philip, to place the responsibility for their lives in his hands.

A long, shuddering sigh escaped her, and she forced herself to turn away and begin to walk. She could not, she must remember that; she could not destroy Charles. Whatever else she did in her life, she must not ruin that man, that life, that precious, shining love that had glowed for a brief while between them.

The next evening, Lettice listened intently to the conversations of the officers, her interest no longer feigned, and concentrated hard to remember anything that might be important. Much of what she heard was useless, but now and then an interesting tidbit cropped up.

As she talked with two men, making witty sallies and appearing charmed by them, she heard a conversation begin behind her and she focused her attention on it.

"Well, damme," one gruff voice said, obviously far gone in drink, "I think Gage is acting like a bloody coward, running around digging up every spare soldier he can find."

"Well, we are a small force among a rather large potential enemy," his companion returned calmly.

"Enemy!" the other man snorted contemptuously. "A cowardly mob, that's all these people are. It wouldn't take half the men Gage has to put down one of their riots. But he's pulled every available soldier in all the colonies into Boston and is still crying for more from home."

"That's not what he needs most from home," the sober voice replied. "What he's really asking for is guidance. How should he treat these people? Are they enemies? Countrymen? Outlaws? Gage doesn't know whether to placate them or make war on them, and that's the truth. But the ministers won't give him any guidance."

Lettice tucked that information away in her head, along with the slip an earnest young Lieutenant made later when she asked if he would return to her house the following evening: "Oh, no, milady," he replied ingenuously, "I wish I could, but we're marching out tomorrow to seize a munitions dump the colonists have."

"Oh?" Lettice replied, keeping her tone light, despite the way her stomach fluttered at his words. "Will it be that far away?"

"Oh, yes, milady. In Medford."

"That's too bad," Lettice pouted prettily. "I shall miss you terribly."

It was all she could do to stay in the room, laughing and playing her role, until most of the soldiers had left, leaving only the serious card players behind. Then she slipped upstairs and quickly undressed and removed her makeup, forcing herself to stay calm as her maid took down her hair and combed it out.

Becky helped her into her nightgown and left the room, and Lettice lay down in her bed, impatiently waiting until the girl was back in her room and safely in bed. After she judged enough time to have passed, Lettice left her bed and quietly dressed in the dark, putting on a simple dark-blue dress and sturdy shoes. Then she slipped on a woolen mantle and pulled the hood over her hair.

On tiptoe she crept down the back stairs and out the rear servant's entrance, shivering a little in the predawn chill. Pulling her cloak tight around her, her face hidden by the hood, she hurried through the streets toward Jonathan's house.

"Hey, you there!" A voice rang out through the still-dark night, and Lettice froze, her heart pounding.

Slowly she turned and saw a red-uniformed soldier walking toward her. Her mouth went dry with fear—was she to be discovered so easily?

"Now what's your business that you're sneaking through the streets so early and so quiet-like?" The man reached out to push the hood off her face. Amazement flickered across his face when he saw her. "My, you're a pretty one, aren't you? Tell me, what's a sweet lass like you doing out here this time of night?"

Nervously Lettice wet her lips and stammered, "Beggin' your pardon, sir, but I wasn't doing nothin' wrong." She lowered her eyes from his gaze, striving to look like a frightened, naïve serving girl.

"And what was this nothing you were doing?" he continued remorselessly.

Lettice cast him a pained glance and whispered, "You won't be telling my mistress, will you?"

"No." A faint smile touched his lips.

"I was going home, to my mistress's house, where I'm supposed to sleep. She's a fearful stern woman, sir, and she would toss me out for sure, if she knew where I'd been. I was—" she paused as though embarrassed, then continued in a rush, "I was with my Johnny. I swear it weren't wrong, sir. He loves me; truly he does, and he'll marry me as soon as he gets the money to buy his own shop. But Mistress Fletcher don't believe that. She won't let any of us maids see any boys. If she knew I'd sneaked out to meet Johnny, she'd pull my hair and call me a slut and throw me out the door. Please, sir, promise you won't tell her. I need the job awful bad; times are so hard right now."

The soldier chuckled indulgently. "A little romance, is it? Well, I promise I won't tell your Mistress Fletcher. But you be careful in these streets, understand? Sometimes they're not safe at night for a lass."

"Oh, yes, sir, thank you, sir," Lettice said breathlessly and bobbed him a curtsey. Pulling her hood back up to conceal her face, she hurried away before he could get to thinking about the cut and material of her cloak and wonder where a lowly maid obtained such an expensive item.

She reached Baker's house without further incident and tapped softly at his side door. Finally, after her persistent knocks, the door opened and a tousled, sleepy Jonathan appeared at the door. He yawned and motioned her inside. However, when she told him her information, the sleep quickly disappeared from his face, and he took a quill and a scrap of paper and wrote down what she had said.

"Thank you, Mistress—that is, milady," Jonathan said, "I will pass your information along immediately."

A faint, cold smile touched Lettice's lips. She could see the distrust in Jonathan's eyes. He had not expected her to be of use, and was still uncertain whether her information was correct, or some devious plot by the British to ensnare him.

"Good day, Mr. Baker," she said and stood. "I shall see you again whenever I have further information."

As the spring came slowly upon them, Lettice continued her spying, though rarely did she come upon any information as important as that she had gleaned the first evening. Sometimes it seemed rather a chore, in fact, to have to listen so intently to the boring conversation that swelled around her.

One evening as she stood, waving her fan languidly, her thoughts a million miles away from the conversation she was supposed to be a part of, the most important information that had come her way almost passed her by. She seemed to come awake as a Lieutenant said, chuckling, ". . . and take the rascals by surprise! Good idea, don't you think?"

"I *am* sorry," she said, smiling at the man radiantly, "I'm afraid I missed what you were saying. I scarcely know where my thoughts were."

The boy blushed under her smile and stammered, "Oh, nothing, milady, nothing. I was just blathering on about the colonials."

"You must think me terribly rude," Lettice said sweetly, cursing herself for her inattention. "Please, I really am most interested."

Fortunately, George Hunter was eager to seize her attention for himself and he continued what the other had apparently thought better of blurting out. "What he said was that the General has heard of large munitions stores in Lexington and Concord, and he plans to march out of Boston and seize them."

"Oh, my," Lettice said, hoping she sounded sufficiently brainless, "how terribly exciting! When?"

"Why, tomorrow night, I hear."

Lettice felt as though her heart had leaped up into her mouth. Tomorrow night! That left so little time to get word to Baker. He must know at once, so that word could be sent to Lexington. There was only one thing she could do, and that was to somehow get out of here and run to Baker with the news.

Excusing herself from the group, Lettice went to her husband and begged his attention for a moment. He turned from the table, irritated at the interruption, but at the sight of her pale face, his eyebrows shot up.

"What is it, Lettice? Are you ill? You look damned pale."

Gratefully, Lettice seized on the excuse, "Yes, please, I feel suddenly quite nauseated. I have to go up and lie down. Please, I must leave."

"Well, of course." He waved her away impatiently. He certainly had no desire to hear any further details of her illness.

Managing to keep her steps slow and weak-seeming, Lettice climbed the stairs; then, grabbing a light shawl, she slipped down the servants' stairs in the back and out the back door. Almost running, she hurried to Jonathan's house and up the walk to the dark side door. Her gentle tap brought no response, and she pounded louder, still to no avail. In desperation, she circled back to the front door and pounded until the dour housekeeper opened the door a crack and peered out.

She frowned at the sight of Lettice and said sourly, "What are you doing here? 'Tis the middle of the night, when folks should be home in bed asleep."

"I must see Mr. Baker. It is dreadfully important, or I would not be here at this hour," Lettice snapped. "I have to see him! Please inform him that I am here."

"Well, I can't," the woman said with smug satisfaction, " 'cause he ain't here."

"Where is he?" Lettice asked, her voice rising in alarm.

"Out of town. His brother in Salem is ill, and he went up this morning to visit him."

Lettice slumped and walked away from the door, appalled at this turn of events. What was she to do now? She must get word to someone; it was far too important to just let it go. Dr. Warren? But she did not know where he lived, and he had met her only once or twice. Would he even remember who she was? And why should he believe what she said?

In despair, she walked back out to the street, choking back the sobs that threatened to fill her throat. She had only one recourse, but everything in her rebelled against it. She should go to Charles. He knew her and would believe her; Baker might even have told him of her spying efforts. But to see him again, to have to speak to him and be with him, look at him, just as if nothing had happened . . . that was too awful to contemplate.

Yet, there was nothing else to do. Either she faced Charles, or she let the British soldiers get their hands on the munitions depots so valuable to the colonials. Reluctantly, her steps turned toward Charles's home.

The Murdock house was dark when she approached, but when she looked down the narrow passage between Charles's house and the one next to it, she saw that a light still burned in his study. She forced herself to go down the walkway and approach the window. Through a small crack in the draperies, she could see that Charles was slumped forward at his desk, his head in his hands. A faint, tender smile touched her lips; he had fallen asleep at his desk. Softly she tapped at the window, and his head snapped up. He looked around the room, blinking, and she tapped again. This time he came to the window and pulled aside the curtain to look out, and she found herself staring into the face of the man she had loved and abandoned.

For a moment, Charles stood looking at her in disbelief, thinking that he was still dreaming, or at least muddled by his sleepiness. But the apparition did not go away; instead, she motioned to be let in, and Charles was forced to admit that it was Lettice herself who stood outside his study.

For weeks now he had lived in a desert of loneliness and despair, his brief dream of love ripped from him. Now, looking out at her, he knew that she had never left his heart. Damn her husband, for returning. Damn her, for going back to him. A flood of conflicting emotions rushed through him, pulling him in a thousand different directions. He hated, loved, feared her, dreaded facing her, and could not stand to send her away.

Charles let the curtain drop and strode to the front door to admit her. Silently she slipped inside and followed him back to his study, not speaking until the door was shut behind her. Charles turned to her inquiringly, his face cold and remote, though his heart pounded against his ribs and his hands ached to reach out and touch her.

Lettice blushed, uncertain before his clear, cool gaze. She wanted to cry out to him not to look at her like that. Instead she said as coolly as she could, "I had to come here. Mr. Baker was not at home, and I had to bring him some urgent news." Charles was silent, and she said anxiously, "Did he tell you that I was helping him, that I spied on the soldiers and brought him reports?"

"No." Charles shook his head, taken aback by her words. He did not know what he had expected, but it certainly was not this.

"Well, I have been. You see, Philip wanted me back so that I could attract the officers to his card games, and it gives me a great deal of opportunity to find out what is going on. Tonight I heard something most urgent, and I pretended to be sick and went up to bed, then slipped out to Jonathan's with the news. But he is in Salem, and I had to tell somebody!"

Her words ended almost on a wail. Lettice could read doubt in his eyes, and suddenly she was frightened that even Charles would not believe her, that all her efforts would all be for naught.

"I swear to you, Charles, I am not lying; it is the truth. I have no reason to lie."

"And what reason do you have to spy on your own countrymen?" he replied coldly.

"Charles, do you think I returned willingly to that creature!" Lettice gasped. "Do you think I have any care for Philip or my past life or even my countrymen? Well, I don't! I still believe in freedom! Helping your cause is the only thing I have left in my life. I am not lying to you; I gladly spy on my countrymen and inform on them. They mean nothing to me. You, and your people, and this city—they mean everything to me."

Tears gathered in her eyes, and it was only with the greatest difficulty that Charles refrained from taking her in his arms. "All right," he said wearily, "I believe you. What is this news that is so urgent?"

"Gage is marching tomorrow night to seize the munitions supplies at Lexington and Concord."

"What! He's never yet done anything so openly militant! Why, he is declaring war on us." With a sigh, he rubbed his hand across his forehead and was silent for a moment, digesting this new idea. At last he smiled at her weakly and said, "Thank you, Lettice. You are right; it is vitally important. I must tell Dr. Warren and Revere. Do they sail or march across the Neck?"

"I don't know."

"Well, no matter, we'll set a watch and find that out. Thank you, Lettice, I will send the alarm to Lexington and Concord."

For a moment they looked at each other, Lettice knowing that she needed to hurry back to the house before Philip might discover her absence, Charles knowing that he must leave and find Revere to set in motion their warning system. Yet, for a moment they could not move, could only gaze at each other, their love burning deep in their eyes. It was gone, lost, they told themselves, and yet, in that one instant, when time hung motionless, they could not deny the desire that surged between them.

Suddenly everything snapped, and Charles stepped forward as Lettice threw herself into his arms. For one long, passionate moment, they clung to each other, the flame of their bodies searing through their clothing, their lips blending in an agony of love.

Charles tore his lips from hers to move down her neck, murmuring, "My love, my love. Oh, God, Lettice, I love you. Please, please, stay with me."

Wildly Lettice returned his kisses, sobs choking her throat, thrusting herself against him, molding her body to his. "Yes, yes," her voice was soft and quavering, "Take me, Charles, take me. I love you. Please, please."

His hands tore demandingly at her stiff bodice, delving down to caress the quivering softness of her breasts. His mouth was like flame upon her breasts, his kisses branding her with his desire. They sank together to the floor of his study, tearing at their encumbering clothing, and there, locked together in a rage of desire, once more he possessed her. He drove into her with all the frustrated love and anger and loss he had felt since she left, and she responded in kind, writhing beneath him, glorying in the feel of him and crying out against the irrevocable loss. Finally she arched against him as wave after wave of release washed over her, and he cried out hoarsely and came to his own fulfillment.

Afterwards, exhausted, they lay entangled on the floor, dazed by the onslaught of passion. Silently, regretfully, Lettice pulled away from him and began to dress. She felt as though it tore her very soul from her to leave him, and yet she knew that if she did not leave now, she would never be able to.

Charles turned his head to watch her and closed his eyes wearily. She was going. Dear God, how could she go after that? He tried to resign himself to it; he rose and began to dress, as she did, telling himself that he would set out for Revere's house, that it would be as if this interlude had never happened. That was what she wanted.

But finally, his voice split the silence, drawn and hoarse in his agony. "Lettice, my God, don't leave me again! Sweet Jesus, can he give you that? Can he give you what I just did, for all the jewels and fancy clothes?"

She whirled, angrily. "Do you think that is why I left? Do you think I went with Philip because I missed the life I had? How can you say you love me and think that!"

"I don't know what I think!" he roared back. "I hardly know who I am or what I am doing, ever since you left. I cannot bear life without you, Lettice. Please, I beg you, don't go back to him."

"He is my husband; I have to. He has rightful 'claim' to me," she replied bitterly.

"He has no claim to you," Charles said, his face thunderous. "All he ever did was abuse you. No just God would force you to remain with a man after what he has done, merely because some minister spoke a few words over you."

"God does not force me. My marriage vows do not force me. Don't you know even yet how slender my moral thread is? If I could have kept the knowledge of his reappearance from you, I would have. I would have stayed silent about my husband and married you, against all laws and religion!"

"Then why go back to him? Stay with me, Lettice."

"And destroy you? I cannot. Philip told me that if I didn't come back to him and join in his schemes once again, he would tell all of Boston that you and I tried to kill him, that we were lovers and you stole me from him!"

"That bastard! I'd *like* to kill him! If he were here this moment, I'd cut him down, I swear. Oh, Lettice, my love. I'm so sorry." He reached out and pulled her into his arms, softly cradling her against his chest. His breath stirred her hair as he spoke. "I love you, Lettice. I love you more than reputation or Boston or religion or—or anything. I don't care what Philip says; let him shout it from the highest treetops, let him tear my reputation to shreds. I care not. All I want is you."

Lettice looked up at him, tears shining in her green eyes. "But don't you see, Charles? It would not be just your reputation. Gage would seize on this to arrest you and ship you back to England for trial for attempted murder. It would be a perfect opportunity for him."

"Then we will leave here, escape. We will run to the southern colonies tonight, leave all of this behind us."

With her whole heart Lettice wanted to cry out that she

would accept his offer. Oh, to flee with him and live with him forevermore. To wake every morning by his side . . . for that she would count the world well lost. But gently she drew back from him, blinking away her tears.

"No, Charles, I cannot let you do that for me. I love you; I would like nothing better than to be with you. But I am married. All the rest of your life you would be committing adultery by living with me; you would be giving up your life, your home, your law, your principles, everything you have always held dear. You would be sacrificing your very soul for me by living in a way you knew to be wrong, and you would regret it always. I cannot do that to you." Her smile was brief and faint. "I will not destroy your goodness, Charles; I'd rather die than do that."

He swallowed against the rage and love that filled his throat, choking him; tears misted his eyes so that he could hardly see. Lettice was a blur as she stepped through the door and out of his life.

Seventeen

$\mathcal{L}$ettice spent the next two days in an agony of waiting, her mind worrying over the outcome of Gage's attempt to seize the munitions while she struggled to maintain an appearance of innocence and unconcern. She knew it would arouse suspicion if she showed interest in the British soldiers' marching to Lexington. So she waited, praying she would glean information from the soldiers' conversations. Even then she could not ask eager questions, but merely bide her time until one of the officers brought it up.

Fortunately it was a topic of great interest to the men, and they spent the evening discussing little else. "Eight hundred men marched to Lexington," Leon Dalworth said. "And when we got there, we found a line of colonials drawn up across the town square. Of course, we were shocked. It was an open act of rebellion against the Crown! The yokels were hopelessly outnumbered, but defiant. Tempers flared—as you might imagine with the colonials defying the King's own soldiers. Someone shouted 'Fire!' or thought that it was shouted, and we opened up. Several colonials fell."

At that news Lettice gasped and had to fight for control to return her face to its former expression of faint interest. She looked down at her hands for a moment, then up, and saw that Philip was watching her, a puzzled, calculating look upon his face. For an instant she felt a tiny stab of fear, and then the look was gone, replaced by his usual indifference. Lettice pushed her husband from her mind; she had to find out more about the battle.

"But what happened then, Leon?" she asked the man telling the story. "Did the soldiers kill them all?"

"No, the colonials turned and ran, of course," another officer interrupted, expressing the typical British view of the colonials' courage.

"Yes, they broke, and we marched to Concord and met resistance again." The man shook his head in ponderous disbelief. "I never thought I'd see the day fellow Britons would be firing at one another. All the way back from Concord, the colonials fired at the soldiers from concealed places—trees and rocks and ditches. They fought like Indians—savages!"

"Yes, hiding safely behind their rocks!" the other officer said with a contemptuous smile.

"Yes, well, it would not have seemed so amusing to you if the entire regiment had been wiped out, which there was every danger of. If Earl Percy had not arrived with reinforcements, it would have turned into a rout!"

"You mean the colonials won?" Lettice asked innocently.

"Of course not! Lady Lettice, how could you even think such a thing? We held the day, even though we lost many men."

"And we'd have had no casualties at all if those colonials hadn't skulked around like cowards, instead of coming out and facing us like gentlemen."

"You mean they don't fight according to the rules?" Lettice asked, her eyes round and guileless. "But how wicked—especially since our men are still dead, even if the others *were* ungentlemanly."

Leon smiled indulgently. "Lady Lettice, you are a lovely, charming female, but, pray, don't try to be a military expert."

Lettice laughed and cast her bright green eyes up at him through her thick lashes. "Leon, please, don't even say such a thing! Nothing could be more deadly dull than armies and battles. The only thing military I admire are the officers."

She made it through the rest of the evening calmly enough, though whenever her mind returned to the battle her heart began to thud irregularly. She shuddered at the thought that the colonials, people like her friends here in Boston, had fallen before her countrymen's guns. Worst of all, she worried that Charles might have been one of the ones who rode out to raise the alarm in the countryside, might have stayed with the Minutemen and fought . . . and been hurt.

It was not likely, she told herself. Charles was no great horseman; surely someone else would have been sent to the villages. And yet what if, desperate from their last meeting, he had wanted to throw himself into danger? That thought gripped her heart like a cold hand and kept her wide awake after she went to bed. She longed to run to Jonathan's house and ask for news of Charles, but doubtless he was still absent.

As often as she could in the next few days, she walked

past the Murdock house, but she was never rewarded by a glimpse of any occupant. She kept her worry to herself, smiling as always at the men who flocked to her home, listening intently as they talked of the unexpected flood of colonials who had rushed to Cambridge, just across the Neck from Boston.

Their numbers were a shock to all the British; until now they had never fully realized that the opposition consisted of many colonials, not just a few radicals. The fact that troops from all the surrounding colonies, fifteen thousand strong, had flocked to defend their Massachusetts brethren stunned the army.

"Why, it's as though they were laying siege to the army," cried George Hunter in a shocked tone. The very idea was almost unthinkable.

"Rag-tag and bobtail," William Evelyn said, predictably contemptuous. "At the first sign of advance from us, they'll turn tail and run."

But the British did not advance. General Gage, with less than five thousand men, his reinforcements from England consisting of more officers, not fighting men, proceeded to dig in at Boston and barricade the Neck. With the port closed and the Neck barricaded, the city was completely cut off.

In May, Gage proclaimed that if the citizens of Boston would give up their arms, he would allow any who wished to leave to do so. Upon the advice of Dr. Warren, the citizens agreed, and deposited thousands of firearms in Faneuil Hall. In just four days, four thousand Bostonians then swarmed across the Neck to the peninsula. With clenched hands, Lettice watched the steady progress of people through the streets and wished desperately that she could go with them. Then Gage clamped down on the exodus, and the stream thinned to a trickle before ceasing altogether, and the people of Boston cried, "Foul!" but were trapped within the city.

The atmosphere in the city grew tenser daily. Suddenly the ugly specter of war loomed large and real on the horizon.

One evening in early May, not long after the Lexington and Concord incident, as Lettice sat before her mirror carefully attending to her face and hair for the evening, the door to her room opened and Philip stepped in. Lettice stared at him in the mirror, surprised at his presence, then swung around to face him.

"It is customary to knock," she said icily.

Philip shut the door and leaned languidly against it, the careful mask of his face revealing nothing. Disgust curled in his stomach as he looked as his coldly beautiful wife. He did not love Lettice, of course, but he never forgot the humiliation of knowing that she loved someone else—and someone so far beneath himself in every way!

"There are times," he said smoothly, his expression bland, "when I would dearly love to put my hands upon your lovely throat and choke the life from you."

Lettice did not even blink at his words, but turned calmly back to her mirror. "Is that what you came in here to tell me?" she asked, dipping her brush into the jar of black and carefully lining her eyelids.

Philip noticed with displeasure that her hand did not tremble in the slightest. Lettice had a trifle too much courage for his taste; he would have been easier on her in the past if she had but cringed sometimes or shown a little fear.

"Hardly," he replied, baring his teeth in a smile. "That feeling is so constantly upon me that it is hardly worthy of expression."

"Then why don't you do it?" Lettice asked indifferently.

"Because you're far too valuable to me, my dear. You would not attract so many customers as a corpse."

"Probably not."

He waited for a moment, observing her go about her work, ignoring him completely. "I've been watching you lately, Lettice."

Her hand tightened fractionally on her brush, but she said merely, "Oh?"

"Yes. You seem different, changed."

"I told you that I had changed, Philip. I am not the woman you knew in London."

"No, I don't mean that. Since you've come to the house, you've changed. Why is that?"

"I didn't know I had," Lettice said, carefully laying down her brush and putting the top on the pot of black.

"Yes. At first, you were quite stiff, full of tears and hardly charming. But the past few weeks, you seem to have perked up. Your cheeks are brighter, your eyes more luminous; you flirt and chatter with merriment. What has wrought such a change?"

"Perhaps I am beginning to become accustomed to my old life again." Lettice suggested, not looking at him, her heart pounding in her chest. Did he suspect her spying activities?

"Somehow I don't think so. You don't seem happier, simply more interested in something."

Lettice shrugged. "One can't go about cast down in gloom forever, I suppose."

"Are you seeing Murdock?" he lashed out, coming to the real purpose for his visit. "Is that the reason for your bright eyes? Are you sneaking out during the day and coupling with that merchant?"

Lettice rose to her feet and turned to face him in one quick, angry movement. "How dare you accuse me of that!" Her eyes flashed fire and her hands were clenched at her sides. "I am not carrying on an affair with Charles."

"How moral of you," Philip sneered.

"No, not moral, but I would not involve him in something like that. He is too good a person! Charles is not an adulterer."

"He seems to have managed that roll quite well in the past."

"He thought you were dead!" Lettice spat. "I only wish you had been."

"Such tender wifely feelings," Philip mocked.

Lettice sucked in a deep breath and controlled her anger. Tightly she said, "I'm going to ring for my maid and get dressed. I suggest that you leave now."

"What? So modest? Surely, as your husband, I at least have the right to watch you dress."

"You have no husbandly rights over me, Philip," Lettice said flatly. "That is, if you wish me to continue gracing your card games. Of course, if you would rather stand there and look at me than have me come down to the gaming room, feel free to. It makes no difference to me."

Philip's nostrils flared—the little bitch! How dare she threaten him? She was up to something, he knew, but she wasn't going to reveal it voluntarily. Well, he could wait and watch, and before long, he would find out what it was she was doing.

He swept her a mocking bow. "Dear wife, your request is my command, as always."

He opened the door and left, as silently as he had entered. Lettice stood staring after him in impotent fury for a moment, then sat down angrily and rang for her maid.

Two days after her encounter with Philip, Lettice had enough information to take to Baker, and so in the early hours of dawn, she slipped out of her house and took off at a rapid pace. So anxious was she to see Jonathan and inquire after Charles that she did not even glance around her and so did not see Philip step out the back door moments after she did and leisurely follow the direction she took.

Her husband followed her through the streets of Boston to the block that Baker's house sat in. He stared with narrow eyes at the house she entered, then turned and slowly, thoughtfully made his way back to his own abode.

As soon as Lettice gave Jonathan her information, she asked anxiously, "Jonathan, please, how is Charles? Did he go to Lexington? Is he all right?"

"Yes, he's fine. Of course he did not ride to Lexington; you know Charles is not a horseman." He smiled indulgently. "By the way, thank you for what you told us. I must admit at first I had strong doubts about you, but I think you proved quite clearly where your loyalties lie."

Lettice shrugged. His opinion of her was of little concern to her. Her mind was all on Murdock. "Have they—are they still in Boston? The Murdocks, I mean."

"No, they left when Gage opened the Neck. Charles has gone to join the army, and Molly and the others have gone to her cousin's farm." He paused and colored a little. "Before she left, Molly and I became betrothed."

Lettice smiled. "Why, Jonathan, that is wonderful! But what did Marian say about that?"

He chuckled. "Oh, she was none too pleased, but Charles approved and he, after all, is the head of the family. Besides, all this fighting and moving to the country and confusion had thrown Mistress Murdock all cock-a-hoop. I am afraid she was too unsettled even to keep up her complaints for long."

"Well, good, I'm glad you and Molly are to be married. I know she adores you."

Baker's blush deepened. "She is too young for marriage now, of course—not quite seventeen—but with all this going on, I wanted to get things settled between us. I don't know what is ahead, but I'm afraid it's open war, maybe something that will drag on for years. By the time it's over and things have returned to normal, I imagine Molly will be old enough to marry."

"Why did you not go, Jonathan?"

He sighed. "God knows, I wanted to, but I think I'm more needed here. The British don't suspect me; I'm not famous. Therefore I can get information in and out more readily than someone they had a watch on. There are others who have chosen to stay and spy, thinking themselves more useful in this capacity. James Lovell, for instance; he longed to go fight, but his health is poor and, being the son of a staunch loyalist, he has great opportunity to gather information. So he stayed. And I shall stay, too, until they come to suspect me, and then I have an escape planned."

Lettice smiled weakly. Charles was gone; she would never see him again. If there was war, he might be killed, and she would not even know it. Doubtless she and Philip would leave if war came, and she would never again see Boston. Her heart felt suddenly torn and bleeding, and she knew that part of her was gone, dead, vanished with Charles.

May crept dully on, enlivened at the end by the pride-puncturing battle known as Noddle Island. Lettice was given the details of the fight by an Army officer who was not above finding glee in the Navy's embarrassment.

"You know that Admiral Graves keeps his livestock for his men over on Hog Island," Major Rodgers began, smoothing down his elegant mustache. "Well, it seems the colonials thought it would be a good trick to raid the island and steal the cattle out from under Graves's nose. When the Admiral heard what was going on, he sent a schooner to protect his property. But the schooner was hopelessly outnumbered by the Americans and they could do nothing but watch helplessly as the colonials drove off hundreds of horses, cows, and sheep."

"Oh, no," Lettice said, a bubble of laughter rising from her throat.

"But, even worse," Rodgers went on with a sardonic smile. "The fools drifted into a treacherous channel as they watched, and it started pulling them to the colonists' shore! Next an armed sloop and barges were sent to tow the ship out, but they could not correct her drift."

Lettice covered her mouth with her fan to hide the giggles that welled in her; she must not seem to get too much enjoyment out of this. "What happened then? Surely they managed to get out."

"Not with their ship," the man said. "The colonials opened fire on them while they were trying to tow her out, which made it even more difficult, and by nighttime, the schooner went aground and had to be abandoned by her crew. The colonials stripped the schooner and burned her to the shoreline, while the sloop that was set to rescue her was so badly riddled by shot that they had to tow her off!"

"That incompetent fool," a Colonel snapped, his face livid. "Dammit, Rodgers, I don't see how you can find amusement in a thing like that, even if it was the Navy. After all, they were Englishmen, and they made us look like idiots. Graves is incompetent. God help us with him in command of the naval forces. A simple thieving raid by the colonials, and he manages to turn it into a defeat and the loss of two ships!"

Lettice had to glance down at her hands to hide her dancing eyes. She wondered if the arrogant officers were beginning to feel any pinpricks of doubt.

When at last everyone left and she was free to retire to her room, she quickly scribbled down exactly what had been said about Graves. Jonathan would no doubt like to know that Graves's own people thought him incompetent. She put the slip of paper in the locked drawer with her other papers and began to prepare for bed. With the comments about the Admiral, she thought she had information enough to take to Baker.

She forced herself to lie down and close her eyes. She had found over the weeks that it was better to go at daybreak, when there were more people about and she would not attract so much attention scurrying along. The night visits were far too dangerous for anything but the most important messages.

Lettice slept lightly, as she always did when there were messages to take at dawn, and awoke as the pale streaks of light lifted the dark from her room. Quickly she rose and dressed in her simple old clothes, pulling on a large, frilly mobcap to hide her gleaming hair and conceal her face a little. Then she slipped down the stairs and out the back door and went hurrying on her way.

Soon after she left, she began to get an uneasy, prickling feeling along the back of her neck, and she realized that she felt as if someone were watching her. That was ridiculous, she told herself, but she couldn't keep from glancing over her shoulder. About halfway down the block behind her, a nondescript man walked. He was dressed like a laborer, and she reasoned that doubtless he was on his way to work.

However, the uneasy feeling would not leave her, and soon she stopped in front of a shop window, pretending to be interested in the goods. From the corner of her eye, she saw the same man stop and look into a store. Her heart began to pound furiously. It might not be the same man; it might be coincidence. But what if it were not! What if he were following her!

She wet her lips and began to walk on, forcing herself to remain calm. After all, his following her, if that was what he was doing, might not mean that the army suspected her of spying. He might simply be a man following a pretty girl, hoping for a chance to talk, or worse. Still, she could not afford to lead him to Jonathan's house; there was too great a chance that he was spying on her for the British.

So, aimlessly, Lettice began to walk, leaving the path she was taking and crossing into the business center, where there would be more traffic. The marketplace was coming alive—shopkeepers were sweeping off the sidewalks and clerks were hurrying to their work. Continuing quickly, Lettice made her way to a millinery shop where she had been before, and went inside. The woman behind the counter looked up with a smile for her early customer, recognizing Lettice.

"Please, mistress, is there a back door to this building?"

"Yes, but it opens onto the alley."

"But I could get out that way?"

"Yes . . ." she said doubtfully.

"May I please use it? There is a man outside who has been following me. I think he wishes to make unwelcome advances," Lettice explained with a modest blush.

"Of course," the older woman replied indignantly and shooed Lettice behind the counter and through the back rooms into the alley.

Lettice waved her thanks and hurried down the alley to the side street. The man was nowhere in sight, and she scurried around quickly to the cross street and started back toward Jonathan's house. Every now and then she stopped and looked cautiously around her, but she did not see the man again, and so she went on to Jonathan Baker's house.

* * *

The rest of May and early June passed, with nothing to relieve the monotony of the closed city, and to make things worse, the summer heat set in, making everyone even more irritable and uncomfortable. Lettice cursed her heavy dresses and innumerable petticoats and the weight of her powdered hair and hairpieces, padded out with rags and wire.

One morning, in the middle of June, when Lettice lay in her bed asleep after a wearying night of cards, the sudden boom of cannon woke her rudely. Blinking, she sat up, wondering what on earth had happened. Just as she shrugged and lay back down, a roar of cannon shook the windows, and she jumped from her bed and rushed to look out. All up and down the street, her neighbors leaned out their windows or poured into the streets, looking all around them in dismay.

"What was that?" a woman shrieked to a man below in the street, and everyone began to babble.

One voice rose above the others. "It must be the whole bloody fleet opening fire!"

The hideous booming continued as Lettice retreated from the window and began hurriedly to dress. She had to find out what was going on, and obviously she would not discover anything hanging out the window listening to others as ignorant as she. When she was dressed, she rushed downstairs and sent a servant out to find out what had happened. Then, after gulping down a cup of tea and a few biscuits, she darted back upstairs and, lifting her skirts with one hand, climbed the ladder that led to the flat roof.

From there she had a commanding view of the Boston

harbor and, across the water, the peninsula of Charlestown, which hung down from the mainland above Boston. Her eyes narrowed as she looked, and she shaded her eyes with her hand to see better. Something was different on the other peninsula. Charlestown had been abandoned by its citizens, and the streets still looked quiet and empty, but outside of the town, on one of the hills, there were strange mounds of dirt. What in the world, she thought, and then it came to her: Those were earthworks, fortifications. The colonials must have decided to fortify the hill—what was the name of it? Bunker? No, that was the one behind it. Breed's Hill, that was it.

She swallowed. Suddenly war became very real. That was what the fleet was firing at. Their shots fell short, however, merely gouging out huge chunks of dirt before the breastworks. Now the whole building shook beneath her feet as the army battery on Copp's Hill opened up on the dirt fort, joining the steady din of the fleet's poundings.

All over the city, people poured from their houses, climbing like Lettice to the flat roofs to watch, or streaming up to Beacon Hill or Copp's Hill to view the phenomenon on the other peninsula. As the morning passed, the summer heat grew, and ladies returned to their homes for hats and fans to guard against the sun. Companies of soldiers formed and marched through the streets to some unknown destination.

By noon, Lettice had grown tired of the waiting and watching, with no sign of movement on the opposite shore, and nothing but the ceaseless, steady boom of the cannons. Tiredly, she climbed down the ladder and went to eat lunch. The noise of the guns dwindled away to nothing, and she guessed that the stir was over. Apparently the British had decided to do nothing about the fort, since their guns seemed unable to hit their mark. Lettice was just about to undress and go back to bed for a nap when the thunder of the guns crashed out again, as loud as ever. Her heart leaped into her throat, and she knew that something was different now.

Quickly she scrambled up the ladder and ran to the edge of the roof. And there, crossing the Charles River, which divided the two peninsulas, she saw a fleet of large rowboats, filled with red-coated soldiers, the sailors pulling steadily at the oars. Above them, the shot from the ships spewed through the air as cover, and Lettice realized with a gasp how open the soldiers were to any return fire from the fort. But it did not come, and the first boat reached the shore. Its passengers disembarked safely.

It seemed to take hours for the boats to unload their cargo, and then for a while the soldiers sat around on the beach, apparently eating their lunch, before at last they began to form up and move forward. All the time Lettice watched, her fists clenched, fear tightening her stomach. There was going to be a battle, and she wondered desperately if Charles was out there on the other side of the earthen fort. Her throat felt as dry as dust, and she found herself praying that he would be all right.

Suddenly flames shot up in the vacant town of Charlestown, and Lettice gasped. Seemingly in an instant the entire city was on fire, a vision from a nightmare, a scene from a story of some long-ago barbaric time and place. And then magnificently, the staunch red line moved forward, a few coming toward the fort from Charlestown on the left, the rest stretching out on the right-hand side of the fort, apparently to march around it. At the site, the soldiers struggled under their heavy packs, stumbling over hillocks, blocked by low stone walls that divided one property from another, wading through tall grasses and weeds and rivulets of water. But from the city, where Lettice stood watching, it was a steady movement of bright red, topped by the glittering metal of the bayonets, an awesome, overwhelming force. They began to run toward a shallow breastwork of earth and logs that stretched across their path from the fort to the sea and were almost upon it when suddenly fire belched out from the earth wall.

Lettice's hand flew to her mouth to stifle her scream as she saw the ranks waver, crumple, and reform. Miraculously the fire belched again, stripping through the ranks, and Lettice could not imagine how they could have reloaded so quickly and fired again. It took even the most experienced soldier over a minute to load his gun with cap, ball, and powder. Even more amazing, a third volley came only a few seconds later, shattering the already decimated British ranks. What she and the British soldiers, panicking at the speed of the fire, did not know was that the backwoods colonial Rangers were manning this breastwork, men who had been taught by the finest British officers during the French and Indian War, and they were trained to fire in three separate groups, thus keeping up a constant volley while the other two groups reloaded.

For a moment the red forms that remained wavered, then dissolved and ran back to the beach. Lettice closed her eyes and let out a sigh. The colonists had repelled the soldiers. Thank heavens! But she felt slightly sick at her stomach. All those crumpled little splashes of red all over the ground were British soldiers, dead and wounded. Never in her life had she seen anything so gruesome.

Three times the British soldiers rushed the breastworks, and their ranks dwindled horribly. Lettice clenched her skirt in her hands, tears streaming down her face, begging them to retreat, to return to Boston and leave the Hill in the colonials' hands. But then fresh troops arrived on the Charlestown side, and once more they massed for an assault. This time as the right line ran, it suddenly changed course and charged not the thin line of deadly Rangers but the more imposing central breastworks. Here, at last, they broke through, scrambling over the sides of the earth fort and dropping inside. The fort inside was thinly manned, and the troops on the line to the sea could not reach it in time to save it. The colonials were now the ones who broke and ran.

It was dusk as Lettice stumbled back down the ladder from the roof. Her head ached violently from lack of sleep, the glare of the sun, and the monotonous pounding of the guns; there was a worse ache inside her as she thought of the red-coated troops streaming over the fort. The colonials had lost finally; the might of the British Army had won the day at last. Had Charles been there? How many Americans were slain? Did Charles lie inside the fort, a crumpled figure leaking out his life's blood like the rag-doll British soldiers? Lettice felt bitter bile rise in her throat as she stumbled to her room and sank down on the bed.

She could not sleep, just lay numbly, reliving the scenes of horror she had witnessed that day, plagued by anxiety for Charles. Was he dead? Wounded? Had he even been in the battle at all? Or was he, miracle of miracles, still peacefully in Cambridge?

A strange, wild crying in the streets below finally brought her to her feet, and she looked out the window. It was already dark outside and she could see little. The high, piercing keening continued eerily, and she shivered.

Her maid entered to help her dress, and Lettice looked at her wildly, hardly understanding the meaning of the words the girl spoke, her mind as disheveled as her dress and hair. "What? No! No, I will not dress tonight! My God, who could come to play cards on such a night as this? What is that noise, girl?"

"Oh, that, milady," the girl said, her face carefully blank. She was a loyalist herself, but tonight she found it hard to approve of the British victory, with her own countrymen lying dead out there on Breed's Hill. "Those are the women of the common soldiers, milady. Camp followers. You know, many of them are Irish, and they go through all that papist moaning and crying and rattling their beads when someone dies."

Lettice shivered again and said hoarsely, "It sounds like all the souls in hell."

"They're bringing over the wounded soldiers from Charlestown and unloading them. A powerful lot of them, there are. That's why the women are all running down to the docks, crying and moaning over their dead."

Lettice thought that was what she would do, if she found Charles dead. It would be like having her heart ripped from her chest, to see his lifeless form; she imagined she too would break into wild, insane sobbing and screaming. As though escaping that thought, she rushed from the room and down the stairs, colliding with an immaculate Philip at the bottom.

"Good God, Lettice!" he exclaimed, catching her as she stumbled against him and holding her away from him, his fingers digging into her arms. "What in the world is the matter with you? You look like a witch, your hair every which way and your face white as a sheet. What is it?"

She looked at him blankly, almost wondering who he was, and an insane giggle rose in her throat. "Don't you know? Didn't you see? My God, Philip, are you that self-centered? The army just attacked colonial troops on Charlestown peninsula and wiped out the majority of their men! British subjects, Philip, were fighting and killing one another in droves out there!" Her voice rose hysterically. "Does that mean nothing to you?"

"What should it mean?" he said coolly. "Soldiers kill and are killed all the time; that is their occupation. Am I supposed to fall apart because of it?"

Lettice stared at him, horrified, seeing his cold, arrogant face and superimposed over that the lifeless, bleeding body of Charles Murdock. "I hate you!" she spat. "You are a vile, loathsome creature. I wish to God I'd killed you! Now, get out of my way!"

She shoved against him hard and, surprised, he dropped his hold of her. Lettice rushed out into the street. There carriages, wagons, and litters toiled from the docks in a macabre procession. All around the vehicles staggered dirty, bleeding men, some with vacant eyes, others holding their arms or dragging useless legs.

"Oh, my God!" Lettice cried.

A portly harassed gentleman, dressed in civilian

clothes and hurrying toward the docks, turned to her, his face a hard mask. "Don't just stand there, woman, fetch some water and linen for bandages. It looks as though I might as well begin my work right here." He set down his doctor's bag and began to dig in it.

Lettice turned at his words and ran back into the house, calling to the maids. Soon she and her women were on the doorsteps with pails and buckets and pans of water, ripping sheets into strips for bandages. For long, aching hours she worked beside the doctor, trying to staunch the awful flow of blood, to cleanse and bind wounds, to help ease the soldiers down onto the ground for the doctor to work on them.

"Insanity!" the Boston doctor muttered. "Sheer insanity! Do the British have nothing to do but slaughter each other? Over a thousand dead, and that's only the British. God knows what we colonials suffered. There are only four men left in the King's Own Grenadiers, only eight in the Fifty-Second Grenadiers. Slaughter, pure slaughter."

Wearily Lettice toiled through the night, finally staggering up to her bed in the early hours of the dawn. There she stripped off her gown, ruined from the dirt of the street and the blood of the soldiers, and dropped it on the floor, then scrubbed frantically at her face and hands and arms, trying to remove every last trace of blood, but still the sickening stench lingered. She tumbled into bed and slept the whole day through.

Lettice went through the next two days in a state of numbness. She could think of nothing but the horror of the battle and the fate of the man she loved. She longed to run to Baker's house and find out how Charles was, whether he had participated in the battle, but she knew that would be foolish. Jonathan would not yet have heard anything of what had transpired among the Americans.

Lettice could hardly eat, and she did not even bother to dress up and attend Philip's games. There were a few hardy souls who came despite the decimation of their comrades, but Lettice refused to be there.

Philip stormed up to her room the first evening she did not come down, rigid with anger. "What the hell do you think you are doing up here? Get dressed and come down at once!"

"I am not coming to your games again," Lettice said dully and returned to staring out the window, too full of stunned anxiety to quail before Philip's rage.

"Damn you, Lettice, there are men down there who are asking about you. I insist that you come down immediately. What is the matter with you? Have you gone mad?"

"No," Lettice retorted, "though it seems everyone else has. How you or any of them can play cards and make merry when half the ones who used to come are dead or dying is beyond me. I, for one, cannot do it."

"They're soldiers," Philip said with an impatient shrug. "That is simply part of their job."

"Dying?" Lettice said scornfully. "Well, even if it is, I don't care. I refuse to come down. I am tired of your nasty games, and I refuse to take part in them."

Philip's eyes went cold and opaque, and once Lettice would have shuddered with fear to see him look at her so, but now she did not care. "Have you forgotten about your precious Murdock and what I could do to him? One word to the army, and his life would be forfeit."

Lettice leaped to her feet, her eyes blazing. "Good

God, Philip, are you that blind? Don't you realize what is going on? War has started between Massachusetts and England. Beside that, all your vile threats seem incredibly puny. What would the army care or be able to do if you did tell them that a rebel soldier tried to murder you? His life is forfeit already; he is an enemy to England! He isn't in Boston. My God, I don't even know if he is alive!"

"I can still inform them of your plot to murder me."

"Go ahead!" Lettice snapped. "I no longer care. Charles is lost to me, I am trapped here in this city. He may be dead. I don't care about it anymore! Do it; inform on me. I don't care!"

Philip's lips went white with rage. "Oh, no, Lettice, you have not escaped me that easily. Don't come downstairs; that's fine. But you will rue this day, I promise you."

Lettice turned away and resumed her study of the street below. Philip slammed out of the room and ran down the stairs. Lettice leaned her head against the glass, her turbulent emotions roiling inside her. Finally she turned and ran lightly down the stairs. She had to see Jonathan now; she simply could not wait any longer to hear news of Charles.

So great was her anxiety as she hurried out her front door and down the street that she did not see the man who disengaged himself from the shadows and slipped quietly after her.

Baker could tell her nothing for certain. "I cannot swear whether or not he was in the battle, Lettice!" he cried in frustration. "We have a war on our hands, and I am now a spy in enemy territory. I know nothing! How can I know who was in the battle on our side? I have heard that it is ironic that not one Massachusetts company participated, so I presumed that Charles was not there. But I know nothing definite. Our communications are destroyed; Dr. Warren was killed on the battlefield; everything is in chaos. Lord, we don't even know if the rest of the colonies will support us, or if we shall be crushed like bugs by the British Army, with no one coming to our aid."

"I know," Lettice said, joy breaking over her. There was hope for her now; at least she could believe that the chances were that Charles was still alive. Baker's other tense, angry words hardly touched her. "I know how desperate you must feel, how much you want to join the others. But I had to come. I had to know something. I was almost crazy with fear. Thank you for telling me what you know. Shall I continue to do my work?"

Baker sighed and rubbed his hand wearily across his forehead. "Yes, if you wish. But I am leaving tonight. I'm taking a boat across the Neck to join the others. It's no longer safe for me here. I've told Lovell about you, and if you wish to continue, you may take your information to him. I—I'm sorry I snapped at you."

Lettice smiled. "That's all right, Jonathan. I understand your feelings. Good luck, and, if you see Charles, tell him I love him. I shall continue my work. I think I can now feel that there is a good chance Charles is alive. After all, there must have been no troops from Boston there, or they would not have mistaken Breed's Hill for Bunker Hill. So I shall go back to Philip and tell him that his threats tonight have frightened me sufficiently, and I shall return to the games."

He took her hand in parting, and when she returned to her house, her steps were light and even cheerful. There was still a smile on her lips when she stepped into her house. Then she stopped with a jolt.

Four men faced her in the hall—an officer, two enlisted men with guns at their sides, and the nondescript laborer who had followed her that day. Lettice gasped at the sight of them, her frightened eyes going from the officer to the spy.

"That's her," the spy said. "She went to Baker's house all right."

Lettice's heart began to pound violently in her chest, and her throat went dry. She wet her lips and said, "What—what are you doing here?"

"I am sorry, milady, but it has come to our attention that you have been engaged in some very questionable activities," the officer said.

"What?" Lettice tried to summon an innocent look of disbelief to her face, stalling frantically for time. "You must be mad. Whatever are you talking about?"

"I regret that I must arrest you for spying and informing to the rebelling colonials."

"Sir," Lettice said haughtily, pulling up every scrap of dignity she possessed. "Do you realize to whom you are speaking? How dare you accuse me of such things? I am Lady Lettice Kenton. I am a Delaplaine, and my husband is the grandson of a Duke!"

The officer cleared his throat with embarrassment and was silent. Lettice looked past his shoulder to the door of their drawing room and saw Philip lounging there gracefully, a cold smile playing on his lips. Even before the officer spoke, Lettice guessed instinctively what he would say.

"I know, milady. But, you see, it was Lord Philip who informed us of your spying activities."

Eighteen

*L*ettice walked numbly between the soldiers, horrifying visions of a filthy, crowded jail cell flooding her brain. It was a great relief when they went up the steps of a respectable-looking red brick house, and she realized that her incarceration would be more civilized. The officer opened the door for her, and there was an uncertain, slightly embarrassed look in his eyes as he stepped aside for her to pass. For the first time since she saw the soldiers in her house, a flicker of hope pierced the haze of shock that she had been in. She was a British lady, the descendant of a long line of nobility, and the wife of a future Duke. Surely the man must wonder why it would be at all reasonable to think that one such as she was engaged in spying for the rebel colonials. Added to that was the fact of Philip's rather unsavory reputation; the army could hardly be unaware of his dishonest card games, which siphoned money from its men, and they must disapprove of such a practice. It was simply his word against hers; perhaps she could bluff her way out of this.

She almost smiled. There was hope, after all. What proof could they have of her spying? Baker would not confess, she was certain; and then she made a fervent prayer that he had gotten wind of what had happened and had managed to escape to the mainland. If she just maintained a cool air of innocence and righteous indignation, never confessing to their accusations, it was possible she could create enough doubt in their minds to let her go. It would not hurt, she thought, to cast a little suspicion on her husband as well. Philip was a vicious sort, but she suspected that he had not informed on her merely out of spite; he must have hoped to gain something from the army. The only reason Lettice could think of was that the military had threatened to close down his games to prevent the shearing of its soldiers.

Haughtily, Lettice surveyed the hallway in which she stood, and then turned back to the officer. "Is this where I am to be jailed?" she asked imperiously.

The man cleared his throat a trifle nervously. "Yes, milady."

"Why, how kind of the army," Lettice said bitingly. "I thought such a 'dangerous criminal' as I would be thrown in the deepest dungeon."

The man flushed and avoided her eyes, and Lettice knew that she was striking home. She continued her attack. "Whose house is this?"

"Why, it is Colonel Hempstead's headquarters, milady."

"Indeed." She allowed one eyebrow to float questioningly upward. "And am I to share a house with a man – several men, for all I know—unaccompanied by a female?"

He stared, obviously struck for the first time by the social impropriety of the situation, and Lettice pressed home her advantage. "Really, sir—what is your title, by the way?"

"Lieutenant Devlin, milady."

"Well, then, Lieutenant Devlin, I must point out that when Colonel Hempstead comes to his senses and realizes what a mess of self-serving drivel he has swallowed from Philip and lets me go, my reputation will be in absolute shreds. I simply must have a female companion—a *proper* female companion, not one of these common camp followers."

"Yes, milady, I quite see the problem," he said, gulping. "I will speak to the Colonel about it right away. Now, I am sorry, but you will have to accompany these men to your room, and I am afraid that I shall have to insist that you stay there. A man will be stationed outside your door."

Lettice smiled indulgently, allowing her dimple to deepen prettily. "Yes, Lieutenant Devlin. I promise I shall stay in my room and not make an attempt to overpower my guard and escape."

Lettice spent a few boring hours in her new quarters, which turned out to be a large, comfortable room, adequately furnished, but with only one window. She quickly determined that the window offered no possibility of escape, being three stories up, with no tree or drainpipe or even vines clinging to the brick upon which she could climb to freedom. Having established that, she sat down to draw up her battle plans against Philip and the British Army, and then just sat, staring out the window, until at last a knock sounded on the door.

Lieutenant Devlin entered and informed her that the Colonel would interview her now. Lettice favored him with a smile and swept past him, hiding her sweating, clenched hands in the folds of her skirt.

Colonel Hempstead was a middle-aged, portly sort, who turned around to face her with a stern expression on his face. But the nervous clenching and unclenching of his fists betrayed his uncertainty. "Milady," he said and cleared his throat.

"Colonel," Lettice returned coolly, assessing him. "We have never met in London, have we?"

"Oh, no, milady," he returned, a flush beginning at the base of his neck and creeping upward. "My family—that is to say—we would hardly be in the circle that you—"

Lettice smiled graciously. "Of course." It was obvious that the man was awed by her birth; and that would be her strong suit against him.

"Have you found a companion for me?" Lettice said, deciding to begin the confrontation on the attack, and using a tone she might employ with a servant.

"Oh, yes, milady, a very proper woman, the widow of Captain Wilson, who fell at Breed's Hill."

"Good. I do hope you are not planning to keep me cooped up in that little room the whole time I am here. It could be days before you realize that my husband has fed you a story, and I know I shall die of boredom if I am locked up in there by myself."

"Oh, no, milady, you may take your meals with my staff and myself, and of course, you and Mistress Wilson will no doubt wish to use the sitting room and the music room. And there is a library, if you care to read."

Lettice let her expression show that such delights hardly interested her, but thanked him for his kindness. She then fell silent, and the Colonel scratched his cheek and straightened his wig and cleared his throat, so patently ill at ease that Lettice could barely suppress a smile.

"Milady, you realize the seriousness of the charges against you . . ." he began questioningly.

"Yes, and the absurdity, as well," Lettice answered promptly. "Why on earth should I spy for the colonials?"

"Why should your own husband inform against you if it were not true?" the man countered.

"If you knew Philip, you would not ask that," Lettice said drily. "Come, Colonel, it must be clear to you that he did it to curry favor with the army, to distract the army's attention from his rigged card games. I imagine he realized that the army was on to the fact that he cheats soldiers out of their pay, and he must have felt that they were going to ship him out of the city." She shrugged. "Besides, I had refused to appear at his tables recently; ever since the battle, I just did not have the heart. So he was quite angry with me, and no doubt hoped to kill two birds with one stone."

Hempstead frowned and looked down at the carpet, then admitted uncomfortably, "We had heard and disapproved of your husband's card games. However, one of our men did follow you to Jonathan Baker's house."

Lettice raised her brows coolly. "I was not aware that that was a crime."

"He is a colonial, and one we suspect of being engaged in spying activities."

"Surely, Colonel Hempstead, in this city filled with colonials, if Mr. Baker was spying, he could have found more likely prospects to give him information. Why on earth should I help the rebels?"

Hempstead bit his lip, and Lettice surmised that it was

a question that had worried him as well. After a few more inquiries concerning her meetings with Baker and her opportunities to gather information at her husband's tables, which Lettice met with a sophisticated air of nonchalance, he let her return to her room.

After that, her incarceration began to take on the makings of a farce. The widow arrived that evening, after Lettice spent her evening meal flirting and laughing with Hempstead and his staff. Mistress Wilson was smothered in widow's weeds, a frail, helpless woman with red-rimmed eyes and a tendency to burst into tears at inappropriate times. Lettice felt a surge of sympathy for the woman and went to her and put an arm around her, at which Mistress Wilson leaned against her and began to sob. After that, it was Lettice who was the comforter and the companion, until no one would have suspected that Lettice had been imprisoned on suspicion of treason.

But Mistress Wilson did not arrive alone. She was the mother of three boisterous children, all under the age of six, and she exercised almost no control over them, particularly in her present bereaved state. The house was in chaos after their arrival, with the guards spending most of their time keeping the youngsters out of trouble, and the halls ringing with the sound of their laughter and loud voices and running feet, until Colonel Hempstead locked himself up in his study all day long to avoid them, coming out only for meals.

Lettice did not hesitate to use her charms on her captors, smiling and flirting with them at meals and in the evening. Daily the number of officers who found an excuse to visit Hempstead's headquarters grew, until her jailing took on the aspects of a social gathering. Mistress

Wilson turned out to be able to play the piano passably, and often there was singing, or Lettice danced with her swains. She had to hide a smile at the harassed expression in Hempstead's eyes.

After a week had passed, a guard interrupted Lettice and her companion in the sitting room and said that Lettice's presence was required in the study. Her stomach tightened as she rose and followed the man, dreading an announcement that she was to be tried and hoping for her release. When she stepped inside the room and saw Hempstead standing by the window, looking affronted, and a stern-looking Colonel seated behind his desk, her heart dropped at her feet. This new man did not look at all lenient, and to make matters even worse, Philip rose from a chair by the desk and made her a mocking bow.

Lettice kept her face carefully blank and cool, and sketched a curtsey to the men. "Have you come to apologize and set me free?"

The stranger did not smile. "Not exactly, milady. I would like to ask you a few questions about your association with the rebels."

"I beg your pardon," Lettice said smoothly, though her heart took up a rapid beat within her chest. "I am afraid that I have no association with any rebels."

"Please, milady, don't play your games with me. Lord Philip Kenton has informed us of your activities."

"A rather strange thing for a husband to do, don't you think?" Lettice interrupted.

"Not if he is a loyal Englishman and his wife is a spy."

"And not if he is fleecing British soldiers at his card tables, and wishes to keep in the army's good graces, and so throws his wife as a sop to the wolves?"

The Colonel's rigid face shifted for an instant, and Lettice knew that the same thought had crossed his mind. However, he went on without expression. "Your argument would have more merit, milady, if a soldier had not followed you to the house of Jonathan Baker, based on your husband's information."

"As you may know, Colonel, I was in this city some months before my husband arrived; we had to leave England because our creditors were at our heels, and he went to the Continent and I to the colonies to confuse our pursuers. I lived here with a family named Murdock, and Mr. Baker was a frequent visitor to their home. We became friends; I see nothing wrong with visiting a friend."

"Alone? Your husband informs us that you often sneak out of the house at strange hours to meet with him."

"Philip is a famous liar," Lettice said with a curl of her lip.

"Your mysterious exits from the house in the early morning hours for several weeks now were confirmed by the servants in your house."

Her heart leaped up in her throat, and Lettice had to fight down a moment of panic. He had no proof, she reminded herself, and decided to switch tactics.

She allowed a rueful smile to curve her lips and said, "Well, I am caught, I see, and must confess." She raised her clear green eyes to look straight into the Colonel's eyes. "Yes, I sneaked out of my house and visited Mr. Baker alone. But it was for a much simpler reason than spying for the rebels. During the time I was here in Boston alone, I formed an affection for the man; in short,

Colonel, I was having an affair with Jonathan. You can understand, I'm sure, why I was secretive about the matter, and also why my husband would like to have his revenge. But the fact of the matter is that we are talking about adultery, not treason."

The Colonel studied her for a moment, a grin tugging at the corners of his mouth. Lettice could feel him softening, and apparently Philip detected it as well, for suddenly he leaped to his feet and confronted the colonel, rage in every line of him.

"Dammit, man, you can't let her wriggle out of it like this. She was spying for the rebels; I am positive of it. She was no more interested in Baker than I am. The truth of the matter is that she was Charles Murdock's mistress. She ran away with him when he was visiting England, and lived with him openly for several months. And when I found them and made her return to me, she began to spy for the rebels, out of love for that fool Murdock!"

Lettice stared at her husband in surprise. She had never seen him so livid, so outraged. Never would she have imagined that Philip, who had gladly given her to men he wished to favor, would be jealous of her sharing a bed with another man. She had thought he had acted only out of cold self-interest in having her arrested, but now it dawned on her that it was hate and hurt pride that drove him. He hated her for preferring a common colonial like Murdock to his own handsome, aristocratic self. Philip did not simply wish to distract the army's interest from his card games; she knew now that he wanted vengeance, that he would not rest until he saw her punished.

Desperately Lettice let out a short, scornful laugh. "Colonel, have you ever met Charles Murdock?"

"Yes, I saw him once."

"Then it must be obvious to you how ridiculous my husband's accusations are. Do you really think that I would fall in love with a great lump like Murdock?"

"It seems unlikely," the Colonel murmured, but his eyes had turned cold and watchful again. His moment of amused understanding was gone; the rage and jealousy of her husband against Murdock were too real for him to dismiss Kenton's story.

"Baker has fled," the Colonel said. "Why run if what you say is true?"

"Why stay?" Lettice countered. "What can a Bostonian, after the losses at Breed's Hill, expect from a jealous husband who is an English lord, and backed in his revenge by the British Army?"

The man stared at her icily, drumming his fingers on the desk. At last he spoke. "There is something to be said for your story. However, I think that there is sufficient suspicion that we should turn the matter over to a martial court."

The blood drained from Lettice's face, and her voice came out a whisper, "You mean, I am to be tried for treason?"

"Exactly."

Shakily, Lettice rose to her feet, summoning all her pride to support her before her enemies. "May I return to my room, then, if your questioning is over?"

He nodded his head, and just as she turned to walk to the door, the door opened, and a man quietly stepped inside. He was inconspicuously dressed in the leather vest and cloth breeches of a laborer, but there was nothing ordinary about his huge frame, or the blue eyes and large nose that dominated his face. Lettice stopped dead still and stared at him, and all the heads in the room swung to look at him.

"Murdock!" Philip hissed.

The man strode to the desk in two quick strides, pulling out a pistol from inside his vest, and unceremoniously jerked the startled Colonel to his feet. He twisted the officer's arm behind his back and shoved the mouth of the pistol against his temple.

"Colonel, I have come here to ask you to release Lady Lettice," he said in solemn lawyer's tones.

"It seems I have little choice," the Colonel said drily.

"Good, I am glad you see reason so quickly. I suggest you and I and the lady take a stroll outside."

"Charles," Lettice breathed, unable to do anything but stare at him in amazement. He had come to save her, had entered an enemy city and walked right into the very jaws of the lion to rescue her. Her eyes misted with tears, and her love choked her so she could not speak. Never would she have believed that she was capable of inspiring such love, and never would she have thought that she would rather take her punishment than have him place himself in such danger.

"Good God, Colonel, you can't mean to let her go!" Philip raged, his face insane with hatred for the man before him. "This proves what I told you—they are in league; she is spying for him!"

"And just how do you suggest I stop him?" the Colonel snapped at Philip, and Kenton's eyes bulged with fury.

"Lettice, you go first, and, Colonel, you will follow her. You will pretend that she is in your custody, and that you are taking her away. I will walk beside you with this gun against your side under my vest. Should you call out or betray us in any way, you will be a dead man," Charles instructed coolly.

The Colonel nodded briefly, and with trembling fingers, Lettice turned the doorknob and walked out of the study. All the way down the hall and out the front door past the guards, she walked stonily, acutely conscious of her unprotected back and expecting a bullet in it at any moment. But, miraculously, they were out on the front stoop and walking down the sidewalk, and still no shot was fired.

"Stop them!" Suddenly Philip's voice rang out, high-pitched with mindless fury, and Lettice whirled to see her husband running out onto the stoop, shouting and gesticulating at the guard. "You fool! Shoot them! Shoot them! He is a rebel!"

"Run, Lettice!" Charles hissed, and she took off on winged feet.

The soldier stared stupidly at Philip, who had lost all reason, his eyes wild, and flecks of spittle at the corners of his mouth. With a cry of exasperation, Philip seized the soldier's gun and raised it to fire at Murdock, and Murdock's pistol boomed. Philip stood for a second, stunned, his hands clutching at the gaping hole in his chest, and then toppled to the ground.

His weapon now a useless threat, its single shot spent, Charles swung it against the Colonel's temple, knocking him unconscious, and raced after Lettice.

Quickly he caught up with her, and taking her arm, propelled her rapidly through the streets of Boston, dodging down narrow alleyways and through winding streets. His superior knowledge of the town soon put them out of sight of their pursuers, but they did not pause to talk. Instead, Charles led her through the streets and down to the shore not far from the Neck. On an isolated strip of beach, a small rowboat awaited them, and beside it sat Jonathan Baker.

It was almost dusk by now, but they could not wait for dark. They tumbled into the boat, and the two men began to row steadily across the strip of water to the mainland. Lettice prayed that the British soldiers on the Neck would not chance to look across the water and see them. Softly the oars dipped into the water and swooshed through it; quiet was as important as speed. Lettice huddled in the front of the boat, her head on her knees, eyes closed, with all her might willing them to succeed.

At last there was a jolt and a scrape, and then Murdock's calm voice came to her through the dark. "We are here."

Then his hand was under her elbow, and he was helping her jump out of the boat into shallow water. Her shoes and skirt were soaked, but she hardly noticed as she struggled to the shore. Freedom! She was gone, safe from the British soldiers and the trial, and Philip—Philip was dead. Murdock's arm went around her shoulders, firm and strong, and she leaned against him.

"Charles." Her tongue caressed the name. "Charles."

And then the darkness seemed to close in, and she felt herself sliding down into peaceful oblivion.

When Lettice awoke in a warm, dark place, stretched out on a soft bed, for a moment she was afraid that she was back in her room at Hempstead's house, and that the entire scene with Charles had been a dream. She closed her eyes and opened them again and in the dim moonlight could see that this was a different room from the one at Hempstead's headquarters.

"Charles?" she called softly, struggling to sit up, and immediately his form loomed up out of a nearby chair, and he came quickly to the bed, taking her hand.

"Oh, Lettice, thank God," he said fervently, and squeezed her hand.

"Charles, I—I can't believe it's really you," she whispered, and to her dismay tears began to roll down her cheeks.

"Who else could it be?" he chuckled warmly. "Do you know another with a face like mine?"

"No! There's no other so good, so kind, so dear to me. Oh, Charles!" She flung her arms around his neck and buried her face in his shoulder.

His arms tightened around her, and he laid his cheek against the silken softness of her hair. When Baker had come to him and said that Lettice had been arrested, he had thought he would go mad. Now it seemed a miracle that they had both come out safely, alive—and together.

"I'm sorry I had to shoot Philip," he said awkwardly.

Lettice gave a short laugh. "I can hardly pretend to be sorry he's gone," she said. Suddenly shy, she did not add that now they could be married.

The silence stretched awkwardly between them, both of them so full of love and joy that they feared the other might not feel as much. Lettice lay back against the pillow, and Charles rose to stand by the window, looking out into the night.

"General Washington has arrived to take over the command of our Army," he said at last.

"Who is he?"

"A Virginian, a strong man with experience in fighting in the French and Indian War." He paused for a moment, "It means a great deal that he has come. For one thing, it means a commitment to war; there is no turning back for us now. Never again can we be British subjects. Now it will be either freedom or death. But by Washington's coming, we know that we are not alone. The rest of the colonies are behind us; the Continental Congress sent him to take over the army. We are united now, and I am convinced that we shall lay the British low!"

Lettice stared at his profile, wondering what that meant for them.

"Charles, are you going to fight?" She asked, her voice faint. "Charles, what about us? I love you!" Her words tore through the night, fierce and desperate.

Instantly he was back at her side, sitting on the bed and holding her close in his arms. "And I love you. I love you more than anything. But I must fight. There is a new world before us, Lettice, and we shall be part of it. We're going to defeat the mightiest kingdom on the globe, and set up here on this continent an example for all the world, a model of freedom the like of which no nation has ever seen. It will take courage and hardship, I fear. We may be parted; I may be killed; I don't know. But I want us to be married, Lettice. I want us to face this new life together. We can take what comes and wring our joy from it, I am convinced. Lettice, when Jonathan told me that they had captured you, I knew that I would die without you. You are everything to me. I don't care about Philip or your past or what has happened to us. I only know that without you I would be destroyed, and with you, I feel I could accomplish anything! Will you marry me?"

"Oh, yes," she cried, giving a shaky little laugh, "I will."

COMING NEXT MONTH

INDIGO BLUE by Catherine Anderson

The long-awaited final installment of the Comanche trilogy. Indigo Blue Wolf, a quarter-breed Comanche, has vowed never to marry and become the property of any white man. When tall, dark and handsome Jake Rand comes to Wolf's Landing, Indigo senses he will somehow take over her life.

THE LEGACY by Patricia Simpson

A mesmerizing love story in the tradition of the movie *Ghost*. Jessica Ward returns to her childhood home near Seattle to help her ailing father. There, she meets again an old friend, the man she's secretly loved since she was a teenager.

EMERALD QUEEN by Karen Jones Delk

An exciting historical romance that sweeps from the French Quarter of Antebellum New Orleans to the magnificent steamboat *The Emerald Queen*.

THE STARS BURN ON by Denise Robertson

A moving chronicle of the life and loves of eight friends, who come of age in the decadent and turbulent '80s.

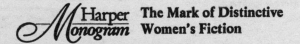 **The Mark of Distinctive Women's Fiction**